BLACKBALL

Also by Jimmy Sangster

The John Smith Series
The Spy Killer
Foreign Exchange

The Touchfeather Series
Touchfeather
Touchfeather, Too

The James Reed Series
Snowball
Blackball
Hardball
Fireball

BLACKBALL

JIMMY SANGSTER

Copyright © 2019 Jimmy Sangster. All Rights Reserved.

The characters and events portrayed in this book are fictitious. Any similarity to real persons, living or dead, is coincidental and not intended by the author.

No part of this book may be reproduced, or stored in a retrieval system, or transmitted in any form or by any means, electronic, mechanical, photocopying, recording, or otherwise, without express written permission of the publisher.

ISBN: 1941298559
ISBN-13: 978-1-941298-55-8

Published by
Brash Books, LLC
12120 State Line #253
Leawood, Kansas 66209
www.brash-books.com

FOR JAMES
(at last)

CHAPTER ONE

Los Angeles, 1987

"Rape is an extremely serious charge."
"No shit," said James.
"Five years in the slammer. I hope it was worth it."
"I didn't rape her."
"Guilty until proven innocent."
"It's the other way around."
"Not with rape, pal. Culpability is assumed. Especially when the jury is made up of horny, red-blooded males like yourself. They take one look at the chick in the dock and all they can think is there 'but for the grace of God go I, if I'd had the chance.'"
"Some attorney you're turning out to be," said James.
"I'm a good attorney," said Simms defensively.
"You'd better be. That female barracuda out there just told me what you're going to charge."
"Only if I get you off," said Simms.
"How much if you don't get me off?"
"It's on the house."
"Meaning you expect to get me off."
"Meaning if you're sent up for five years I probably couldn't collect anyway."
Charles Simms tipped back in the oversized executive chair and planted his Gucci loafers on his immaculate leather desktop. Behind the tinted lenses of his heavy tortoiseshell glasses,

his eyes showed a faint gleam of anticipation. James wondered if he'd come to the right attorney.

"Tell me about it," said Simms. "Spare none of the juicy details."

"I suppose we couldn't make a deal," said James, wondering where he was going to find the ten thousand dollars Simms was asking to take his case.

"We already have a deal," said Simms. He glanced at the Patek Phillipe on his wrist, a move designed to show James that he had excellent taste and that he probably had a dozen more lucrative cases waiting for him in the outer office.

What the hell, thought James. In for a penny, in for ten grand.

It had been a bad time at the beach. All the pundits had predicted it. There was a big storm mixing it up three hundred miles out in the Pacific. This, coupled with the conjunction of Earth, Sun and Moon (and, according to some, Mars and Jupiter as well) affected the tides all along the Southern California coast, raising them three feet above normal.

It was especially bad along the stretch between Long Beach and the Ventura County line. This golden strip of coast was, for the most part, lined with private homes. It was okay if your house was built on pilings that raised the building ten feet above the beach, providing, of course, that the pilings were solidly sunk in cement. But for the inhabitants of that section of Malibu known as the Colony, it was a disaster. These homes, whose starting price was in the region of two million dollars, were built directly on the beach. A normal high tide they could cope with. But not this one.

James joined other beach dwellers spending the weekend helping his rich neighbors fill and stack sandbags in a futile attempt to stave off the inevitable. Later, when the sandbags proved ineffectual, and the sea started to flood across patios, tennis courts and freshwater swimming pools, he helped them move their Picassos and Hepworths and Warhols from the ground floor up to the bedrooms.

There had been a time when James had been a welcome, even desirable guest in these houses. But that was when he was married to Katherine Long, superstar. Three years is a long time in Los Angeles, where memories are as short as the grosses of your last movie or hit record. Katherine's career might be in temporary limbo, but she was still a star. James was just an ex-husband. Ex-anything didn't rate in the Colony. Consequently, the only familiar faces were those of his immediate neighbors who were also helping out. These were the people with whom he had a nodding acquaintance, the people he met while jogging on the beach. They lived in the houses a mile on either side of his, where the property values were a quarter of those in the Colony, but where the houses weren't in imminent danger of being washed out to sea. The other people out that weekend, those they were trying to help, were strangers.

The whole area looked like a night location for a disaster movie. Floodlights, normally reserved for illuminating pools or tennis courts, had been switched on. They had been backed up with portable lighting systems provided by the local fire department. Upwards of 150 people were milling around moving in and out of the houses, filling sandbags, moving furniture, tripping over each other and generally creating chaos. Occasionally an efficient group would be working under the guidance of a self-appointed leader. But these small parties were the exception. For the most part disorder reigned supreme. The noise was monumental. Apart from the shouting and the yelling and the crying, there was the ever-constant sound of the breakers coming in at a height of eight or nine feet, dumping their load of devastation before making way for the next one.

James spent twenty minutes trying to help a hysterical woman in curlers find her dog, an over-fed, bad-tempered poodle who turned out to be sound asleep in the woman's closet. She grabbed up the animal and then pushed James out of the house before he could make off with the family silver. As he moved along to the next house, he saw Harry Davis, who lived with his wife Beth, four houses down from James. He was supervising a group of students from Pepperdine University, instructing them on the best way to stack the sandbags they were filling. He had a large drink in one hand and, by the extravagance of his gestures, four or five more inside of him. The students, a bunch of good-looking kids, were fortunately taking no notice of him, going about their voluntary task with diligent enthusiasm. Harry waved in James's direction and shouted something. Whatever he said was lost beneath the sound of the breakers as they demolished the newly placed sandbags, splitting them open and sucking the sand back to where it originally came from. James waved a general response in Harry's direction as he moved along the beach, knee-deep in water, to the next house.

This was one of the last houses in the Colony, set back deeper than its immediate neighbors on a lot narrower than the others. Because of this it was easy to overlook unless one was actually level with it. Maybe that was the reason that people weren't swarming all over it. That, and the fact that the whole place was dark. The occupants were probably out of town or they would certainly be here trying to keep the elements from destroying everything. James sloshed across the patio, staying well clear of a diving board that marked the edge of a swimming pool now invisible under two feet of seawater. He reached the back of the house and peered through the glass doors. The water inside was also two feet deep. A newspaper bobbed gently in the center of the room, jostling an empty whiskey bottle. The water level wasn't high enough yet to have covered the furniture, but it wouldn't be long now. Although the house was set back from its neighbors there was still enough leak light from the floodlights next door for James to have a pretty clear view into the room.

There didn't seem to be anything irreplaceable, nothing that couldn't be taken care of by the owner's insurance or personal bank balance. The paintings that James could identify were reproductions and the furnishings, though expensive, were contemporary. If the owners couldn't be bothered saving anything inside, James could see no reason why he should. He was about to move on when somebody next door moved one of the floodlights and the far corner of the room was suddenly illuminated. There was a man there. He was lying on a couch with his back to the room. The level of the water was just two inches from him. He wasn't moving. Five more minutes and he was going to be submerged.

James tried the door. It was unlocked. Pushing hard against the water, James forced it open and waded into the room. As he crossed toward the motionless figure, James hoped that he wasn't dead. In his experience, corpses invariably turned out to be problems for the individuals who discovered them. Then, just before James reached him, the man groaned loudly, rolled onto his back, slipped off the couch and disappeared under the water. He emerged a moment later, spluttering and coughing.

"Jesus H. Christ!" he said. Then he saw James. "Hi, buddy. Have a drink."

He tried to get to his feet, fell back and disappeared once more. This time when he resurfaced, he spouted a jet of water like an exuberant whale.

"Women and children first," he said. James reached down and, taking the man's hand, dragged him to his feet. The man stood unsteadily, trying to focus on James. Then he gave up and looked around the room.

"Holy shit!" he said finally. He looked terrible. There was a three-day stubble on his face and his eyes were red-rimmed inside and out. There were dark blue smudges beneath them, so pronounced they resembled a couple of black eyes. He smelled of a three-day bender, stale booze and vomit.

"You okay?" asked James.

The man swung his eyes back to James. "I feel like somebody just peeled me from the inside. My house looks like Jacques Cousteau just moved in and I nearly drowned on my living room floor. And you ask me if I'm okay! What are you, crazy?" He shook himself like a large dog coming out of the water. "I'm okay," he said finally. He looked around the room again.

"Holy shit!" he said.

"You already said that," said James. "Look, they estimate the water's going to rise a couple more feet in the next hour. Anything down here you want to move upstairs?"

The man was still looking around the room. James estimated he was about forty years old. He had thin, fair hair which, right now, was plastered to his scalp giving him the appearance of being totally bald. The face beneath the stubble was well formed. Maybe when he was clean and sober, he'd be a reasonable-looking guy. In his present state, he looked like the ultimate wino. He looked back at James.

"What did you say?"

"The water, it's going to get higher. Anything need saving?"

He looked around the room again. "It's all shit," he said. Then, back to James. "Who the hell are you?"

"James Reed, neighbor."

"Okay, James Reed, neighbor. Have a drink." He started toward the bar at the far end of the living room, forgetting the water was up to his knees. He fell, face forward, disappearing beneath the water for the third time. He was learning. This time he managed to get to his feet unaided.

"The hell with it," he said. "I'm going to bed." He changed direction and lurched toward the stairs. "Help yourself to booze." He missed the first step, falling over once more. This time he didn't get to his feet. He lay on the bottom stairs, the lower part of his body submerged. James considered leaving him. Providing the forecast was right and the water only rose another two feet, he'd be okay. Any higher, and he'd probably drown.

Cursing himself for being such a Good Samaritan, James waded over to him and grabbed him under the armpits. He started to drag him upstairs.

"Yo ho ho and a bottle of rum," said the man before passing out again. James knew it was going to be for some time. He'd had enough experience with drunks to know the symptoms. The man would be unconscious for the next few hours.

He weighed about 175 pounds, but it was dead weight and by the time James had dragged him up as far as the landing, he was exhausted. Providing the whole house wasn't washed away, he'd be safe here. He half propped him against the landing wall and started to leave. It was then that he heard the noise. He couldn't identify it immediately. It took him thirty seconds to work out what it was and from where it was coming. Someone was singing. A woman's voice. It was coming from a room two doors down the passage. Obviously, the drunk had a companion who was similarly afflicted. Best to leave her, thought James. Providing she didn't go downstairs to fetch another bottle, she'd be okay up here. Let the two of them take care of each other.

Even as he was formulating this line of reasoning he was moving along the passage toward the open door. It wasn't much of a voice and the tune was unidentifiable. It was the kind of sound a person made when he or she was alone and happy or drunk or stoned. James reached the door and looked in. The room was large and faced out onto the beach—probably the master bedroom. For a brief moment he thought he had interrupted an orgy. There were at least half a dozen people in the room, all of them on their hands and knees and all of them stark naked.

It took him a second to realize that the room was mirrored on three of its four walls and he was looking at multiple reflections of one person. She was on all fours at the far side of the bed. She had a corner of the carpet rolled back and was busy going through the contents of the small safe that was set in the floor. Anything that interested her she was putting in a transparent plastic shower cap. Her face was masked by a heavy curtain of long, very blond hair. She was facing away from the door, and a flash of pubic hair beneath the crease of her skinny backside was the same color blond.

A natural blonde was the first thing that came to James's mind. The second was that it was none of his business. Obviously, the girl belonged in the house. If she were a burglar, she'd be wearing clothes. He had just made up his mind to fade quietly away when she caught sight of one of his reflections in a mirror. She stopped her singing and tried to locate exactly where he was, not an easy feat as she could see at least five of him. He helped her out.

"Over here," he said.

She finally located him, brushing back her curtain of hair. "Hi!"

"Need any help?"

She looked back toward the safe she was rifling, then back up to James. "Where's Charlie?" she said.

James assumed Charlie was the drunk. "Sleeping it off." Then, because her nakedness was starting to get to him, "You want to put some clothes on?"

She remained on all fours considering this for a moment. Then she stood up and turned to face him, putting her hands on her hips.

"You want me to?" she asked.

She was extremely pretty, with that fresh-faced California complexion which would later turn to parchment if she continued to expose it to the sun and the dry air. She was too skinny for James's taste, but, as he had no intention of tasting, it didn't bother him.

"Well?" she said, finally.

James had forgotten what she had asked. "Well what?"

"Do you want me to put some clothes on?"

"Suit yourself," he said. He turned to go.

"Hey! Wait a minute." He turned back to her. "Where's Charlie?"

"Passed out at the top of the stairs. Gone for the night."

"Charlie doesn't drink."

"Then I don't know where Charlie is. But there's a guy passed out at the top of the stairs. See you around."

The drunk had slipped sideways so that he was now sprawled on the landing floor blocking the stairway. James stepped over him and went back downstairs. The water had risen a couple of inches in the past few minutes and was now beginning to engulf some of the lower-built furniture. James waded across the living room and went out the same way he had come in. He closed the door behind him and went back toward the beach, where the noise and the confusion hadn't diminished.

"That's it?" said Simms. He was obviously disappointed.

"That's it," said James.

"When did you see the girl again?"

"I didn't."

"What do you mean, you didn't?"

"I saw her for two minutes that night and that's it. I didn't even know her name until I heard it from the police."

They'd knocked on his door four days later. James had been jogging on the beach and was in the shower, so he didn't hear them arrive. He came out of the shower, and still naked he walked through to the living room on his way to the kitchen to pour himself a cup of coffee. Two men were poking around the living room. They stopped what they were doing as James came in.

"James Reed?" said the older of the two, a craggy-faced man whose nose marked him as a serious drinker.

"Who wants to know?" asked James, reaching for the pants he'd thrown over the back of the couch. He knew the answer already. They had fuzz written all over them. The younger one edged forward as if he was hoping James would make some kind of desperate move. He was sharp-faced and pale-eyed with fair hair. He looked like a person Central Casting would send around to audition as a Gestapo officer.

"Are you or are you not James Reed?" he asked. It was plain he already knew the answer.

James finished climbing into his pants and admitted he was indeed James Reed.

"She was right," said the young one. "He does look like Michael Caine."

"Who was right?" asked James.

"The girl you raped."

"Allegedly raped," said the older one, who had been a cop longer than his partner.

James walked through to the kitchen to pour his coffee. As far as he could recall, he hadn't raped anyone in months. He'd recently broken off an affair with a thirty-five-year-old divorcee who lived in Brentwood. The affair had lasted for three months and the lady had been as relieved as James when it came to an end, tears notwithstanding. Still, there was no point in speculating. He finished pouring his coffee and came back into the living room area.

"Who did I allegedly rape?" He directed the question to the older cop. The young one looked as if he was about to reach for the rubber hose.

"Charlotee Fisher."

"I don't know any Charlotte Fisher."

"Not Charlotte. Charlotee," said the older cop.

"Come on," said James. "Nobody's called Charlotee."

"Miss Fisher is. They misspelled the name on her birth certificate and it stuck."

"I've still never heard of her," said James.

"She's heard of you, pal," said the younger cop. "Now finish getting dressed. You're coming with us."

"Read him his rights," said the older cop.

"Bastards like him don't have any rights."

The older sighed gently. He'd had previous dealings with his partner. "Read him his rights, Al," he said.

The younger cop rattled off the formula quickly, at the same time pulling a pair of handcuffs from his back pocket.

"I want to make a phone call," said James, who had only now begun to realize that this whole thing was for real. A mistake, certainly, but one that wasn't going to go away by itself.

"You can make a call from downtown," said the older cop. "Now finish getting dressed like Al says or we'll take you in like you are."

James had finished dressing. He'd allowed the enthusiastic Al to cuff him, and he'd been driven downtown. There he had been booked. Only then had he been permitted to make a phone call. He had called Ziggy Lehman, an attorney who had last acted for him when he was divorcing Katherine. Ziggy had not been pleased to hear from him, even less so when James told him what the charge was. But he had dispatched one of his juniors downtown. Bail had been arranged and James had been turned loose.

Ziggy hadn't even wanted to see him. His office handled divorces and tax problems. Rape came into an area that Ziggy only read about in the newspapers. He arranged for James to see Charles Simms of Banks, Balkin and Simms, and that's what James had done.

This was their first meeting. James had spent the last forty-eight hours trying to find out all that he could about Charlotee

Fisher. It turned out to be nothing. There was a name and an address in Glendale. James had gotten the telephone number from Information and called. There was no answer. He had called every hour on the hour and there was still no answer. After twelve tries, he had climbed into his car and drove to Glendale and found the address. It was a small house in the hills at the back of the town and there was nobody there. He had rung the bell and banged on the front door. He had walked around to the back and tried banging on the kitchen door. Nothing.

"Just as well," said Simms. "What would you have done if Miss Fisher had answered the door?"

"Not recognized her," said James. "Unless she'd been naked."

"You didn't look at her face the night you... the night you were supposed to have raped her?"

"I saw her face. I was looking elsewhere. She's a natural blonde. You don't see many of them nowadays."

"I've never seen one," said Simms with a tinge of regret. "But you haven't answered my question. What would you have said to her?"

"That's a dumb question," said James.

"I don't ask dumb questions," said Simms. "What would you have said to her?"

James shrugged. "I'd have asked her what the hell she thought she was going to gain by accusing me of a rape I didn't do."

"Maybe you would have threatened her," said Simms.

"Maybe."

"Which would have strengthened the evidence against you. Not only did you rape her but a week later you threaten her with physical violence."

"I didn't look at it that way," said James, who had, but who had decided that it was worth the chance if it would have helped him uncover anything of value.

"You were a policeman once," said Simms.

"A long time ago," said James.

"As an ex-cop didn't it occur to you that it was a stupid thing to do?"

"It occurred to me."

"So...should it ever come up, I want you to deny trying to make any contact with her whatsoever. Understood?"

James accepted that he understood and promised he wouldn't try to contact the woman again.

"Now we get to the nitty-gritty of the whole affair," said Simms. "Why?"

"Why what?"

"Why is this woman you have never seen before or since accusing you of a rape that you say you didn't commit?"

"It's a good question," said James.

"That's exactly what the jury is going to say. Look at it from their point of view. Why should this innocent young lady, and believe me, that's what she'll look like in the dock, why should this innocent young creature accuse a complete stranger of rape unless the rape actually took place?"

"That's what I was trying to find out," said James.

"I mean, like what has she to gain?"

"Maybe that's how she gets her jollies. We could try asking Charlie."

Simms glanced at some notes he had made. "Charlie's the name of the person she asked about that night?"

"I thought she was talking about the guy I dragged upstairs. But she said Charlie didn't drink, and that guy was legless. So I assume Charlie's someone else."

"Who wasn't in the house?"

"He might have been in the house. I didn't see him."

"Who was the man you dragged upstairs?"

"I've no idea. I can't find him either."

After his fruitless trip to Glendale, James had gone back to the house in Malibu Colony. The place had been locked up tight. The floods had receded by then, but no attempt had been made to clean up the inside of the place. The living room looked like the bottom of a swamp. The seawater, true to the forecast, had risen to a height of three feet, just high enough to completely submerge most of the furniture. He had banged on the doors, front and back, to no avail. He had considered breaking into the place, then decided better not. An inquiry next door as to who owned the house came up blank. The neighbors knew nothing other than that the house remained unoccupied most of the time, and no, they didn't know who the owner was and no, they didn't know what he looked like.

Simms made a note. "We can find out," he said. "Maybe he'll be able to tell us something about Miss Fisher."

"That's why I wanted to see him," said James.

"On the other hand, she may have been in the house uninvited."

"Stark naked?" said James.

Simms agreed it was unlikely. He made a couple more notes. "I'll put a private detective on it."

"I'll do it," said James. "I've got nothing else to do. Besides, I can't afford a private detective. If it comes to that, I can't afford you either."

Simms exposed his immaculate teeth in a semblance of a smile. "You own a house on the beach which is worth close to four million dollars. You have no mortgage on it."

"I can't afford a mortgage," said James. The house had come to him out of his divorce from Katherine. She had never particularly liked it, and she had assuaged her guilt about the divorce by deeding the property free and clear to James. He lived in the guest house and rented the main property whenever possible. It was his only source of income. He had no intention of saddling himself with mortgage payments.

"As you please," said Simms. "I suppose there can be no harm in you trying to locate the owner of the house in question. But let me repeat what I said earlier. If, in the course of your investigation, you happen to come across Charlotee Fisher, back off. Stay away from that lady. Clear?"

James agreed to behave himself, and Simms announced that the meeting was over by picking up his desk phone and asking his secretary if his next client was waiting.

It took James twenty minutes to locate his car in the underground parking lot of Century City's twin towers. He had forgotten the color code of the floor he was parked on, and even after he had found the correct floor it took him another five minutes to find the bay where he had left it. As usual, it was a bitch to start. It was a fifteen-year-old Corvette. The odometer had given up at around 200,000 miles. The bodywork matched the engine, both having been thoroughly neglected during the time that James had owned the vehicle. His attitude was that it was so far gone it wasn't worth having fixed. One day soon it would quietly expire. When that happened he would buy a new one. Until then, why spend the money? Just as James was deciding that he was going to have to call the auto club, the engine fired spasmodically. He revved it for a couple of minutes, creating clouds of noxious fumes, before easing it out of the parking bay, up the ramp and out onto Santa Monica Boulevard. There he turned left, heading toward the beach.

At Pacific Coast Highway, he turned right and fifteen minutes later he had put the car in the garage and was letting himself into the guest house. Just as he was going in, he heard his name called. It was his current tenant, one half of the couple who were renting the main house. Amy Darwin was an extremely beautiful woman of thirty-eight very generous years. She had taken the house for three months. She wanted to get away from the rat race of New York, she had told James when she had first come to see the place. She and her friend needed some peace and quiet. Her friend had turned out to be even more beautiful, a striking redhead named Carlotta. James had spent a couple of days wondering which one of his new tenants he might make a play for. He had just decided that Amy would be the lucky girl when, one morning, he had gone into the main house to collect something he had stored in the cellar and stumbled across the two girls making love on the living room couch. He had apologized for the intrusion but they hadn't seemed to mind. In fact, they gave the impression that they were glad he knew about them. At least now there would be no necessity for explanations. They paid their rent on time, they rarely asked him for anything, they stayed indoors most of the time and they never had any parties. All in all, they were perfect tenants.

"Someone was looking for you earlier," said Amy. "I told them I didn't know when you'd be back."

"Any message?" asked James.

"No message. He said he'd be back later."

"Thank you, Amy." He turned to go inside, but she hadn't finished.

"He said he was a friend of yours. I don't think he was." Something had unsettled her.

James closed the door of the guest house and walked over to Amy who was standing just outside the front door of the main house. She was wearing a bikini that must have cost $150 at about $10 per square inch. Not for the first time, James was unable to repress his chauvinism. Looking at her magnificent body, all he could think was what a waste.

"Why don't you think he was a friend of mine?" he asked.

"He looked like a man who wouldn't have any friends. Tell you the truth, he scared me. Carlotta too."

James grinned. "He didn't make a pass at you, did he?"

"Good God, no. That we could handle."

"So, how did he scare you?"

"I think it was the way he looked. I shouldn't admit it, but I don't like deformity, physical or mental."

"Which was he?"

"Both. One of his legs was... I don't know... kind of twisted. His arm too. One side of his face was badly scarred. Okay, okay, I know what you're going to say..."

James hadn't been going to say anything, but he knew what she meant. She was feeling the guilt of her own intolerance. He waited for her to continue. She said nothing for a moment. When she did finally speak, it was almost a plea.

"I'm right, aren't I? He's not a friend of yours?"

"I don't know anybody who looks like that."

Amy continued quickly as if she was trying for some kind of expiation. "It wasn't just the way he looked, it was the way he behaved. I mean, he wasn't so much asking for you, he was... he was... *demanding*. Like it was my fault you weren't here. He looked like he was about to explode." She paused a moment as if what she was going to say next was going to be difficult. "Listen, you say he's not a friend of yours. Okay, I believe you, but if he's going to be around at all... Carlotta feels the same way... well, we'd just as soon not stay on. I know we've got a lease and everything but... hell, you know what I'm talking about."

"Don't worry about it," said James. "I'll take care of it." She looked at him for a moment, then without another word she turned and went into the house, closing the front door behind her.

James walked back to the guest house and let himself in. His answering machine was blinking at him. He'd had a couple of calls while he'd been out. He switched off the machine without picking up the messages, then started to make himself a cup of coffee. The hell with it, he decided. He poured himself a drink instead. He had been trying to cut down on the booze. When a guy lives alone, doesn't work for a living and spends each day wondering how he's going to fill it, he's inclined to set up disciplines for himself, if only to keep from turning into a vegetable. Right now his discipline was to cut down on the booze. It was pathetic, he decided as he downed a shot of Scotch. He poured himself another before going through into the bedroom to change into his jogging suit. He thought about what Amy had just told him. She had been really shaken up by the visitor. It wasn't like her. She struck James as being a very capable, self-sufficient lady, Carlotta was the same, soft and luscious on the outside, solid steel underneath. Who the hell was the guy who had affected them this way? And what did he want?

He finished his second drink as he climbed into his jogging suit. Without bothering to lock up, he went out to the beach. It was one of those late spring afternoons when the air is clear and sharp and yachts two miles out at sea look close enough to wade to. The sun had started to dip but it still held a lot of warmth, the gentle warmth of a Southern California spring which, in a couple of months, would turn to the searing heat of summer. The aftermath of the storm was still evident. Sand had piled up high under the houses. Some of his neighbors had their heating systems located beneath their houses; these had been torn out by the high seas. One place, a few hundred yards from James's, had been knocked off its main supports and was now leaning drunkenly against its neighbor. It would probably have to be rebuilt from scratch.

Everywhere the beach was strewn with the flotsam thrown up by the storm. Nevertheless the regulars were all doing their thing, walking the dog, jogging or just passing the time of day. They were a strange bunch, these beach people. If their houses weren't being pounded by the sea, they were threatened by the shifting hills on the land side. Mold proliferated in their closets. Sand invaded every corner of their houses. Three months a year they never saw the sun at all. Even in midsummer it often stayed cloudy until past noon. Still they considered they lived in the best place on earth. Houses that had been bought fifteen or twenty years ago for around fifty thousand dollars would now fetch a million or more. Some of the residents were sorely in need of money. If they'd been prepared to relocate, they could have cleared small fortunes. But they stayed on, smug and satisfied. James stayed on because he could think of nothing better to do. He'd been advised to sell the house, pocket three and a half million dollars and move someplace else, back to London perhaps, or Mexico where he could live like a prince, maybe the South of France or Spain. But moves like that took decisions, and he wasn't into making decisions right now. He hadn't been for the past four years. Besides, he was a writer, and the best place for a writer to be was Los Angeles. That's where all the markets were. The fact that he rarely wrote any longer, and that when he did, he didn't sell anything, didn't alter his point of view.

He jogged his compulsory mile along the beach before turning and heading back toward the house. Vague gestures of recognition passed between him and other regulars. Never more than a nod or a "nice day" or "going to be a hot one tomorrow." Confidences were never invited. Most of these people he saw every day of his life, but he knew nothing about them, not even their names. That's how they liked it on the beach. Anyway, right now he had too much on his mind to be sociable. First there was the rape charge hanging over his head, and now the problem of his mysterious visitor, a man capable of scaring his tenants out of their lease, thereby cutting his income to zero. He needed the money from this rental to fix a section of the roof of the main house. If he didn't fix it, come next winter the rain would get in and he'd be landed with a bill for ten times the amount.

As he jogged back toward the house, he kept an eye out for the stranger. If Amy's description was anything to go by, he sure as hell wasn't going to be difficult to recognize. But if he was anywhere around, James didn't see him. He came through the gate that led directly from the beach. Before going back into the guest house he took a look in the road outside. There were no strange cars parked and nobody hanging around. He went into the guest house, poured himself another drink and finally picked up the messages from his answering machine. The first call was from the divorcee in Brentwood who felt that maybe they had made a mistake ending their affair and would he like to talk about it. The second was from the offices of Banks, Balkin and Simms. Would he be kind enough to mail them a check for five thousand dollars as a fifty-percent deposit on their anticipated fee? James wiped both messages without making a note of either. Then he started to plan how to go about locating the owner of the house in the Colony where everything had started. Simms had wanted to hire a private investigator. There sure as hell was nothing a PI could do that James couldn't do—if not better, then certainly cheaper. He looked up the number of the property tax office and called it. He told the girl who answered the phone that he had a complaint about his tax bill. She asked him to hold and then connected him to another extension.

"Marcy Ryman. How can I help you?"

"My tax bill's out of sight."

"What exactly is your complaint?"

"I just told you. It's out of sight. Too high."

"What is your name and address please?"

"Harvey Wilcox." He gave the address of the house in the Colony.

"Hold the line please." He listened to Mantovani over the line before she came back on.

"Sorry to keep you waiting. Wilcox, did you say?"

"Harvey Wilcox."

"The property address you gave me is registered in the name of Harold J. Everly."

"Guess I must have the wrong address," said James. "Sorry." And he hung up.

Okay. Now he had a name. He wrote it down and looked at it for a minute. Harold J. Everly. It meant nothing to him. There was no reason why it should. But it was a start. He looked up the name in the local telephone book. It wasn't there. A lot of people who lived in the Colony had unlisted numbers. There had been a time, when James first came to Los Angeles, that he had thought there were more unlisted numbers than there were numbers in the phone book. But that was when he was married to Katherine. Their circle of acquaintances considered an unlisted telephone number as mandatory as a charge account at Tiffany's.

He called the Malibu office of one of the large real estate brokers and asked to speak to Gloria.

"She's busy right now, can I get her to return your call?"

James left his name and number and hung up. Less than a minute later Gloria called him back.

"That isn't the James Reed who once bedded me," she said in the husky smoker's voice James had used to find so sexy.

"It was more than once."

"It was so long ago I've forgotten."

"It was six months."

"Whatever," she said. "You want to take up where we left off?"

"Do you?"

"I asked first."

"I want to pick your brains," said James.

"Darling, you can pick any part of me."

"Brains first," said James. He arranged to meet her in the Randy Tar, a local watering hole, at six thirty. It was already five forty-five. He poured himself another drink, then went to shower and change. Knowing Gloria, she would be late, so he didn't hurry.

He arrived at the Randy Tar at six forty-five to find Gloria waiting for him.

"You're late," she said, kissing him with a lot more ardor than he was expecting. Sure, they'd had a brief fling, but James had the impression that when it ended, it was because she wanted it that way. "Unpunctuality wasn't one of your shortcomings."

"It was one of yours," said James. He ordered himself a drink.

"I've changed my image," said Gloria. "Nowadays I'm always on time, I keep the apartment tidy and I jog every morning before breakfast."

"It looks good on you," said James. He meant it. When he had been dating her she had been at least twelve pounds heavier. The weight had come off in the right places.

"I had my eyes done, too," she said. "Tops and bottoms."

Another thing James had become accustomed to since he had been living in Los Angeles was the way the women spoke freely about their cosmetic surgery. Nose jobs, tummy tucks, tit jobs, full face-lifts, skin scrapes, all were discussed as casually as the location of the latest "in" restaurant.

James couldn't see the difference. "He did a good job," he said.

"I'd have killed him if he hadn't," said Gloria. "It cost me three thousand dollars."

They moved from the bar to a booth at the back.

"Why the reunion?" she asked when they were settled.

"I told you. I want to pick your brains."

"And I told you, you can pick any part of me."

"Later," said James. He meant it. She really was looking very good, and he hadn't gotten laid for over a month.

"So...pick away," she said, putting her hand on his leg beneath the table.

"Harold J. Everly," he said.

"What about him?"

"Do you know him?"

"I sold him his house."

"The one in the Colony?"

"A couple of years ago. I haven't seen him since."

"So tell me about him. What does he look like?"

"Fair, nice build, around forty."

"A drinking man?" asked James, just to be sure.

"You could say that."

"What does he do?"

"He has mucho bucks. He paid the asking price. No haggling. Then he spent half as much again doing the place over."

"He shouldn't have bothered," said James, remembering the decor of the house.

"What's your interest anyway?" asked Gloria. She moved her hand a little further up his leg.

James ignored the question, just as he tried to ignore what she was doing with her hand. "I need to get in touch with him," he said. "Do you have another address?"

"Maybe the office does. I'll check it out for you." She moved her hand a fraction higher. One thing about Gloria, if she wanted something she didn't waste time going for it.

"How about we have some dinner?" suggested James.

"Your place or mine?"

"I was thinking about right here."

"Your place would be better," she said. She did something with her hand which nearly brought tears to his eyes.

"My place it is," he said.

He settled the check and they walked out to the parking lot together. On the way out she suggested that they use his car. Afterward, he could drive her back to pick up hers. Then she saw what he was driving.

"I don't believe that thing's still on the road."

James had long ago given up trying to defend his car. "So we'll use two cars."

"You just don't want to get out of bed to drive me back here," she said.

She headed toward a white Mercedes 450 SL. As she did so, she reached into her purse, pulled out a remote control box and buzzed a signal at the car. The car buzzed back at her as it unlocked its doors mechanically. James climbed into his own car, and as he pulled out of the parking lot, she was right behind him.

By the time he had put his car in the garage alongside the rented Cadillac belonging to his tenants, Gloria was waiting for him at the front door of the guest house. He went straight to the bar. She stood in the center of the room looking around.

"You've redecorated," she said.
"No I haven't," said James.
"It looks different."
"I moved the desk," he said.

Three months ago, he had bought himself a word processor in the mistaken belief that it would help his creative writing. After some thought, he had moved his desk to the place in the room he considered would be most conducive to writing with a word processor. He had then started to write his first novel. At least, that had been his intention. The problem was, his "user-friendly" word processor had turned out to be an obstacle that he still hadn't overcome. Words that he put in somehow managed to disappear forever into the electronic maw of the computer. After a couple of weeks, he had given up on the novel and started to use the computer part of the word processor to play interminable games of chess which he invariably lost. He hadn't yet got around to moving the desk back to where it belonged.

"What would you like to drink?" he asked.
"Whatever you're having," she said.

By the time he had made their drinks, she had disappeared into the bedroom. He carried the drinks through. Her outer garments were on the floor and she was in the bathroom doing whatever it is that women do in bathrooms just before climbing into bed with nothing more on their minds than a therapeutic fuck. James had no illusions about her motives, and it suited him just fine. A couple of old friends getting together to help each other out. The good old days, when one's urges could be satisfied by a visit to a singles bar, had long gone. Herpes and AIDS had closed more bars than prohibition.

He climbed out of his clothes quickly and was in bed by the time she emerged from the bathroom. She didn't look quite as good without her clothes on. The weight she had lost had left some sags and creases where once had been smoothly rounded flesh. But she was a nice person, warm and generous, and James wondered vaguely for a moment why he had let her go. Then he remembered, she was the one who had let go. It had been something to do with wanting to settle down. There had been some guy she had mentioned. Obviously it hadn't worked out. He pulled back a corner of the sheet and she climbed in beside him. He reached for her drink, which he had put on the bedside table, but she didn't want it. Instead she burrowed down under the sheet like a mole returning to its hide. James glanced at the bedside clock as he put her drink back on the nightstand. It was seven thirty. He wondered for a moment what he was going to do with the rest of the evening. Then he started to enjoy himself.

Three minutes later, there was a knock on the front door. Gloria was still busy beneath the bedclothes. Either she didn't hear anything or she was choosing to ignore it. James decided to ignore it too. But whoever it was had other ideas. The knocking continued. Finally James reached down and dragged Gloria away from her current preoccupation.

"Someone's at the door," he said.

"They'll go away," said Gloria, huskily. Her face had that soft, vulnerable look that some women get when they are feeling particularly sensual. Before James could tell her he didn't think they'd go away, the knocking started up again, this time with a persistence that even Gloria recognized couldn't be ignored. She sighed loudly and reaching across him she took the drink he had made for her.

"Get rid of them, darling, before I go off the boil."

James climbed out of bed and into a robe. Just before he headed out toward the living room she nodded toward the bulge in the front of his robe.

"Better pour cold water on that before you answer the door," she said.

He crossed the living room and opened the front door.

"Hi, man!" said the guy standing outside. Amy had been right. He was scary. First there was his physical appearance. Amy

25

had called it "twisted." James classified it more as "lopsided." His left leg looked as if it had been twisted out of joint, losing a few inches in the process. He supported himself on that side with the aid of a crutch tucked securely in his armpit. His left arm too was twisted and he was wearing a black leather glove on his left hand. The left side of his face was badly scarred as if he had been burned and nobody had bothered with skin grafting. The damage to his face included his left eye, which was plainly artificial. But his other eye made up for it, it made you forget everything else. Words that immediately came to mind were *psychopath* or *sociopath* or any other *path* you could think of. It gleamed dully, and with a malevolence that was almost palpable. Whoever the guy was, he was well aware of the effect his physical appearance had on people seeing him for the first time. He stood looking at James, waiting for the reaction.

"You want to call again later?" said James. "I'm busy right now."

"That's cool, man. I'll wait." He started in, obviously expecting James to step aside.

James didn't move. "Tomorrow would be better."

"Right now would be best," said the man.

James looked at him for a long moment. "Tomorrow," he said. He closed the front door. He was heading back toward the bedroom when the knocking started again.

"Do me a favor and beat it," he called. At the same time, he moved behind the bar and picked up an unopened bottle of Coke. When the knocking persisted, he headed back toward the door, slipping the Coke bottle into the pocket of his robe.

Gloria called from the bedroom. "Who is it, honey?"

"I won't be long," he called back. He opened the front door once more. "You want me to call the police," he said.

"You wouldn't want to do that," said the guy.

"You're right," said James. "So make your pitch and make it fast. If it costs more than five bucks, I don't want it."

"It's not going to cost you a cent," said the man. "And you'll want it, Mr. Reed, take my word for it."

Gloria's voice came from the bedroom. "Are you coming back to bed or am I going home?"

The man grinned. His teeth were crooked and neglected. James decided that if he looked the way the rest of this guy did, he wouldn't worry about his teeth either.

"You wanna get rid of the broad," said the man.

"The only person I want to get rid of right now is you," said James.

"I'll hang around outside for ten minutes. That should give you time to get rid of her. Then we'll talk."

"What are we going to talk about?"

"My sister," said the man.

"Do I know her?"

"Sure you do. You raped her, man."

James looked at the guy for a long moment. "You're Charlie," he said finally.

"Got it in one," said Charlie.

It didn't take ten minutes to get rid of Gloria. As soon as James came back into the bedroom and told her she would have to leave, she was out of bed and into her clothes in three minutes flat. There were no reproaches, no scenes, nothing. Just a tight-lipped silence. James pulled on his clothes as she went into the bathroom again. When she came out three minutes later, she walked out of the guest house slamming the door hard enough to dislodge a section of ceiling plaster. James peered into the bathroom. She had written on the mirror with lipstick. *Shithead!!*

Exactly ten minutes later, Charlie knocked on the door again. This time when James opened it, he stepped aside and Charlie came in. He stood just inside the door, looking around.

"Cozy," he said. He spotted the word processor and hobbled over toward it.

James decided that the crutch was more of a prop than a serviceable piece of equipment. Charlie seemed to move pretty well without putting any weight on it at all. He moved like a crab, traveling half a pace sideways for every one he took forward.

Charlie stood looking at the word processor for a moment. "I've got one of these," he said. "Same make."

James wasn't interested. He watched Charlie move back to the center of the room.

"You auditioning for Richard the Third?" he asked.

"Lucky for you I'm not sensitive," said Charlie.

"You're not particularly crippled either."

Charlie bared his ugly teeth again. "I got blown up in Nam," he said.

"Tough," said James.

"Broke my leg in a couple of places, broke my arm and singed my face."

"How did you lose the eye?" asked James.

"In a bar fight," said Charlie. He put his crutch down. Sure, he still walked with a limp, but James had been beaten on the tennis court by guys with greater handicaps.

"So what's with the Quasimodo act?" asked James.

"It intimidates people," said Charlie.

"Not me," said James.

"That's why I quit," said Charlie. "You want to hear about Charlotee?"

"Is that really her name?"

"So help me. The guy at the birth registry was drunk. He wrote it down wrong. My parents were too dumb to argue with him. Couple of real assholes."

"That figures," said James.

Charlie fixed his good eye on James. The glass one had more life in it. "Meaning?"

"Dumb parents. Dumb kids."

"You're the one who's going to jail."

"I didn't rape her," said James.

"Tell that to the judge."

"I intend to."

"She'll be dolled up in a pretty new dress. No makeup. She'll say 'Yes sir' and 'No sir.' She might even cry a bit. You'll get five to ten."

"I bet she'll tell them she was a virgin."

"Rape is rape man. Virgin or hooker, makes no difference."

"I'll see you in court," said James. He turned back to open the front door.

"They're not going to believe you," said Charlie. "You know it and I know it."

"Sure they will," said James.

"Then I guess I'm wasting my time," said Charlie.

"You were there that night. You know I didn't touch her."

"I know. She knows. You know. As far as everyone else is concerned you banged her brains out … against her will."

James moved over to the bar to pour himself a drink. He didn't offer one to Charlie.

"So what's the deal?" he asked. "I assume there is one or you wouldn't be here."

"It's easy," said Charlie. "You don't tell anyone she had her nose in the safe, and she'll drop the charges."

"I already told my attorney," said James.

"So tell him different. Tell him you made a mistake. Tell him whatever you want, but forget the safe."

"What was in the safe?"

"What do you care! A couple hundred bucks."

"She'll drop the charge?"

"You'll be clean as a whistle," said Charlie. "Charlotee tells the DA she made a mistake, like she won't be able to stand up in court and identify you for sure, and even if you were the guy who banged her that night, it was mostly her fault because she egged you on. The DA's not going to court with a case like that, and you know it!"

"So why did she bring the charge?"

"What difference does it make! We gotta deal?"

"Maybe," said James.

"What do you mean, maybe!" said Charlie.

James now understood Amy's description of Charlie when she said he looked as if he was about to explode. He had tightened up physically, like a steel cable that somebody forgot to loosen as the ship went out. Any moment now and the cable was going to snap and cut somebody in half.

James wasn't impressed. "I mean maybe we've got a deal, maybe we haven't."

"Listen, asshole," said Charlie. "Charlotee will go to court looking like a fifteen-year-old nun. She's a good actress. The jury won't even need to retire. You any idea what happens to guys in the slammer for rape? You'll be lucky to last six months."

James went to pour himself another drink. He took his time, aware that Charlie was watching him carefully.

"Okay," he said finally. "We've got a deal."

The tension in Charlie eased. "Good decision, man," he said.

"Sure," said James.

He watched Charlie pick up his crutch and tuck it under his armpit. Just before he walked out, Charlie turned back to James, who had remained behind the bar.

"You want to ball her?" he said.

"Who?" said James, thinking perhaps Charlie was referring to Gloria.

"Charlotee. She said she fancies you. You look like Michael Caine. I can fix it for you."

"No," said James. "I don't want to ball her."

"Just asking," said Charlie. "See you around." And he walked out, leaving the front door open.

James finished pouring his drink and walked over to close the front door. He carried the drink into the bedroom and started to get dressed. The room still smelled of Gloria. He went into the bathroom and wiped *Shithead!!* off the mirror. Then he called Gloria's home number. It rang half a dozen times before she picked up.

"Someone wrote 'shithead' on my mirror," said James. She hung up the phone. He dialed again. This time it only rang twice. When she answered she pretended she didn't know it was James.

"Hello!"

"I'm sorry," he said. "This guy wanted to make me an offer I couldn't refuse."

"I thought I was doing that," said Gloria.

"You were. I want to make it up to you."

"How?"

"I want to buy you a very expensive dinner."

"Tonight?"

"It's only eight o'clock."

"Where?"

"You name it," said James.

"Gaston's in Santa Monica," said Gloria.

"We'll never get a table," said James.

"I'll take care of it," said Gloria. "Nine thirty." She hung up. James was regretting his impulse already. Dinner at Gaston's was going to cost him around two hundred dollars. He hated to spend that kind of money in a restaurant where the prices seemed to be in inverse ratio to the amount of food and the quality of the service and where wine that he could buy in his local liquor store for ten bucks a bottle was priced at seventy-five. He tried consoling himself with the thought that he owed Gloria for the way he had treated her. In fact, he still needed something from her. Also he was still feeling horny.

He decided to change his clothes, dressing in something more suitable for one of the most expensive restaurants in town. Anywhere else in the world this would have meant a jacket and tie. In Los Angeles, it meant designer jeans, a silk shirt and a cashmere sweater draped over your shoulders. James didn't own designer jeans. But at least he had a decent pair of pants. He dug them out from the back of his closet. They were still in the polythene wrapping from the cleaners. It was a Beverly Hills cleaner. He hadn't had stuff cleaned in Beverly Hills since he left Katherine. He didn't own a silk shirt either, and his cashmere sweater was in the car where he used it to wipe down the windshield because the demister didn't work.

This time, Gloria was late. James arrived at the restaurant at nine twenty-five. The place was full, as usual, and noisy. It was as if the diners had decided that if they were paying these prices, they were going to make as much noise as possible to prove to themselves what a good time they were having.

James asked if a reservation had been made in the name of Reed.

"Most certainly, my lord," said the maître d'hotel. "This way please."

He led James to what was obviously the best table in the place.

"Shall I open the champagne now?" he asked, as James sat down. It was Dom Perignon. At about fifty bucks retail, James reckoned the price here would be around $175.

"Did I order that?" said James.

"Your secretary ordered it when she made the reservation, my lord."

"What name did she make the reservation in?"

"Yours, sir. Lord Reed."

"Thank you," said James. He pronounced the champagne fit to drink and the maître d' left with a flourish, no doubt to inform the rest of the clientele that they were fortunate enough tonight to be dining in the same place as a real live English aristocrat.

Gloria arrived fifteen minutes later. "Lord Reed's table," she said in a voice loud enough to turn every head in the room. The maître d' bowed and scraped her over to James's table and poured her a glass of champagne. James asked to see the menu.

"Your secretary already ordered for you my lord," said the maître d'. "Unless of course you'd like to change?"

James flashed a look at Gloria. She smiled at him sweetly across the top of her champagne glass. He told the maître d' that he'd stick with whatever his secretary had ordered.

First there was the caviar. This was followed by fresh Maine lobster, "flown out today" according to the maître d'. The soufflé was delicious, and the cognac to finish up was thirty-five dollars a glass. Gloria had two.

Throughout the meal, Gloria managed to steer the conversation into the mundane. How had he been? What was he doing with himself these days? Did he ever see Katherine? And wasn't the real-estate market going through a slump? Only as she ordered her second glass of cognac was James able to bring up what he wanted to.

"You won't forget about Everly," he said.

"Who?"

"Harold J. Everly. You were going to ask at the office."

"I won't forget," said Gloria. "Don't you want another cognac?"

James told her that he didn't want another cognac and asked for the check. It came to $438 plus tip.

They walked out to the parking lot together.

"Your place or mine?" asked James.

"I'm tired," said Gloria. "And I've got a headache." She smiled at him. "Thank you for a lovely dinner," she said. She buzzed her car open, climbed in and started the engine. Just before she drove away, she lowered the window. "Now we're quits," she said. "I'll call you tomorrow."

It was just past midnight as James put the car away. The lights were on in the main house and he considered for a moment whether or not to bang on the front door and ask for a drink. Then he decided the hell with it. He let himself into the guest house. His answering machine was flashing at him. He flipped the switch to Playback and went into the kitchen to pour himself a glass of milk.

"It's all taken care of," said the voice of Charlie. "You'll most likely hear from your attorney tomorrow. Ciao, man." The machine went dead.

James moved over and switched it off. Okay, so he was off the hook. All that remained now was to find out why.

CHAPTER TWO

Gloria called him at ten thirty.

"How did you sleep?" she said.

"Caviar gives me indigestion."

"How about dinner again tonight?"

"I'll have to get a mortgage on the house," said James. "I don't know if I can manage it in one day."

"On me," said Gloria. "My place."

"Did you find out about Everly?"

"Yes."

"Tell me."

"Tonight. Seven thirty. Same address."

"Can I bring anything?"

"Just a toothbrush," said Gloria.

Obviously honor had been satisfied and Gloria was willing to start afresh. James wasn't sure he wanted to start afresh, but he needed to know about Everly. Also, he had been having a very good time when Charlie had banged on the door last night. He called one of the guys he played poker with and told him he wouldn't be able to make it for this evening. Then he called the offices of Banks, Balkin and Simms and asked to speak to Mr. Simms.

"I was just going to call you," said Simms. "I arranged to get the charge dropped."

"How did you do that?" asked James.

"The DA's office owes me a couple of favors. Listen, did you mail me that check yet?"

"No I didn't," said James.

"Be a pal. Drop it in the mail today, and we'll call it quits. I'll settle for the five grand."

"Tell me something," said James. "What do you estimate your time is worth on an hourly basis?"

"A couple of hundred," said Simms. "Why?"

"We spent about fifteen minutes together the other day. I'll mail you a check for fifty."

"I don't think you heard me right. I got them to drop the charges, pal. You're free and clear."

"It feels great," said James and hung up.

He wrote out a check for fifty dollars to Banks, Balkin and Simms and stuck it in an envelope. He addressed and stamped the envelope and put it in his mailbox to be collected. Then he went for a run on the beach.

Everly's house was still closed up as tight. Peering through the window, James could see that nothing had been touched since the flood. The patio doors were locked. So too were the front and back doors. He was contemplating breaking in when he noticed one of the neighbors eyeing him from the terrace of the next-door house. James waved the man a cheerful good morning and started to jog back toward his own section of the beach.

He had blocked out a scenario for Harold J. Everly and he badly wanted to confirm its accuracy. Everly…a rich drunk, picks up a pretty chick, one Charlotee, and brings her back to his pad. Maybe he even moves her in for a few days. Long enough for her to become thoroughly acquainted with the house. Where the safe is, where he keeps the keys or the combination to said safe, cozy little domestic details. When she's thoroughly familiar with the place, she calls brother Charlie and tells him she's ready. No problem getting Everly drunk, he gets drunk all the time. Everly passes out, Charlotee opens the safe and rifles it. Meantime Charlie pulls up outside in some form of transport just in case there's anything bulky worth stealing—pictures, objets d'art, the family silver. Maybe Charlie brings a friend, someone to help him move the heavier stuff. That's why Charlotee wasn't too surprised when she first caught sight of James, why she asked him where Charlie was. The truck or the station wagon is loaded, Charlotee packs her suitcase and by the time Everly gropes his way out of the booze, they are long gone together with half the contents of his house and everything in the safe that is negotiable. Very neat, very tidy, not a bad scenario at all, so far.

Then must have come the questions from Charlotee. If the guy who saw me in the bedroom isn't one of us, who the hell is he? Charlie finds out. Not too hard for someone as bright as Charlie. And how are we going to keep him quiet? Simple. Charge him with rape and offer to drop the charges if he keeps his mouth shut.

Fade out. End of scenario. Put it down on paper and he could sell it to any cop show in town. Except then the producer would start to ask questions.

Why didn't the Everly character go to the police and report the burglary?

Maybe because he didn't want it known he was shacking with a young chick.

Come on! The guy's about forty years old. Everyone who's forty years old shacks with a young chick at some time or another.

Okay, maybe he's married and he doesn't want his wife to find out.

There isn't any wife. The neighbors would have known if there had been. So would the real-estate lady who sold him the house.

Maybe he was so drunk he didn't know he'd been burgled.

They emptied his safe, for crying out loud. Helen Keller would have known she'd been burgled.

Unless there was something in his safe that he just can't report stolen. Something he's not supposed to have in the first place.

Now you're cooking. Find out, and you might sell your scenario. On the other hand, why bother? What's it to you? You're off the hook, clean as a whistle. Why get mixed up with the problems of some drunk you don't even know and can't find?

Right about there, James came up against what he had often considered a serious flaw in his own character. When he wasn't being too self-analytical, he was able to convince himself that it was a matter of pride. He didn't like being used. Okay, a lot of people felt that way. It happened all the time. Socially, professionally, at home, at work, people were always getting their pride hurt. Most of the time, they shrugged it off, telling themselves that they wouldn't allow it to happen again. James had been like that once. It had to do with his divorce from Katherine. He had been the injured party. He had wallowed in self-pity for a time until somebody had pointed out to him that the real thing he was hurting from was his pride. He'd given this diagnosis some serious thought and eventually accepted it. From then on, screw hurt pride, it wasn't worth the angst. Somebody uses you, don't sulk, get even. *Vindictive* was a word that came to mind. And *implacable, retaliatory,* or just plain *bloody-minded.* They all fit. What it boiled down to was don't stick it to James Reed, because, one way or another, he was going to stick it right back to you.

He considered buying a bottle of wine to take to Gloria's for dinner. Then he remembered what the meal last night had cost. His credit-card company was going to be on his back next month asking why he had exceeded his spending limit. He decided to let Gloria pay for the wine. And because he was still pissed off at what she had done last night, he decided to arrive late for dinner. In fact, he nearly didn't arrive at all. His car had one of its periodic fits of temperament and wouldn't start. He ran the battery flat trying. Eventually he was forced to go to the main house and ask for a loan of his tenants' Cadillac.

While Amy fetched him the keys from upstairs, Carlotta asked him in for a drink. He decided that perhaps Carlotta wasn't as completely bent as he had first thought. She was definitely putting out signals. But Amy was paying the rent and one of the first rules he had set for himself when he had started to lease out the main house was never to make a pass at the lessee's live-in companion, be it wife or girlfriend. That was the fast way to the bread line. He declined Carlotta's offer of a drink and waited at the front door until Amy returned with the keys.

"Did your friend show up?" she asked as she showed him out.

"You won't be seeing him again," said James.

Driving along Pacific Coast Highway on his way to Gloria's, James gave serious thought to getting himself a new car. It invariably happened when he borrowed somebody else's. Especially when it was a car where the radio, the air conditioner and the fuel gauge all functioned as they had been designed to and you could barely hear the sound of the engine when traveling at seventy.

He turned left on Sunset Boulevard and then left again almost immediately. He drove through rolling hills for a mile until he reached the development where Gloria lived. It was barely a mile from the ocean, but as far as the homeowners here were concerned they could have been a thousand miles inland. There was no sight, sound or smell of the sea. They were separated from it by high hills that stretched from here as far as the steep escarpment that lined the east side of Pacific Coast Highway. Every house looked the same. It was difficult to know where one left off and the next began. The developer had obviously given instructions that as many units as possible should be stacked into the available space. If everything hadn't been painted white it would have looked like a high-class slum. As it was, the starting prices were in the region of a quarter of a million dollars.

James located Gloria's house at the second try. He parked the car and knocked on the door he thought was hers. It wasn't. But the noise the homeowner made telling James he was at the wrong place was sufficient to set Gloria's dog barking next door. He remembered the dog well, a fussy little poodle who, like its mistress, had a proclivity for nuzzling the crotches of male visitors. By the time James had apologized to the wrong householder and gone next door, Gloria was waiting for him on the doorstep.

"You're late again," she said as he came in.

"The car wouldn't start."

"Surprise, surprise," said Gloria.

She looked very attractive this evening. She had obviously taken considerable care over her appearance. James knew right away that he wasn't expected to go home tonight. Nobody dressed like that just to cook dinner. By way of confirmation she asked him if he'd done what she'd told him and brought his toothbrush.

"I'll borrow yours," he said, accepting the glass of champagne she handed him.

It wasn't Dom Perignon, but then it wasn't American champagne either. As far as James was concerned, champagne was a morning drink. But she'd spent the money and made the effort. There was no point in appearing churlish. Besides, he needed something from her.

After a couple of minutes, she excused herself to go into the kitchen to stir a couple of pots. James looked around the living room. It hadn't changed in the six months since he had last been here. The same white on white carpets, wall covering, drapes and soft furnishings, interspersed with large chunks of glass and chrome. There was track lighting mounted on the ceiling designed to illuminate half a dozen paintings whose only virtue seemed to be their size and lack of color. James had been in a dozen similar living rooms. Sometimes he believed that the divorced women of Los Angeles setting up house on their own all went to the same interior designer, who provided everything down to the expensive art books arranged neatly on the coffee table gathering small rings where guests put their drinks.

She called to him from the kitchen.

"Help yourself to another glass of champagne."

He went to the sideboard and poured half the contents of his glass into the ice bucket.

"Make yourself at home," she called again. "I won't be a minute."

James sat down, choosing the large, overstuffed settee. Immediately the poodle, whose name he'd forgotten, was on his lap sniffing at his crotch. He pushed the dog away as Gloria came back in and poured herself another glass of champagne. She came and sat beside him on the settee. James caught a whiff of a heavy perfume. It was very sexy. So too was her outfit. It could best be described as diaphanous, cut low in the front so when she leaned toward him, as she did now, he could see clear down to her navel.

"I apologize for last night," she said.

"Don't worry about it."

"Was it a great deal of money?"

"I said don't worry about it. You were entitled."

"I'm not used to being tossed out of a man's bed."

"It won't happen again," said James. "Tell me about Everly."

She pulled back slightly, looking at him.

"That's the only reason you're here, isn't it?"

"If it was, I could have called you."

She thought about this for a moment. She decided to give him the benefit of the doubt.

"There's not much to tell. I dug out the files. But they didn't come up with much. Then I had an idea. I called the broker who brought him to me. I remember, at the time, they seemed to be a bit of an item together."

"Anyone I know?" asked James.

"Bee Kendrick. She works out of Beverly Hills."

"Never heard of her."

Gloria smiled sweetly. "You don't know all the female brokers in the city, just most of them." She continued before James could comment. "Anyway, not only did she know him, but she thinks he's a shit."

"What did he do, dump her?" said James.

"That's what I figured. Hell hath no fury... as well you know after last night."

"What did she tell you?"

"First, he's rich. Rich *rich*. Family money that goes back forever. So much money even he can't spend it. Although, according to Bee he doesn't give up trying. Apart from the house in the Colony, he has a duplex in New York, an apartment in London, and a hundred thousand acres of horses in Nevada."

"Nobody has horses in Nevada," said James.

"Most of the property is in Utah, but it overlaps into Nevada. He gets some kind of a tax break that way."

"Where does he spend his time?" asked James.

"He's got no schedule. He goes where his fancy takes him and where the action is."

"Female action?"

"To hear Bee tell it, and I quote, He'd fuck a puddle in the road, unquote. Bee has a quaint way with words."

"Does she know where he is right now?"

"She hasn't seen him for eighteen months."

"Could she find out?"

"I could ask her."

"Why don't I ask her?"

"Two reasons. One she probably wouldn't tell you. Girl talk is for girls. That's what we had, a girl talk. And two, as long as you've decided to sample my home cooking again, I'm not going to let you get within ten miles of Bee Kendrick."

It wasn't going to be difficult to locate Bee Kendrick, so James let it slide.

"Talking of home cooking...," he said.

She stood up and headed for the kitchen again.

"Two minutes and you're going to get the best meal you've had since I last cooked for you." She disappeared into the kitchen.

As far as James could remember she'd never cooked for him, but it wasn't important. He'd got the information he wanted and tomorrow he could start acting on it. Meanwhile, he had the evening ahead of him. He pushed the dog away again and went to pour himself another drink.

He turned the keys of the Cadillac back to Amy at nine o'clock the next morning.

"Any time," she said as he thanked her for the loan. He caught a glimpse of Carlotta who was oiling her lean, tanned, topless magnificence on the patio. Again he suspected she was sending out signals. But right now he wasn't in a receptive frame of mind. Gloria had put him through the wringer last night.

She had cooked him breakfast before he left. Eggs, bacon and hotcakes. He didn't eat breakfast normally, but like the dinner last night, which had been pretty ordinary, he felt the effort she'd made required a measure of appreciation in return. So he had eaten everything. Then had come the part he had been dreading. The good-bye. He knew that she was expecting their new relationship to blossom. For his part, he didn't want any kind of relationship with anyone right now. He didn't know how he was going to let her down lightly. She was dressed for her day at the office when she walked him out to his car, looking very yuppie.

Outside, she eyed the Cadillac skeptically. "When I said you needed a new car, I meant a proper one," she said. As far as Gloria was concerned, if it wasn't a Mercedes or a Jaguar, it had no business being on the highway.

"It belongs to my tenant," said James. "I borrowed it."

"Take it back, honey. It doesn't suit you," she said.

She reached up and kissed him lightly, like a longtime wife sending her husband off to work. "I'll call you sometime," she said.

That had been it. Not "Please call me," which was the standard opening gambit for a new relationship. Then she had patted him lightly on the cheek and gone back into the house.

James had driven home in two states of mind. One, he was glad to have gotten out of the whole affair so easily, and two, he was a little pissed off that Gloria should have let him go without a struggle.

After making himself a cup of coffee, he started calling the real estate brokers in Beverly Hills. He was lucky with the fourth call.

"Hold the line for Ms. Kendrick," said the operator. A moment later Bee Kendrick came on.

"What took you so long?" she said, after James had identified himself. She had a Southern accent, which a lot of men found attractive, but which never failed to grate on James. "Gloria said you'd be calling ten minutes after she called me."

Another point for Gloria, thought James. Since he'd renewed their friendship two days ago she'd been four steps ahead of him all the way. Maybe he *would* call her after all. "She said you might be able to help me," he said.

"She told me it was the other way around," said Bee. "When can we get together?"

"It's nothing we can't handle over the phone," said James.

"Then you know some tricks I don't," said Bee. "How about lunch?"

There was no alternative. James agreed to meet her for lunch. He hung up and called Gloria at her office.

"I feel like I'm talking to my pimp," he said to her.

"Don't knock it until you've tried it," she said.

"You told me last night you didn't want me going within four miles of Bee Kendrick."

"Things often look different when the sun comes up."

"Meaning you wouldn't care if I take her to bed."

"Why should I?"

"Does she feel the same way?"

"Honey, she's banking on it. Have a nice day." She hung up.

Either Gloria was playing some complicated game, the rules of which he couldn't even begin to understand, or she had decided that her friends should share in James's prowess beneath the sheets. He had long considered himself a minor leaguer in that department. He decided that Gloria was setting an extremely complicated trap designed to ensnare him. Meanwhile, he had to arrange transport to get himself up to Beverly Hills where he had a lunch date with Bee Kendrick.

Using Amy's Cadillac, he jump-started his own car and left the engine running to charge the battery while he went to change. At a quarter past twelve, he was on Sunset Boulevard heading into town. The traffic was thin that time of day and he made good time. He passed the sign which told him he was entering the city of Beverly Hills, and, as he always did, when he entered her territory, he thought briefly of Katherine. She had been a big star when they married, one of the biggest. He'd still been a cop working out of Scotland Yard when she'd had her first big hit. Afterward, when he left the police force under a minor cloud, he had gone to work for a private security firm where one of his assignments had been to act as bodyguard to Katherine Long, movie star. She had been shooting a movie in England at the time. From bodyguard to lover to husband to ex-husband, all in a matter of three years. Most of the time they'd been good years. They'd had fun and they'd loved a lot. At least, James had loved a lot. He assumed Katherine had felt the same way. For two and a half of those three years, she had. Then, needing some assurance of her continued desirability, she'd moved on, and James had moved out. She was still a big star, but she didn't work too often now, not since the scandal over the death of her daughter Caroline.

James drove down the ramp of the Rodeo Collection and handed his car over to a parking valet who recoiled in horror at having to take James's place behind the wheel.

"I get in there, who's gonna pay my cleaning bill, man?"

"I'm a big tipper," said James.

Bee Kendrick was waiting for him under one of the huge umbrellas outside Pastels. While not quite an "in" restaurant, it wasn't far enough out not to be busy with the Beverly Hills lunchtime crowd. Bee had obviously been told how to recognize James because she started yoo-hooing while he was still on the escalator. Even if she hadn't identified herself, James would have known her. First, she was sitting alone, obviously waiting for somebody. Second, she couldn't have been anything else except a Beverly Hills real estate broker. James sometimes thought they cloned them. Age, between forty and fifty; marital status, divorced; children, two teenagers at Beverly High; financial status, precarious; physical appearance, blond, good figure and incredible teeth; dress code, smart, fashionable and never bought retail.

James squeezed between the other diners until he reached Bee's table. He would have taken money on what her first line was going to be.

"Gloria was right. You do look like Michael Caine."

He slipped into the seat opposite her. She already had a glass of champagne in front of her, the bottle in an ice bucket close at hand. That could have been Gloria's doing, but equally, Bee might have ordered it on her own initiative. Another characteristic of the type was a complete disregard for money, providing it was someone else's.

"Champagne?" she said.

James assumed he was paying for it. "Please."

She only had to reach out for the bottle but instead she started to semaphore for the attention of one of the waiters.

"Allow me," said James. He poured himself a glass and topped up Bee's. He put the bottle back into the ice bucket just as the waiter answered Bee's summons.

"Can I help you?" he asked politely.

She flashed her magnificent teeth at him. "We'll order later," she said.

The mystified waiter walked away, as Bee took a sip from her glass and eyed James speculatively across the table.

"What's the big interest in Harold J. Everly?" she asked.

"I need to get in touch with him," said James, delighted that she had come straight to the point.

"Good news or bad for Mr. Everly?"

"Does it make any difference?"

"Certainly darling. If it's bad news I'll tell you where to find him. If it's good, then you'll have wasted the very expensive lunch you're about to buy me because I won't tell you anything."

Right about here, James considered forgetting the whole thing. It was starting to cost him too much money. Dinner with Gloria and now lunch with Bee. He'd blown his budget for the entire month. But she looked like a lady who had to watch her figure. He hoped she'd order just a salad, and as he was already liable for the champagne, he plunged on.

"Bad news," he said.

"Then I'll tell you," she said with a smile. "After we've had lunch."

He was wrong. She wasn't watching her figure, or she wasn't watching it today. She didn't even look at the menu as she ordered the two most expensive items it contained. It was James who settled for just a salad.

During lunch she refused point-blank to talk about Everly. Maybe she thought that when James had learned everything he needed to, he would up and leave her with the check. Instead, she wanted to know what it had been like being married to one of the biggest stars in the business, and did James still see Katherine, and wasn't it terrible the way the economy wasn't picking up, and had he been to that great new restaurant that Wolfgang Puck had opened and wasn't it a shame that the old Ma Maison had closed, still it never had been the same after Wolfgang had left and how long had he known Gloria and wasn't she a marvelous person and had he met her new boyfriend, the jealous one with all the muscles. James interjected the right sounds into the monologue, had another glass of champagne, and declined a cognac with his coffee as Bee ordered a second.

Sometime during the past half an hour, as the champagne had taken effect, Bee had started to lose some of her polish. As her second cognac arrived, she pulled a makeup compact from her purse and tried to repair her lipstick. She didn't make a very good job of it. But she was beyond caring.

"Hey ho," she said as she put away her compact. "What are your plans for this afternoon?"

"I have to take a meeting with my agent," said James. He didn't have an agent. But if he had told her that he'd an appointment with his doctor or dentist she would have suggested he cancel it. In this town, one always kept appointments with one's agent. She pulled a business card from the Gucci note case in her Louis Vuitton purse and circled one of the telephone numbers.

"That's my home number," she said. "Please call me … soon."

James promised that he would and Bee started making preparations to leave.

"You haven't told me about Everly," said James.

"Silly me," she said. "I wonder, could I have just one more tiny little cognac?"

James waved at the waiter, pointed to Bee's glass, and signaled for a refill.

"Lucky me," said Bee. "I don't have to go to the office this afternoon."

Lucky office, thought James.

The waiter brought her brandy and she drank half of it in the first swallow. "Now, where were we?" she said.

"Everly?" prompted James.

"Bastard," she said.

"In what way?"

"You name it," said Bee.

This was going to be hard as well as expensive, decided James.

"A drinking man, right?"

"He's got hollow legs," said Bee.

"Married?"

"Once. A long time ago."

"What happened?"

"She died... I think."

"Children?"

"He can't get it up."

"Maybe he could once," said James.

"No children. Not that he told me about."

"Gloria said he was rich," said James.

"Be careful with Gloria. She's got this boyfriend who's insanely jealous. He's an ex-prize fighter."

"I'll be very careful," said James. "Rich?"

"Filthy rich. I mean, Getty-type rich. Family money."

"What did the family do?"

"Made money."

"I know. But how?"

"Why don't you call your agent and we'll go home and fuck."

"I'd love to," said James. "But you know what agents can be like."

She nodded carefully. "Bastards," she said. Then she started to get to her feet. "I think I'm going home anyway." She tried to push the chair away, failed, and sat down again quickly.

"What does he do with himself?" asked James.

"Who?"

"Everly."

"He doesn't do anything. He's got all this money that just sits around making more money. He likes to shoot things."

"What kind of things?"

"Lions and tigers and elephants, things like that. He's got this room at the ranch full of heads and rugs and stuffed animals and guns and maps of Africa... and heads and stuff... I think I'm going to throw up."

James managed to get her as far as the ladies' room. She disappeared inside. He went back to the table to pay the check. It was as bad as he had thought it was going to be. He used his credit card, hoping they wouldn't call in to check his credit balance. But people who used Pastels, while not necessarily honest, were usually rich enough not to try and swindle the restaurant over something as insignificant as a lunch bill, even if it was for $158. They accepted his card and his signature without a murmur.

He was waiting outside the ladies' room when Bee emerged twenty minutes later. She looked terrible.

"I'll drive you home," he said.

"What about your agent?"

"I called and canceled," said James. She was pathetically grateful.

He didn't want to use his own car in case she threw up again. He gave the parking valet Bee's ticket and a couple of minutes later he was helping her into her white Jaguar. She told him her address. It was a street off Coldwater Canyon which James knew well. Fifteen minutes later, he was unlocking her front door with the key she had handed him. As he opened the door, the alarm went off. She didn't seem to notice.

"Maybe you ought to switch off the alarm," he said. "Before the cops arrive."

"They never arrive," she said. Somehow she managed to hit the right combination of buttons, and the alarm stopped howling.

"Coffee," she said and disappeared toward the kitchen.

It was a pleasant little house if one ignored the interior decoration which looked as if it had been handled by the same guy who'd done Gloria's place. James wandered into the living room. Same art books on the coffee table, same colorless pictures on the wall. As a style, James classified it as "early déjà vu."

She returned with two mugs of coffee, strong and black.

"You want cream or sugar, it's in the kitchen," she said as she lowered herself gently into one of the chrome and cane chairs arranged around the chrome and glass dining table. James didn't push, he knew what was coming next, and he knew he had to let her get it off her chest.

"Oh God," she said finally. "I've never been so embarrassed in my life."

"Don't worry about it," said James. "It happens to everyone."

"Can you ever forgive me?"

"I already have."

"You're very sweet. But if you will ply a girl with liquor, what can you expect?"

"I'm sorry," said James.

"Just so long as you don't hold it against me."

"I won't," promised James. "How are you feeling now?"

"A tidge better, thank you."

"Good." He looked around for a telephone. "May I call a cab? I need to get back to my car."

"You can stay if you like. I'll have a little nap. Then, I'll cook you some dinner and drop you off when I go to the office in the morning."

She was a tryer, thought James. But he detected a small look of relief when he declined the offer. He called a radio cab. They promised to pick him up inside thirty minutes. He thanked them and hung up. That would give him all the time he needed. He poured Bee another cup of coffee and took a chair opposite her across the dining table.

"So tell me more about Harold Everly," he said.

All she really wanted now was to get rid of him. If telling him about Everly was going to do it, then she'd tell him everything she knew. Which, James decided on his drive back to the beach, was a hell of a lot more than he had hoped for.

CHAPTER THREE

At nine thirty the following morning, he was on a flight to Las Vegas. As the plane took off, heading out over the ocean before turning inland once more, James asked a stewardess for something he could write on. She brought him a small notepad with the airline's logo taking up half of every sheet. He had decided to start listing his expenses, which were mounting at an alarming rate.

Gloria's dinner. Bee's lunch. Cab fare. And now a flight to Las Vegas.

He'd have to rent a car when he got there and probably spring for a couple of nights in a hotel.

Shit, he was driving himself into bankruptcy and he didn't even know why. He was going to have to find somebody to pick up the tab somewhere down the line.

Bee Kendrick, it seemed, had been even thicker with Everly than Gloria had thought. It hadn't been just a roll in the hay between a real estate broker and her prospective client. According to Bee, Everly had moved in with her while he was waiting for the escrow to close on the house he'd bought in the Colony. It had been a ninety-day escrow and during that time he had taken Bee to New York for a week and to the ranch for ten days. To hear Bee tell it, the ten days at the ranch was the only time during the three months that he had been sober. In New York, he had asked her to marry him. She had accepted, no doubt unable to believe her good fortune. Then, at the ranch five days later when he had dried out, he told her he'd made a mistake, please would she forgive him, but he didn't think he wanted to marry her after all. She'd reacted in a perfectly reasonable fashion, first bursting into tears, second throwing a screaming fit of hysterics, and third, turning on the sweetness and light in an effort to make him change his mind again. But Everly sober was a different person than Everly drunk. He was polite, good-mannered and completely unshakable. She tried to get him back on the booze, figuring a drunk Everly was better than no Everly at all. But the only drinking he did at the ranch was the odd snort he'd take with some of his ranch hands.

"You should have seen them," said Bee. "Like a fucking Marlboro ad, all cowboy boots, Stetsons and rotgut whiskey."

But it was controlled drinking, he never got drunk. After five miserable days, she had given up and flown home alone. A week later, he had been on her doorstep, drunk as a fiddler's bitch, wondering why she wouldn't let him in. She had threatened to call the police on him, and eventually he'd left. Two weeks later, escrow closed on the Colony house and he had called her and asked if she would help him decorate and, if she was going to be hanging around the house dealing with workmen, why didn't she just move in. She decided to give the whole thing one more try. Maybe if she could get him to propose again while he was drunk, then drag him off to Vegas before he sobered up, she might emerge as Mrs. Everly yet.

It nearly worked, but having got as far as Vegas, Everly had insisted on inviting the guys from the ranch to the wedding. This had involved them driving up there. Once there, he sobered up fast and backed out again. That was it for Bee. She gave up on him entirely.

James had asked her if she could find out where he was right now. By then, all she had wanted to do was to go and lie down. She didn't even ask him why. She picked up the phone and dialed a number in Nevada. James listened to her end of the conversation.

"Mr. Everly, please. When will he be back? This is Los Angeles calling. I see. Do you know whether he plans to come to Los Angeles in the immediate future? I see, thank you very much. No, there's no message."

She hung up and turned to James. "He's at the ranch, and as far as they know, he'll be there for the next week at least. It's 'ropin' an' brandin' time.' He never misses it."

James made her give him directions to get to the ranch. His cab had arrived, and the last he had seen of Bee Kendrick was a very bedraggled figure heading upstairs for much-needed oblivion. She hadn't even asked him to be sure to call.

It was raining when he landed. It often rained in Las Vegas. Nobody minded because nobody went outside. The really important people in Vegas, the tourists, spent their time in hotels trying to lose as much money as they could before their trip came to an end. James thought Las Vegas one of the most depressing places on earth. That was when the sun was shining.

He rented a car at the airport and headed straight out of town. He missed the first entrance to the freeway and found himself driving down the Strip. The hundred-foot-high signs outside the hotels trumpeted names like Sinatra, Wayne Newton, Diana Ross. In smaller billing they also informed passersby that they could get a three-course meal for $6.95, except there were no passersby. Every now and then, crammed between the high-rise hotels, were grouped half a dozen single-story buildings selling liquor, girlie magazines, cheap souvenirs or Chinese take-out food. How these places survived was a mystery. The hotels had long ago worked out that the best way to keep the tourists under their roof and at their gaming tables was to make sure that there was absolutely nothing anybody could want that couldn't be obtained right there in the hotel. That meant that every hotel worth its salt had a shopping mall, half a dozen restaurants and a uniformed bell captain who knew how to come up with hundred-dollar hookers.

James finally found his way onto the freeway, heading north toward Utah. According to the map he'd picked up at the car rental agency, he had an hour's freeway drive ahead of him before turning off. Half an hour later he should reach Everly's place.

He reached the turnoff fifty-five minutes later. He found himself on a two-lane highway stretching ahead in a dead straight line, losing itself in a range of hills about ten miles away. According to his estimation, Everly's place lay just beyond the range of hills. He was going to be there sooner than he'd thought.

He reached the gates of the ranch ten minutes later. He wasn't impressed. Two concrete posts about ten feet high with a battered sign hanging lopsided between them: E-BAR-E. Another sign was stuck in the ground just inside the entrance: KEEP OUT. There was no gate or barrier and James turned off the road and drove through.

He was on a single-track dirt road, bordered on each side by the monotonous scrubland he had been driving through since he left Vegas. After a mile, he came to the first washout. A flash flood, long since gone, had obliterated the dirt track completely, leaving nothing but mud. A four-wheel-drive might have been able to handle it, but James didn't have four-wheel drive. Halfway across, the car slid sideways, lost all traction and came to a dead stop, rear wheels spinning up a cascade of mud.

After a couple of attempts to drive himself clear, he climbed out of the car and, ankle deep in mud, tried to assess the problem. He was up to his rear hubcaps. No way was he going to get out without a tow. No big deal, he thought. He'd already been on the property for a mile. The ranch house couldn't be far away now. Leaving his overnight bag, he sloshed his way out of the washout to where the dirt track started again. The mud reminded him of the inside of Everly's house at the Colony. It also made him wonder, yet again, what the hell he was doing here. Sticking it back to Charlotee and Charlie had seemed very important back in LA. Out here, knee deep in mud, a million miles from anyplace, in the pouring rain, the sweetness of revenge was beginning to taste a little sour.

One hour later, it tasted even sourer. He still hadn't seen anything that even vaguely resembled signs of habitation. Neither had he seen anything to make him revise his first opinion, which had been that only a complete idiot would choose to try to raise anything on land as barren and inhospitable as the E-Bar-E.

Bee Kendrick had said something about horses. James hadn't even seen a gopher. The only sign of life he had come across was a large snake, type unknown, coiled to one side of the track, looking as miserable as James felt. He gave the snake a wide berth. He estimated that he had traveled at least four miles from the point where he had entered the property. It sure was one hell of a spread, even for a guy as rich as Everly was supposed to be. On the other hand, looking at the quality of the land, he'd probably bought it for around ten cents an acre.

The dirt track started to ascend gently toward a line of hills which, to James, looked at least two miles away. In fact, they were three and a half miles. It took him almost another hour to reach them. By now he was in as foul a mood as he could remember. The gradient had become much steeper. He decided that if he didn't see anything promising when he crested the rise, he was going to turn round and go home. Screw Everly, screw Charlotee and her crazy brother, and screw the impulse that had brought him this far. Then he reached the top of the ascent which coincided with a bend in the track, and he saw what E-Bar-E was all about.

The low hill he had been climbing fell away almost vertically. The dirt track skirted the edge in three long, lazy loops down to the canyon floor two hundred feet below. At that point, the track disappeared, swallowed up by trees. There were pines, firs, aspens and blue spruce dotting a landscape which, from here, seemed to be knee high in grass. The whole area was saucer-shaped and James estimated it had to be at least eight miles across. There had to be a pretty major source of water down there because the whole valley was incredibly fertile. James looked back the way he had come, across unlimited desert scrub. He looked out toward the valley again. The contrast was almost indecent. Three-quarters of a mile across the valley floor, almost completely obscured by trees, was a group of buildings. He might have missed seeing them entirely except for the fact that there were a couple of thin plumes of smoke rising almost vertically through the thin rain. Metaphorically girding his loins for the last assault, he started down toward the valley floor.

He was halfway down the second loop of the dirt road when he heard the vehicle. Looking back he saw a jeep heading down toward him. He moved to the edge of the track and waited for the jeep to reach him. There were two men in the vehicle, both dressed like working cowboys. The jeep slithered to a muddy stop, level with him.

The man behind the wheel was one of the thinnest guys James had ever seen. His Levi work clothes looked like they had been sprayed onto a bundle of sticks. He wore the mandatory battered Stetson and well-scuffed Western boots. His face resembled a dried up wadi, all creases and cracks. His eyes were light blue with absolutely no warmth in them. He could have been anywhere between forty and sixty. His companion was dressed the same way with his Stetson tipped well down over his forehead. Both men were wearing slickers over their work clothes. The one behind the wheel regarded James dispassionately for a moment.

"That your vehicle back there?" he said finally. He pronounced it with three distinct syllables, "vee-hick-ul."

James admitted to being the owner of said vehicle.

"How come you didn't see the sign?"

"What sign?"

"The sign that said keep out."

"I saw it," said James. "I'm here to see Mr. Everly."

"Is that a fact. What you want to see him about?"

"It's personal."

The man looked at him a moment longer. He turned to his companion who had taken no part in the proceedings. "You want we should give him a ride?"

The other man shrugged as though it made no difference to him either way.

The driver turned back to James. "Tell you what, son. We'll give you a ride to the bunkhouse. You can make a phone call from there 'bout your car."

"What about Everly?"

"What about him?"

"Is he at the ranch?" asked James, beginning to feel like he'd wandered onto the set of a Western movie.

"Maybe he is, maybe he isn't. We'll find out when we get there. Now get in back, 'cause I ain't waitin' around much longer."

James got in back, wedging himself between a saddle covered with a blanket, and a sack of something that gave off a smell of old manure. Even before he'd settled, the jeep was in motion again. Neither of the men said another word until they reached the buildings that made up the ranch complex.

There were two bunkhouses. There was another building which housed the mess hall and kitchen, and a couple of outbuildings which could have been used for anything. There was a large horse barn and there was the main ranch house, a single-story L-shaped building constructed of logs and adobe. It looked solid and practical, without the frills one would have expected from a man like Everly who, if Bee Kendrick was right, only did his ranching between drinks.

The jeep pulled up outside one of the bunkhouses. The man at the wheel turned to James.

"What did you want to see Mr. Everly about, son?"

"I said it was personal," said James.

"How's he gonna know if he wants to see you if I can't tell him what it's about?"

"Tell him my name is James Reed. I live along the beach from his place in Malibu, and I saved him from drowning last week."

"Is that a fact."

"Yes, it's a fact," said James, who was getting tired of the Gary Cooper act.

"Is that a fact?" said the driver, turning to the other man, who hadn't moved.

"What are you asking him for, for Christ's sake," said James, patience finally exhausted. "Go tell Everly what I said or do you want me to find him and tell him myself?"

"No point losin' your shirt, son," said the driver. "I only work here."

"What at? Making visitors feel at home?" said James.

"He could be right," said the other man, speaking for the first time. "Somebody dragged me upstairs. It sure as hell wasn't the gimp."

"You was drunk?" asked the driver.

"Away from here, I'm always drunk," said Everly.

He tipped his Stetson back on his head and James recognized his very fair hair. That was all he recognized. The man sitting in front of the jeep bore no resemblance to the drunk at the beach. He was clean-shaven, his eyes were bright and he looked as if he had spent the last six months riding the range. He must have the constitution of an ox, decided James. In his experience, anyone as drunk as Everly had been that night should have taken a month to dry out.

"Hi, Everly," said James. "Remember me?"

"Can't say that I do, friend," said Everly. Even his voice was different. He spoke with a slight twang, imitating the cadence of his companion. The man's a fucking chameleon, thought James. He changes his personality as he changes his clothes.

"Tell you what," continued Everly. "Wally will get you fitted out with some dry clothes. Then you come on over the main house and we'll talk." He started to ease himself out of the jeep.

"We'll do something about your car later." A moment later he was striding toward the ranch house. He even walked like a cowboy.

"You heard the boss, son," said Wally. "Let's go."

He raided a couple of lockers in the bunkhouse and came up with a shirt and a pair of jeans which James was able to get into. Boots were more of a problem. Eventually he dug out an old pair of sneakers which James pronounced fit to wear. While he was changing, James tried to ask some questions about Everly. But Wally became even more monosyllabic than before, his conversation degenerating into a series of *yups* and *nopes*, with a lot more of the latter.

Yup, Everly had been up at the ranch a week now. Nope, he didn't say nothing 'bout the flooding. Nope, he don't talk much 'bout what he does when he's off the ranch. And, yup, even if he did Wally wouldn't tell James about it.

"Where are you from, Wally?" James asked as he finished tying his sneakers.

"Right here," said Wally.

"All your life?"

"Not yet," said Wally. "Maybe see you around later." And he ambled out of the bunkhouse leaving James to make his own way across to the main house.

The house consisted of a large kitchen which obviously did service as a general dining/living area as well, a couple of bedrooms, and one huge room at the back where Everly was waiting for James. It was more or less as Bee Kendrick had described it. There were heads lining the walls, deer, buffalo and even a lion. Animal skins were scattered across the tiled floor and one wall held as large a collection of guns as James had seen outside an arsenal. The furniture upholstery looked as if it had been running around the veld at some time in its earlier existence and a huge marlin mounted on one wall was evidence that a creature didn't have to have four legs for Everly to kill it. There was one section of wall devoted to photographs. Everly with a dead lion,

Everly with a dead buffalo, Everly with a bunch of Zulu beaters, and Everly with another man, an older version of himself, the two of them squatting on the huge carcass of a dead elephant. There was Everly on skis, on the back of a polo pony, at the helm of a yacht and shaking hands with Gerald Ford.

The man himself was sitting behind an enormous dark wood desk. He got to his feet as James came in.

"You want a beer?" he asked.

"Do you have any Scotch?" asked James.

"Bourbon?"

James agreed bourbon would do fine. Everly poured him a stiff shot. He didn't pour one for himself. He went back behind his desk telling James to sit himself wherever he wanted.

"Reed? Is that what you said your name was?"

"James Reed. I live down the beach from your place in Malibu."

"I guess you must have something pretty important you want to talk to me about, seeing the trouble you've gone to."

"I rather hoped you'd tell me," said James.

"You're English," said Everly.

"I've been in America quite some time," said James. He liked to think that his accent no longer gave him away.

"So, what's it all about?"

"The night of the flood..." started James.

Everly held up his hand. "Hold on. No good asking me anything about that night. I was unconscious. I didn't even know there'd been a flood till I woke up next morning. Christ, the place was a mess."

"It still is," said James.

"Maybe I'll get some people to go clean it up," said Everly. He didn't sound particularly concerned whether he did or didn't.

"After I dragged you upstairs I heard a noise from the bedroom," said James. "There was this naked chick emptying your safe."

Everly said nothing. He continued to stare at James across the top of his desk. Finally he stood up. "Maybe I'll join you in a beer," he said.

He fetched a can of beer. This time he didn't return behind the desk. He took a seat in an armchair across from James.

"What else did you see?" he asked.

"Nothing. I figured she belonged there and I left."

Everly took a long pull from the beer can, then he peered down at the can like he was seeing it for the first time. After a moment, he looked up at James again.

"Yeah," he said.

James waited for him to continue. He didn't. "Yeah what?"

"Yeah, she belonged there."

"Mind if I have another drink?" said James.

"Help yourself."

James poured himself another bourbon. He knew Everly was watching him. He took his time pouring the drink. "I guess she was entitled to rifle the safe," he said. Everly didn't answer. James carried his drink back to his seat and sat down again. "That being the case, why did she feel the need to keep me quiet?"

"I don't know what you're talking about," said Everly.

James told him. He told him about the rape charge, the visit from Charlie and the deal that had been made for Charlotee to drop the charge.

"Why would they go through that just because I caught her emptying what you're as good as saying is her own safe?"

Everly thought about this for a moment. "What's in this for you?" he said, finally.

"I don't like being fucked over," said James. "I'm dragged downtown. I'm booked for rape. I get involved with an attorney who's a greedy creep, and I've had to spend more time than I can spare right now getting out from under a situation that only came about because I tried to do a shit-faced drunk a good turn."

"According to what you just told me, you're already out from under. She dropped the charges."

"I want to know why," said James.

"No, you don't," said Everly. "You want to get even."

"Bet your ass I want to get even. Wouldn't you?"

"Given the same circumstances, I guess I would."

James swallowed his drink and went to pour another.

"The way I see it, the only way I'm going to get even is to find out what the hell was going on that night. Maybe get them both sent up for burglary. Now you tell me she was entitled to empty your safe. Okay, I don't believe a word of it, but there's nothing I can do about it as long as you sit there lying to me."

"Would you consider yourself a hard case?" said Everly, after another long silence.

"I'm not a hard case, I'm just a vindictive bastard." He walked back to his chair with his fresh drink. "That means if you can't help me, I'm going to have to find another way. Some of it's going to rub off on you."

"What makes you think I'm lying?" said Everly.

"Come on," said James. "Just because you found me wandering around in the desert doesn't mean I've got sunstroke. You want me to tell you how I figure it?"

"Go ahead," said Everly.

James didn't mean to give him the whole scenario, but once he got started he got carried away.

Charlotee was shacking at the beach house with Everly. Right?

Everly said nothing, neither agreeing nor disagreeing.

Okay. She was around long enough to get the layout of the house, locate the safe and figure a way to get hold of the combination. All she need do then was wait around for Everly to pass out, go on a trip, take a walk on the beach ... whatever. Everly obliged. The night of the flood he passed out cold. She called brother Charlie. While she was waiting for him to pitch up, she emptied the safe. They picked up a few hundred dollars cash, not bad for a couple of days sleeping around with a guy who probably never got sober enough to do anything anyway.

And that would have been an end to it. Except they found something else in the safe, something more valuable than a few hundred dollars. And whatever it was, they had to know that Everly wasn't going to report the robbery.

But what about the other guy, the schmuck who saw Charlotee with her sticky fingers in the safe? Can't have him fucking up whatever it is they've stumbled onto. So they come up with this rape scam. That'll keep him quiet while we go about our business with Harold J. Everly, Esquire.

About here, James went to get himself some more ice. Everly hadn't said a word. He just sat in his armchair, motionless, sometimes looking at James and sometimes staring off through the large picture window as though what was going on outside was the only possible thing that interested him. There was nothing going on outside except that it had stopped raining. James turned back from the ice bucket.

"You want another beer?" he asked.

"Nope," said Everly. He got to his feet and walked over to the window. He stood for a short time, his back to the room.

Okay, thought James, he wants some thinking time, that's what he'll get. Maybe he'll think his way into saying something, even if it's only good-bye. Finally, Everly turned back to James.

"You like to ride?" he asked.

James hated to ride. "Sure," he said.

Everly went to the door and opened it to the passage that led to the kitchen.

"Wally," he called. "Saddle a couple of horses."

James heard Wally call back from the kitchen. "Can he ride?"

Everly turned to James. "Can you?"

"Adequately," said James.

"He says he can ride adequately," called Everly.

Wally's voice came floating back over the sound of the back door. "I'll saddle him an adequate horse."

Ten minutes later, James and Everly walked out to where Wally was waiting with a couple of horses. Everly had insisted on lending James a pair of boots. They were as soft as cashmere. They must have cost a thousand bucks.

While James didn't like to ride, he wasn't bad on a horse, providing the animal behaved itself. "She won't give you no trouble, son," said Wally, as James mounted up. A moment later James kicked the horse into following Everly.

"I wish he'd stop calling me 'son,'" he said when he had caught up.

"How old do you think he is?" asked Everly.

"Fiftyish," said James, guessing at a middle point.

"He's seventy-two," said Everly. "I've known him since I was knee-high. He taught me to ride. Taught me other things too."

He didn't teach you how to hold your liquor, thought James. Or how to be a good liar. Or how to stay out of trouble.

It was as if Everly read his mind. "Pity he didn't teach me to stay off the booze," he said.

James didn't feel any comment was called for so he said nothing. He knew that Everly was in the process of making a decision. Either he was going to come clean with James or he was going to kick him out on his ass. Either way, James could do nothing but wait.

Half a mile from the ranch complex, the heavy trees and brush gave way to open meadow. Unfenced, it stretched to the far side of the canyon, nearly six miles away. James could see a couple of small herds of horses grazing in the distance, while over to the east of the canyon, some two miles off, he saw a herd of cattle about fifty strong being driven by four mounted men. It looked as if they were heading for the corral that James had seen as they had ridden out. The "ropin' an' brandin' time" that Bee had spoken about. Again Everly seemed to catch his thought patterns.

"I suppose Bee told you where I was," he said.

James admitted it had been Bee.

"Thought I recognized her voice on the phone last night," said Everly. "Bet you told her you wanted to stick it to me one way or another."

"Something like that," said James.

"Poor old Bee. She wants nothing more than for me to drop dead as painfully as possible."

James didn't argue with him. There didn't seem much point.

Everly pulled ahead as the trail narrowed. After five minutes, as it widened again, he slowed to allow James to catch up once more. The five minutes had decided him.

"I'm going to marry Charlotee," he said.

"Shit," said James. Then, in case he had been too hasty, "What I mean is…" For the life of him he couldn't think of anything else to say except "Shit" once again.

"I take your point," said Everly.

"So what was it all about?" said James. "The whole rape bit?"

"You're a pretty smart man, James. You mind if I call you James?"

James didn't mind and told him so.

"You figured it out almost exactly the way it happened," said Everly.

"I'm sorry," said James. "You're losing me. If you and she are getting married, then everything I figured is hog-wash."

"Now it's hogwash. It wasn't then."

James pondered this a moment. "She did find something other than small change in the safe."

"She did."

"What?"

"That's not important."

"You mean you're not going to tell me."

"That's exactly what I mean. Anyway, their first inclination was straightforward blackmail. Then the gimp had a better idea.

Marry the jerk. He's worth a couple of hundred million. Either he's going to drink himself to death, and we'll get the lot, or you can divorce him and we'll get half. Either way is better than just getting a monthly payment. Good thinking?"

James admitted it was good thinking. "It sounds like something Charlie'd come up with," he said.

"So what the hell," said Everly. "She's not going to hang around playing housewife. It won't make any difference to my life whether I'm married to her or not. As far as the money's concerned, I've got ten times more than I can spend if I live to be ninety."

"That's not the point though, is it," said James.

"Wally wanted to get them both out here to the ranch... just to talk to them, he said. I swear he'd have blown their brains out and buried them out here someplace."

"Wally knows?"

"I tell Wally everything."

"How about what they found in the safe?"

"He knows that too," said Everly. "And before we go any further, don't bother asking again what it is."

"I wasn't going to," said James.

Everly glanced sideways at him. "You're not even curious?"

"Sure, I'm curious. But I'll tell you something, Mr. Everly, the older I get, the less I want to hear other people's secrets."

"Even if knowing them could make you rich?"

"I wouldn't marry you even if you asked me," said James.

Everly laughed. "So what say we forget the whole thing. We'll have some supper and then I'll drive you into Vegas."

"You don't have to do that," said James.

"I know I don't. But right now I feel like getting drunk, and I don't want to do it on my own."

"Wally will keep you company."

"Wally hates it when I drink. That's one of the reasons I stay dry when I'm here."

"What's the other?"

"When I'm here, I don't have any reason to drink."

He pulled his horse around, facing back the way they had come. "I suppose you don't want to race me back to the ranch house," he said.

"You're right," said James. "I don't want to race you back to the ranch house."

He watched as Everly kicked his horse into a gallop, then he let his own mount have its head. It must have been close to feeding time because the horse immediately broke into a gallop which rattled James's teeth.

By the time James reached the ranch complex, Everly had unsaddled and gone indoors. Wally was waiting for him. He took the reins as James dismounted.

"Nice ride, son?" he asked.

James admitted he'd had a nice ride.

"Seems like you're not the trouble I was expectin' you was going to be," said Wally, as he started to uncinch the saddle.

"I'm never any trouble, Wally," said James.

Wally looked at him across the back of the horse who was sweating from his recent gallop.

"Bet you could be if you wanted," said Wally. Before James could say anything, Wally dragged the saddle from the horse's back and started toward the barn. "Better get yourself washed up, son, supper'll be on soon."

They ate supper in the mess hall with the ranch hands. There were half a dozen guys apart from James, Wally and Everly. True to the Western tradition, there was a Chinese cook and the food was pretty terrible. But everyone seemed to enjoy it. The atmosphere around the long, plain wood dining table was one of easygoing conviviality. Everly might have been the owner of the spread and worth two hundred million dollars but it didn't seem to impress anyone at the supper table. James tried to imagine how Bee Kendrick could have fitted in here. He couldn't.

Halfway through the meal, a young, tousle-haired cowboy across the table suddenly pointed a forkful of potato at James.

"I know you," he said.

"Sure you do," said James. "We just met."

"I know you from before. You were a movie star or something. I used to read the fan mags when I was a kid. I seen your picture."

"I'm not Michael Caine," said James.

"You wanna mind your own business, Eddie," said Wally from across the table.

The young guy looked embarrassed suddenly, shoveling the forkful of potato into his mouth. "Sorry," he mumbled. Then it came to him. "You was married to Katherine Long." He blurted it out, took a quick look toward Wally, and then back to James. "Sorry," he said again.

"That's right, I was," said James.

Now the whole table was looking at him. James could hear the unasked questions. What was it like being married to a movie star? Was she as sexy as she is on the screen? How come someone like Katherine Long, who'd been called the thinking man's sex symbol, would marry a limey who obviously didn't have a pot to piss in and how come that limey was dumb enough to let her slip through his fingers? James had been here before, many times. Now someone else's memory was jogged.

"You're a cop," said an older guy further down the table. "I read once you're a cop."

"I was a cop," said James. "That was in London, and it was a long time ago."

"So how come a limey cop gets to…" started the same guy, but he didn't get to finish.

"You brung in all the beef, Hank?" said Wally.

The man who'd fingered James as a cop turned to Wally. "You know I have, Wally. You helped me with the count."

"Seems maybe we were a couple of head short."

"Hundred and twelve head," said Hank. He turned to the table in general. "Am I right? Hundred twelve head?"

Somebody said something from the other end of the table, and in a moment everyone seemed to be talking at the same time. But they were talking about beef, not about James, who caught the wink that Wally gave him.

Five minutes later, Everly nodded toward James and the two of them got up from the table. Nobody seemed to notice as they walked out of the mess hall. The Chinese cook hurried after James.

"I iron your clothes mister. They're over in the house."

James thanked him and walked with Everly back to the main house.

"Meet you out front in fifteen minutes," said Everly as he disappeared into his room.

James changed back into his own clothes. It was just after seven. Supper was eaten early on a working ranch. Fifteen minutes later he was waiting outside for Everly. It was dark already. The rainclouds had long gone, giving way to a clear night sky which, here in the desert, seemed close enough to touch. There was a slight chill in the air and James wished he'd brought a topcoat along with him. Except he hadn't expected to be here this long. Quite what he had expected, he wasn't sure any more.

"Sorry 'bout the boys back there Mr. Reed." It was Wally. James hadn't heard a sound.

"Shit! You scared me," said James.

"Sorry 'bout that too," said Wally, emerging from the shadows. "Strangers come out here 'n the boys just get naturally curious. It ain't none of their business, but they don't mean no harm."

"Forget it," said James. "It happens all the time."

"I s'pose it does," said Wally. "You goin' t'Vegas with Mr. Everly?"

"That seems to be the idea," said James.

"Are you a drinking man, Mr. Reed?"

"Some."

"But not like him."

"No, Wally. Not like Mr. Everly."

"You wanna do me a favor 'n keep an eye out for him," said Wally. "I'd do it m'self, but he don't do no drinkin' when I'm around."

"So come with us," said James.

"Cain't do that," said Wally. "Cain't go into Vegas. There's some fellas layin' for me."

"What about the police?" asked James.

"Them's the fellas," said Wally.

They heard a car engine start up from around back. "He's fetchin' round the jeep," said Wally. "I'll say good night."

"Good night, Wally," said James.

Wally started toward the bunkhouse, then he turned back. "When Mr. Everly's pa died, I promised the old man I'd take care of the boy. Up to now I ain't done much good at it. So's if there's anything you can do 'bout this marryin' business, I'd be mighty grateful."

He was caught momentarily in the headlights as Everly pulled around to the front of the main house. He waved casually toward the jeep before moving on.

James climbed into the passenger seat and Everly took off. For a time they drove in silence. It was only when they were heading up the escarpment out of the valley that Everly spoke.

"Wally fusses too much," he said.

"He promised your pa he'd take care of you."

"He told you that, uh!"

"Is he really in trouble with the police in Vegas?"

"Some."

"Big trouble?"

"He beat up on a couple of cops."

"A seventy-two-year-old man!"

"He pistol-whipped them."

"What were they doing, for Christ's sake?"

"Beating up on me."

Everly drove in silence for a short time. The dirt road was still slippery from the recent rain. Negotiating the hairpin loops toward the top of the canyon took concentration.

"I was drunk at the time," said Everly, finally. "Got myself into an argument with a pit boss. In the old days the casino would have taken care of it themselves. I'd probably be buried someplace out in the desert. Nowadays, they call the law when they have a problem. The cops were cool. They were going to take me downtown and throw me in the tank to dry out. Only Wally had other ideas. He told them he'd take me home and there wouldn't be any more trouble. They told him to mind his own business. Then I threw up over one of them. He belted me across the head with his nightstick and Wally lost his temper. I found out later, one of them got a busted arm and the other had sixteen stitches put in his head. That's why Wally can't go to Vegas."

"You weren't booked as an accessory?" said James.

"I would have been. Wally threw me in the back of the car and drove back here before the cops had got up off the sidewalk."

"So they've got your number in Vegas too," said James.

"I went back a couple of days later and cleared the charge."

"How did you do that?"

"You can buy anything in Vegas if you've got the money."

"Why didn't you buy off Wally's charge too?"

"I did. Officially Wally can go to town anytime he wants. Unofficially, they told me those two cops will beat the shit out of him next time they see him."

"Vegas is a big town."

"Vegas is a village. Everyone knows everyone else. There's got to be a dozen people, dealers, bartenders, pit bosses, cocktail waitresses, you name it. If Wally stuck his head into town, those cops would know about it inside ten minutes."

They reached the top of the escarpment and started down the dirt track to the floor of the desert. Everly drove faster now. James had to hold onto the top of the windshield to avoid being thrown clear out of the jeep. They reached the place where James's car was stuck. James suggested they try to tow it out.

"Forget it," said Everly. "I'll have a couple of the boys pick it up and take it back to the agency tomorrow."

"Let me grab my bag," said James.

Everly pulled over and waited while James fetched his overnight bag from the car. He locked the car and gave the keys to Everly as he climbed back into the jeep. Everly threw them into the glove compartment and drove on.

They swung out of the ranch property onto the highway, turning in the opposite direction from Las Vegas. Before James could comment, Everly told him he needed to pick something up before going into town. Two miles down the highway Everly pulled the jeep into the forecourt of a beat-up gas station. He pulled up close to a ramshackle workshop and sounded the horn. Almost immediately a young guy came out of the workshop.

"Hi there, Mr. Everly. Wally called. She's all gassed and ready."

"Thanks Harvey," said Everly, climbing out of the jeep.

"What time you gonna be back?" asked Harvey.

"No idea," said Everly. "Leave the keys when you go to bed." He turned to James. "Come on," he said.

James followed him into the workshop. Most of it was taken up by a dark blue Bentley Mulsanne which looked as if it had just come off the showroom floor.

"Throw your bag in the back," said Everly. He got into the driver's seat. James did as he was told and got in beside Everly. A moment later they were on the road again.

"It's a nice car," said Everly by way of an explanation. "But it doesn't like the drive to the ranch."

James could see his point. Hundred-twenty-thousand-dollar automobiles weren't cut out for desert driving, wet or dry.

Everly set the cruise control at eighty-five and sat back. For one moment James thought he was going to take his hands off the wheel and leave the whole trip to the car, but he didn't. The inside of the car smelled of new leather. James glanced over at the odometer. It showed just over 25,000 miles. You get what you pay for, thought James.

"You English sure know how to make a nice automobile," said Everly. "You ever drive one of these?"

"My wife had a Rolls," said James. "I used to chauffeur her around in it."

"I met her once, your wife," said Everly.

"Ex-wife."

"Whatever."

"How long ago?"

"Six months. Thereabouts."

"How was she?" It had been almost a year since James had spoken to Katherine.

"I don't know. I was too drunk."

They drove in silence for a few miles, eating up the highway in their soundproof cocoon.

"That right about you being a cop?" said Everly.

"Ex-cop," said James.

"What kind of a cop?"

"Your general run-of-the-mill cop. Drugs mostly."

"What happened?"

"A bust turned sour on me. They allowed me to retire one jump ahead of a court of inquiry."

"It's the same over here," said Everly. "The police take care of their own."

James had always considered he'd been handed a very raw deal by his superiors, but he'd grown used to it so he didn't mention it. Besides, there were other things he wanted to talk about.

"You really going to marry that chick?" he asked.

"One way or another I'm going to have to pay out a lot of money," said Everly. "This way I'm not going to have the IRS breathing down my back wanting to know where it's all going. I'll even file a joint return, get some of it off my taxes. Might even fuck her a couple of times too," he added. "Providing I stay sober long enough to get it up."

"You haven't fucked her yet?"

"I've hardly spoken to her. She wandered in off the beach one day. Before I knew it she'd moved in. Have you?"

"What?"

"Fucked her?"

"No," said James.

They drove another ten miles in silence. This time it was James who spoke first.

"You want out?" he asked.

At first he thought Everly hadn't heard him. He was about to ask the question again.

"That's a dumb question," said Everly.

"Not so dumb," said James. "You might be one of those masochistic guys who just love to screw up their lives. Maybe you even get a kick out of behaving like a prize asshole."

This time Everly remained silent for so long James thought perhaps he'd gone too far.

"There's no way," he said finally.

"Because of what they found in the safe," said James. It was a statement, not a question.

"Forget it," said Everly.

"Suit yourself," said James. "Only trying to help."

"You're trying to get even," said Everly.

"That too."

They didn't speak again until they were coming down the long stretch of freeway that entered Las Vegas from the north. One moment there was the darkness of the desert all around them, then, as they rounded a low series of hills, it was as if suddenly somebody had switched on every colored light in the world. From here, the city looked like a fairyland, a giant Christmas tree, a magic carpet of color. It even looked like a fun place to be heading toward.

"I hate this place," said Everly.

"So why come here?"

"They know me. When I get too drunk to stand up, they check me into a suite and lock the door till I'm sober enough to drive home again."

"Sounds friendly," said James.

"Not really. They know I'll drop a few grand at the tables before I pass out."

"If you're such a high roller how come they called the cops on you that time?"

"I went to the wrong casino. As long as I stick to the Palace, I'll be okay."

"In which case, you can drive me to the airport first," said James.

"Stick around for a couple of drinks," said Everly.

"I can't afford it," said James.

"On me," said Everly. He fumbled in his inside jacket pocket and produced a roll of hundred-dollar bills which, to James, looked as bulky as the Sunday *New York Times*. "Take what you need," he said.

"Thanks. But no thanks," said James.

"Look on it as down payment," said Everly, still holding the roll of money toward James.

"On what?" said James.

"We'll think of something," said Everly. He pushed the money into James's jacket pocket.

James settled back in his seat. It seemed he was going to get even after all.

CHAPTER FOUR

The Bentley was taken from Everly in the forecourt of the Palace. One of the guys in charge of the parking attendants dealt with it personally.

"Good to see you again, Mr. Everly," he said. He handed the keys to one of his minions. "Take care of Mr. Everly's car." Back to Everly. "I'll have it washed and waxed for you, Mr. Everly." The car disappeared before James remembered he had left his overnight bag in the back. He was about to say something to the parking guy when Everly called to him from the main doors of the hotel.

"Come on, buddy. I need a drink."

As James moved up the steps to join Everly, the parking guy picked up his phone and punched an internal number. "Everly's just arrived," he said. He saw that James had overheard him. He grinned. "Have a good time, buddy," he said.

As always, the interior of the casino looked like James's idea of purgatory, that half-world between this and the next where lost souls wander around while the powers that be decide where to send them. The main show was letting out after the first performance, spilling out fifteen hundred people. They mingled with the fifteen hundred lining up for the next show. The tables were all doing great business, as were the rows and rows of slots. Cocktail waitresses, dressed in very short white tunics, moved between the tables taking orders for free drinks from customers who the pit bosses had decided were betting sufficient money.

The noise was built up on three levels, one on top of the other. First there was the steady hum of a couple of thousand voices desperately trying to have a good time. Over that was the noise peculiar to Las Vegas casinos, the clicking of the slots, and the impersonal voice over the public address constantly calling someone or other to the telephone. And over that was the occasional explosion of excitement coupled with the yells of encouragement from the crap tables. As soon as he walked into the place, James felt a headache coming on.

He followed Everly toward one of the bars. Before they reached it a slim, middle-aged guy in a beautifully fitting dark suit cut across toward them, heading Everly off.

"Good to see you again, Mr. Everly," he said.

"Hi, Milo," said Everly.

"They told me you just pulled in. Anything you need, just ask."

"This is a friend of mine," said Everly, introducing James. "I want you to take care of him."

"No problem," said Milo. He turned to James. "Mr .... ?"

"Reed. James Reed."

"Of course. From Los Angeles. Right?"

"Right," said James. Then to make it easier for Milo to check up on him, "Malibu," he added.

"Give him all the credit he needs, Milo," said Everly. "I'll guarantee it."

"Naturally," said Milo. His light gray eyes filed away James's face for future reference. "Enjoy yourselves gentlemen," he said before moving away.

There were two stools available at the bar. Everly grabbed them just ahead of a couple of kids who were too young to be drinking anyway. He ordered two large Scotches, without bothering to ask James what he wanted. The drinks arrived. Everly picked up his and looked at it for a moment. Then, before drinking it, he turned to James.

"Chances are, as the evening develops, I might say a couple of things I don't mean. I won't even remember them when I sober up. So you can do me a big favor by not taking any notice of what I say, and not reminding me about it later. Okay?"

"Okay," said James.

Everly raised his glass. "Mud in your eye," he said.

"Cheers," said James.

That, basically, was the last intelligible conversation James had with Everly until the following morning. He ordered a second drink before the first could hit bottom and five minutes later the Everly of the past few hours had disappeared and been replaced by the guy James had rescued from drowning on his own living room floor.

Four drinks later, at which time James hadn't even finished his first, Everly announced he was going to try his luck at the blackjack tables. He'd been gone a couple of minutes when James remembered the money Everly had stuffed in his pocket in the car. He settled the bar tab and went to look for Everly, his benefactor.

He found him playing at the hundred-dollar blackjack table. Or rather, the dealer was playing, Everly was just providing the money. It was a system that seemed to work. The only decision that Everly was required to make was how many chips to put out on the next hand. James watched him ask for a hit on nineteen.

"You don't want to do that, Mr. Everly," said the dealer.

"Whatever you say friend," said Everly.

The dealer turned a ten to the eight he had showing and Everly won five hundred dollars. The pit boss had his eye on the table so obviously the dealer was acting in accordance with the house rules as they applied to Harold J. Everly.

James watched him empty the glass in front of him. Immediately it was replaced by a fresh drink. Everly tipped the cocktail waitress with a twenty-five-dollar chip. The seat next to him was vacant. James slipped into it just as the dealer started to lay out another hand.

"You playing, mister?" asked the dealer.

James waved the cards away and watched as Everly dropped five hundred dollars. Even the dealer hadn't been able to help him this time, turning up twenty-one to Everly's twenty.

"What do you want done with the money you gave me?" James asked.

Everly looked at him for a moment as though he didn't recognize him. Then he smiled. "It's your money, James old buddy."

There didn't seem much point in arguing about it right now. James went back to the bar where he ordered himself another drink. While he was waiting for it, he counted the money that Everly had given him. It came to $3,200.

A down payment, Everly had said. James pulled from his pocket the slip of paper on which he had been recording his expenses.

Dinner with Gloria, $438 plus tip. Lunch with Bee, $158 plus tip. Cab from Bee's house to pick up his car, $20. He estimated what the car rental would be, then he added in the cost of the airplane ticket and totted the whole thing up. It came to a shade over one thousand dollars. He took ten hundred-dollar bills from what he still considered Everly's money and put them in his wallet. The balance he put back in his pocket. If, in fact, he was now working for Everly, he wanted to keep the records straight. Everly had been extremely vague in the car. "We'll think of something," he'd said when James had asked him what the money was for. It *had* to be in response to James's suggestion that he might be able to extricate Everly from the bind he'd gotten himself into with Charlotee and Charlie. Okay, hotshot, said James to himself, the man's paying you, start earning your money. He ordered another drink. Now that he had convinced himself he was working for Everly, he paid for it with money from Everly's stack of bills. As of now, he decided, he was on expenses.

He should have picked up his bag from Everly's car and taken a cab to the airport. But the fact he was still carrying Everly's money gave him a feeling of responsibility toward his recently acquired benefactor. So he spent the next two hours in the casino, occasionally leaving the bar to discover where Everly had moved to and how he was holding up.

Everly moved from the blackjack table, to the crap tables, to the roulette tables. He tried to get into a high-stakes poker game, but by that time he was so drunk that any game requiring more of him than pushing chips onto the tables was beyond him. Twice, James saw hookers try to attach themselves to him only to be firmly and discreetly driven away by a dark-suited employee of the hotel whose main function, right now, seemed to be to keep Everly free of any distractions which might prevent him losing more money to the house. Also, this man was close at hand every time Everly ran out of money. He would produce a slip of paper from his pocket for Everly to scrawl his signature across and immediately another pile of chips would be handed to him. Sometimes he won, but not very often. James watched him drop sixteen thousand dollars in five minutes on one of the crap tables, tip the table a hundred, move on to a game of roulette and drop another five thousand on two spins of the wheel. All the time he was getting drunker.

The second show turned out of the main showroom and for half an hour there were more people in the casino than it could comfortably handle. Then the crowds started to thin out once more and James went to find Everly for the last time. By now he had a pleasant buzz on. He wasn't drunk, but he wasn't sober either. As far as he was concerned, the evening was over. He didn't fancy the idea of taking a night flight back to Los Angeles and, as long as Everly was going to be provided with a suite by the hotel, James decided he'd use it.

He found Everly back at one of the blackjack tables far too drunk to do anything but just sit there. At the start of each hand, the dealer would ask him how much he wanted to stake and Everly would push a pile of chips into the box. The dealer did the rest, deciding whether Everly should stand or hit, then paying out or raking in depending how the cards came out. And because the dealer was playing strictly according to the book, Everly had started to win. Nobody seemed to mind. At one point, the casino employee who had been watching him all evening reached over and removed ten thousand dollars from Everly's stack of chips and had them returned to the cash desk. James watched the man as he received two of Everly's markers in return and tore them up. The gambler in the large Vegas casinos always got an honest shake. The odds in favor of the house were long enough to make outright stealing unnecessary.

James tapped Everly on the shoulder.

"Put it down here, honey," said Everly, pushing away an empty glass to make room for a fresh drink.

"It's me," said James.

Everly turned, nearly falling off his stool in the process. He stared at James for a moment.

"Who are you?" he said, finally.

"James Reed. Remember?"

Everly groped down into his liquor-sodden mind and managed to come up with a glimmer of recognition. "Hey! Hi, old buddy. You wanna drink?"

James told him he didn't want a drink. What he wanted was to go to bed, and if it was okay with Everly, he'd just bunk down in the suite the hotel was going to provide for their high roller.

"You wanna girl?" asked Everly.

James told him he didn't want a girl.

"Suit yourself," said Everly. Then he called out in no particular direction. "Milo! Hey, Milo, where are you?"

The man who had welcomed Everly at the beginning of the evening appeared almost immediately.

"You gotta room for my ol' buddy here?" Everly asked him.

As far as Milo was concerned, James had dropped no money in the casino, so he was a nonrunner. But evidently Everly's wish was his command. "Of course, Mr. Everly."

"I'll sleep on his couch," said James.

"No need," said Milo. He snapped his fingers and a uniformed bellboy materialized beside him.

"Fetch Mr. Reed the keys to Mr. Everly's suite," he said.

The bellboy disappeared. Milo turned his flat gray eyes onto James once more. "There are two bedrooms in the suite," he said. "You'll find everything you need up there."

"Is he going to be okay?" asked James, nodding toward Everly, who had turned back to the table.

"We'll take care of him," said Milo.

"I bet you will," said James as he saw the dealer rake in a stack of Everly's chips.

"Do you have a problem, Mr. Reed?" said Milo.

"Not me," said James.

"I'm glad to hear it," said Milo. He disappeared almost as quickly as he had appeared.

Everly had already forgotten James and was busy asking the dealer for another drink. James didn't see any point in identifying himself again. He waited for the bellboy to return with the keys and then followed him to the elevators.

"You need a girl?" the bellboy asked as they were waiting for the elevator.

"No," said James.

The elevator arrived. James announced that he was capable of finding his own way to his room and the bellboy handed him the key a shade reluctantly. Conducting Everly to bed was obviously a far more lucrative occupation, a fact confirmed by the expression on his face when James tipped him five dollars.

The suite wasn't so much Arabian Nights as Arabian Nightmares. James felt his headache coming on again as soon as he walked into the place. Through the fourteen-foot-high windows that lined one side of the main room, the Las Vegas strip leered at him so brightly he wished he'd brought sunglasses with him. He spent five minutes trying to drag the drapes shut before he found an electric switch that did it for him. In the center of the room was a circular fireplace blazing brightly without giving off any heat whatsoever. There was a fully stocked bar large enough to seat a dozen heavy drinkers, and more low-slung, overstuffed furniture than James had ever seen outside a warehouse.

As Milo had said, there were two bedrooms that seemed to be competing with each other for a bad-taste award. Eight-foot circular beds with draped canopies, wall-to-wall mirrors, and carpets so thick James felt he was walking through soft sand. The bathrooms stayed in character. Circular baths as large as your average swimming pool bristling with gold-plated plumbing attachments. Twin basins big enough to bathe in, His and Hers lavatories and bidets and enclosed showers which converted into steam rooms large enough to accommodate a football team.

James chose the blue bedroom as opposed to the pink. It seemed slightly less offensive. In the vast closet he found a heavy toweling robe. In the bathroom cabinets were razors, colognes, combs and brushes, hairdryers, toothbrushes, cotton balls, perfume and, in case a guest wanted to be particularly careful, packets of condoms.

James undressed and put on the robe. In the bathroom, he broke the seal on a toothbrush and cleaned his teeth. He broke the seal on a drinking glass and had a drink of water. He broke the seal on a bar of soap and washed. He broke the seal on the toilet and had a pee. Then he went to bed.

He woke up once in the night. It was three A.M. He debated for a moment whether it was worth checking Everly's room. Before he could come to a decision he fell asleep again. The next time he woke it was eight thirty A.M.

He climbed out of bed, pulled on his robe and went to check the other bedroom. Milo had been right when he said the hotel took good care of Everly. A bundle under the bedclothes showed that he had been brought safely to his room sometime in the night. The suit that he had been wearing was hanging in the closet in a plastic bag stamped with the legend of the hotel's cleaning and pressing service and on the nightstand was his billfold, a stack of hundred-dollar chips and a pile of hundred-dollar bills larger than the one he had handed James. Maybe the pile was a couple of hundred short and some bellboy was off having himself a party, but remembering the condition Everly had been in last night, James figured he was entitled.

He closed the bedroom door quietly, waded across the main room to the nearest telephone and called room service for breakfast. While he was waiting, he called the airport and booked himself out on a ten thirty flight to Los Angeles. He called the car rental agency and they confirmed that his car had already been returned and the account settled. That had been Wally's doing, no doubt.

His breakfast arrived, and thirty minutes later he was shaved and dressed. He went back into Everly's bedroom. The bundle was still motionless beneath the covers. James pulled back the sheet and shook Everly by the shoulder. There was no response whatsoever. James confirmed that he was still breathing, rearranged the covers around him and went back into the main room. Using hotel stationery, he made out a receipt to Everly for $3,200. He took it back into the bedroom and put it on the nightstand where Everly would be sure to find it. Back in the main room, he obtained the number of the E-Bar-E ranch from Information and called Wally.

"Your boss is out cold," he said when he had identified himself. "Is it okay to leave him?"

"Where are you?" asked Wally.

"The Palace."

"It's okay," said Wally. "A couple of the guys took your car back this morning. They're hangin' around someplace waitin' for me to call. They'll pick him up and bring him on home."

There was a moment of silence on the other end of the line. James was about to hang up when Wally spoke again. "You fellas talk any last night?"

"Some," said James.
"You wanna tell me?"
"Not much to tell."
"Are we gonna be seeing you around?"
"It's possible," said James.
"Okay, son. Take care of yourself, you hear!" said Wally, and he hung up.

James called him right back.
"I hadn't finished," he said.
"What can I do for you?" asked Wally.
"How much do you know about this marriage business?"
"I figure I know 'bout as much as you."
"When's the happy event?"
"Search me."
"Where do I find the bride-to-be?"
"Don't know that neither. Have you asked the bridegroom?"
"He's a reluctant participant," said James. "Besides, he's unconscious."
"He can't be that reluctant or you'd not be askin' me these questions."
"Okay. Let's say he's ambivalent," said James. "How bad is what they've got on him?"

There was a long pause on the other end of the line, so long that James thought they might have been cut off. "Hello?" he said finally.
"I'm still here," said Wally.
"So? How bad is it?"
"Depends on whose point of view you're takin'," said Wally.
"Make believe I'm a cop."
"Pretty bad."
"Five years bad? Ten years?"
"Could be," said Wally.
"Did he murder somebody?"
There was a fraction's pause before Wally answered. "Would it make any difference?"

"Yes, it would."

"Figured it might," said Wally. "The answer's no. And before you think up anything else to ask me, forget it."

"It could help," said James.

"Is he paying you?"

"I think so," said James.

"You mean you don't know?"

"He gave me some money last night."

"Gamblin' money, drinkin' money, whorin' money?"

"On account, he said."

"On account of what?"

"He said he'd think of something. I'd just asked him if he wanted out."

"Had he started drinking?"

"We hadn't even reached Vegas."

"Then you're being paid, son. That being the case, from now on it's your problem. Have a good flight." He hung up again. This time James didn't call him back.

He checked his bedroom once more to make sure he hadn't forgotten anything. Seeing he had arrived with nothing, it wasn't likely. He came back to the main room to find Everly behind the bar pouring himself a large Scotch. He was draped in one of the sheets from the bed. He looked like a dissolute Caesar.

"Hair of the dog," he said by way of a greeting.

"It must have been a Saint Bernard," said James, eyeing the amount of booze Everly had poured into his glass. Either Everly didn't hear him or he chose to ignore the remark. He gathered his sheet more securely around him and started back toward the bedroom carrying his drink.

"You want to talk to me about anything?" said James.

"No," said Everly as he disappeared into the bedroom.

James followed him in. Everly was just getting back into bed.

"I'm confused," said James.

Everly took a large swallow of the neat Scotch. The fact that he didn't gag was an indication that he was still halfway drunk from last night.

"You know what your problem is?" said Everly.

"Tell me," said James.

"You're so pissed off at those two you can't see straight any more. You want to get even so badly you'd do anything. But you want to dress it all up so's you don't come out looking like the vindictive bastard you are. I've given you that chance and you can't believe your luck." He took another swallow of his drink. "You want some advice?"

"No," said James, who realized that Everly wasn't as drunk as he'd thought.

"So fuck off," said Everly.

"All right. Give me some advice."

"You've got a mean streak in you. Watch out it doesn't screw up your better judgment. Providing you've got any."

"That's it?"

"You're going after those two. Okay, now you can kid yourself you're doing it on my behalf. But if anything goes wrong, and I mean anything, it'll be 'James Reed? Who the hell's James Reed? I've never heard of him.' And don't look for witnesses out at the ranch or here in Vegas because, I promise you, they'll never have heard of you either. So, my advice to you is to tread carefully. Carry a big stick if you like, but don't ever try to tell anyone I gave it to you. You dig me?"

"I dig you," said James. "You want to tell me where I can find them?"

"I don't know."

"You're supposed to be marrying the girl, for Christ's sake."

"My future brother-in-law said they'd be in touch."

"There's an address. A house in Glendale."

"I don't know anything about it."

"When's the happy day?"

"They'll be in touch about that too."

"What are they waiting for?"

"They didn't tell me."

"You're a big help," said James.

Everly grinned without amusement. "Why should I help you? It's got nothing to do with me. Remember?" He finished his drink and held his glass toward James. "You want to get me another drink before you go?"

"Get your own drink," said James.

In front of the hotel, James asked the guy in charge of the parking to have his overnight bag fetched from Everly's car and to call him a cab. Fifteen minutes later, he was waiting to board his flight to Los Angeles, surrounded by departing passengers who were desperately trying to get rid of their last few dollars in the airport slot machines before flying home to Phoenix or Denver or Fort Worth to tell all their friends what a wonderful time they'd had in Las Vegas. Five minutes later, his flight was called.

As usual, he couldn't remember where he had parked his car. He spent fifteen minutes wandering around one of the four-story car parks only to remember, finally, that he had flown out on a different airline than the one he had just come in on. The car was in an identical building six hundred yards away. True to form, the car wouldn't start. He ran the battery flat trying.

He fetched jumper cables from the trunk and, using a trick he'd learned when he was a cop, he unlocked the hood of the car parked next to him and jumped the batteries.

Just as he was beginning to think he'd about run his neighbor's battery flat as well, his engine coughed reluctantly into life. He disconnected the jumper cables and drove off in a cloud of noxious smoke. He felt a momentary twinge of sympathy for the owner of the Mercedes whose battery he had just run flat, but not sufficient to spoil his day.

He found his way out of the airport, no easy feat since they had streamlined the place to handle the 1984 Olympics, and turned onto Sepulveda. He swung left onto Lincoln, drove past Marina del Rey to Santa Monica and onto Pacific Coast Highway. Fifteen minutes later he was home.

There were four calls on his answering machine. One from Gloria, two from Bee Kendrick and one from the offices of Banks, Balkin and Simms saying they hadn't yet received his check. A note had been slipped under his door from the girls in the main house. They were having a party this evening and he would be very welcome. James guessed they planned to make a fair amount of noise and the best way to keep the landlord from complaining was to invite him to participate. He cleared the messages from the machine, changed into a track suit and went for a run on the beach.

As he let himself out of the back gate, Carlotta called down to him from the terrace where she was sunbathing.

"Are we going to see you tonight?"

James said he would try to make it and set off on his run.

He made straight for Everly's house, approaching it from the beach side. He peered in through the doors at the back. Obviously nobody had been here since the night of the flood. Without bothering to hide his actions from any of the neighbors who might have been watching, James knocked out a pane of glass from the door, reached through and let himself in.

The house smelled like the Florida Everglades after a monsoon. The whole of the downstairs was covered with two inches of sand which had only partly dried out. The soft furnishings were still sodden. There was a watermark around the wall at a height of three feet. Anything below that was a complete write-off. Unless somebody did something about drying out the place soon, the same was going to apply to everything else. Already mold had started to form in the corners of the room and at the back of the bar.

James went straight upstairs to the second floor. In the master bedroom, he pulled back the carpet and examined the safe. It fitted flush with the floor and had a single combination dial sunk into the top. An incompetent safecracker could have opened it in five minutes. It took James half an hour. He consoled himself with the fact that he was out of practice. When he finally got it opened, he realized he needn't have bothered. It was empty.

The mirrored closets held some of Everly's clothes. The mold had already taken hold here too. There's nothing like cashmere for growing fungus, thought James. There was nothing of interest on the nightstands other than a couple of half-smoked joints. James figured these had to be a legacy of Charlotee. Everly sought his oblivion in other directions. The other two bedrooms were equally unrewarding. They both looked as though they hadn't been occupied since the house was built.

He went back downstairs. Apart from the living room, there was a formal dining room with seating for eight, a kitchen, and a room next door to the garage which was obviously used as a study. The main item of furniture was a magnificent antique desk that must have cost thirty thousand dollars. One wall was taken up by a stereo and video setup that looked as if a degree in electrical engineering would be needed just to switch it on. Around the other walls there were enough books to stock a medium-sized library.

Here too, the storm had taken its toll. The desk was going to need major restoration work, the electrical equipment was good now only for the junkyard and penicillin was already forming on the book bindings. The wood of the desk, which had, no doubt, survived wars and revolutions, had finally succumbed to the ravages of the Pacific Ocean. It had warped to such an extent that James had to fetch a meat cleaver from the kitchen to force open the drawers.

He found a few papers referring to the buying of the house, an embarrassing letter to Everly from Bee Kendrick, dated six months earlier, some tradesmen's receipts for groceries and booze, and a note to Everly scribbled on the back of a deposit slip torn from a checkbook. The handwriting was sloppy, but the message was clear: *I quit. Mail my money.*

James looked at the printed name and address on the reverse side of the message: *Jaclyn Amway, 2396 W. Beakin, Los Angeles.*

The zip code on the address was for East Los Angeles.

James tucked the slip of paper into the pocket of his track suit and turned to the bookshelves. He figured all the books were ruined by now, so he went through them fast, pulling out each one, shaking it to see if anything fell from between the pages, then dropping it to the floor. It took him twenty minutes to go through the whole library. He found nothing. The kitchen produced nothing more dramatic than a fridge full of bad food. Sometime during the flood the circuit breakers had done what they were supposed to, cutting off all electricity in the house. Nobody had been around to reset them so the house had been without power for eight days. The freezer was worse. There was enough beef in it to supply Lawry's restaurant for a week. It had all gone bad. Lifting the lid was like opening a tomb. James slammed it shut quickly. The crown jewels could have been in there. It would have made no difference. He came back into the living room and tried to think of someplace he might have missed. There was nowhere. Not quite sure what he had hoped to find in the first place, he let himself out and started to jog back to his house.

There was no telephone number on Jaclyn Amway's deposit slip so he called Information. They gave him the number. The phone was answered by a man with the deepest voice James had ever heard.

"I'd like to speak to Jaclyn Amway please," said James.

"She ain't here."

"When will she be back?"

"Who wants to know?"

James gave him his name and number, saying he needed to talk to her as soon as possible.

"You ain't from the welfare?" said the man on the other end. James said he wasn't from the welfare.

The man said he'd give her the message soon as she got in which could be within the next hour or might not be for a week.

"She don't tell me what she's about," he said. He hung up without saying good-bye. James showered, changed his clothes and drove to Glendale.

The house looked the same as the last time he had been here. Locked up and apparently empty. But this time his franchise was different. Last week he had been looking for a girl who had charged him with rape. He had wanted to ask her what the hell it was all about. Now he knew what it had been about.

He didn't bother banging on the back door. Having rung the front doorbell and waited a couple of minutes, he moved round to the back of the house, broke a window and climbed in. The interior smelled musty, like it had been unoccupied for a couple of weeks at least. That figured. If she had been shacking with Everly she wouldn't have been living here. What it didn't explain is where she had been since she disappeared from the beach house.

He went through the place quickly. It was like searching an empty hotel suite. There was nothing personal in the entire place. No clothes, no photographs, makeup, food, liquor, papers or books. In fact, there was nothing that said anybody had ever lived here. There wasn't even a TV set. There was no car in the garage, no garbage in the trash cans.

James tried the telephone. It was still connected, and the electricity was working. That meant that somebody was paying the bills or the utility companies hadn't gotten around to disconnecting their services yet. He went out the same way he had come in, through a window at the back.

Next door, a neighbor had come out of his house and was watering his lawn. He tried to avoid seeing James, conveniently finding a weed in the grass which occupied his full attention while he hoped James would just go away. When he realized that James wasn't going anyplace, he finally straightened up again, turned toward James and tried to smile.

"Nice day," he said.

He was a mild-faced little man who didn't want to deal with guys clambering out of windows of unoccupied houses, even if the house was right next door to his own.

James agreed it was a nice day and asked if the man knew anything about his neighbor.

"We hardly ever see them," said the man.

"Them?"

"They're brother and sister, aren't they? I mean, we don't know them, but my wife spoke to the girl once or twice. She said they were brother and sister."

"You didn't ever speak to them yourself?"

"We don't socialize much," said the man apologetically. Recalling Charlie, James didn't blame him.

"When did you last see them?" he asked.

"Must be a month ago. Looked like they were moving out."

"Is that what they said?"

"We didn't talk to them. We just assumed it. They were loading the car with cartons and stuff." He finally plucked up the courage to ask the question James had been waiting for. "Are you a friend of theirs?"

"An acquaintance," said James. "I need to contact them."

"I'm sorry. I can't help you."

"Maybe your wife knows something," said James.

"She's dead," said the man. "She died last week."

"I'm sorry," said James.

The man looked at him. This time when he smiled, he really meant it. "We all have to go sometime," he said.

As James climbed into his car out front, another car pulled into the short driveway of the little man's house. Out of it got an attractive, comfortable-looking woman in her mid-forties. She was carrying a couple of bags of groceries and wore an expression which announced that, as far as she was concerned, the world was a wonderful place to live in. She smiled happily in James's direction before letting herself into the house with her own key.

James drove down the hill into the town of Glendale. He located a bar, parked the car and went in. He ordered himself a drink and tried to call Jaclyn Amway again. The same deep voice answered the phone.

No, she wasn't home yet, and if James didn't stop bugging him he wouldn't give her the message that he had called in the first place.

James returned to the bar. He downed his drink and ordered another. He was the only customer in the place. Mindful of his calling, the bartender made an effort to start a conversation. He was delighted to discover that James wasn't interested. He retreated to the far end of the bar where he continued to polish the hell out of the glasses. Meanwhile, James peered into his drink rather as though he was hoping that the bottom of his glass might miraculously come up with some answers.

Charlotee and Charlie had apparently disappeared from the face of the earth. It didn't make sense. They'd hooked into a real live one in Everly, and they'd landed him. He'd agreed to make an honest woman out of Charlotee, giving her access to a large share of his $200 million. So where the hell was she? Why weren't she and Charlie dragging Everly up the aisle before he came to his senses and realized there had to be better ways of getting out from under? Deciding the bottom of his glass didn't hold any of the answers, he downed his drink, paid the bartender and headed for home.

He'd chosen a bad time to hit the freeway. It was close to five P.M. and the rush hour was in full swing. The Ventura Freeway is probably the busiest in the city, and it seemed, right now, that every car in Los Angeles was using it. After six miles of being forced to stop and start and never getting above twenty miles an hour, James's car overheated and quietly died on him. He just managed to pull onto the hard shoulder without being hit from behind. There, he got out and opened the hood, fully expecting to be engulfed by flames. There was no fire, but there was enough steam leaking from fifteen different places to power a locomotive.

He walked to the nearest emergency telephone and was told to return to his car and wait. There would be somebody along to assist him at the first available opportunity. They must have been having a field day, because nobody showed up for an hour.

Finally, just when James was seriously considering abandoning the car altogether, a tow truck appeared. It pulled onto the hard shoulder and parked in front of him. Out came a young guy in filthy coveralls with face and hands to match. Beneath the coating of grease and oil, James figured he probably had bright red hair, but he wouldn't have taken money on it. Unlike James, the car had stopped steaming by now. The young guy walked around it once before he said anything at all. Finally he turned to James.

"Sure you want to bother, mister?" he said.

James had worked himself into an extremely bad mood. "Nobody likes a smartass," he said. "Just fix it or tow it someplace they will."

"Got your Auto Club card?"

"I'm not in the Auto Club," said James.

"Fifty bucks," said the young guy. Then, after a second look toward the car. "Up front."

"That's more than the car's worth," said James.

"I know it, mister. That's why I asked if you wanted to bother." He looked as if he had started to enjoy himself. It made a break from his usual routine.

James gave him a credit card which he handled as if he just knew it had to be stolen. He asked to see James's driver's license, and after examining it front and back, he still wasn't convinced. Finally he told James to sit tight, he was going to have to radio in for instructions. He disappeared into the cab of his truck and didn't appear again for ten minutes. It had taken them that long to check the registration of James's car against his driver's license along with the validity of the credit card. James felt like asking whether the kid wanted to count his teeth too, but his initial bad mood had given way to resignation. He helped the kid hitch the car to the tow truck, then he got into the cab for the drive to the service station.

The owner of the station wasn't much older than the boy driving the tow truck, and nearly as dirty. But he was an auto buff. When he first saw James's car being towed in, his eyes lit up with enthusiasm. Then, after he'd had the car unhitched and examined it briefly, he turned on James like a mother who'd just caught a child molester menacing one of her flock.

"You haven't taken care of her," he said.

"Right," said James. "Can you fix it?"

"I can get it started. She's past fixing."

"That'll do," said James.

"Guys like you shouldn't be allowed to own automobiles like this," he said menacingly. He disappeared under the hood for a few minutes. When he emerged, he told James to try the engine. It started first time.

"That'll be fifty bucks," he said to James.

"I already paid," said James.

"That was for the tow. This is for the work."

"Two minutes!"

"Ten years learning how, friend," he said.

James produced his credit card again. The guy started to fill in the details. Halfway through he looked up at James.

"If you'd taken care of her, I'd have done the work for free."

"I'll remember that next time I pass a car wash," said James.

He signed the credit card slip, climbed back behind the wheel and rejoined the rush-hour traffic heading west on the freeway.

He turned off the freeway at Malibu Canyon. Fifteen minutes later, he reached Pacific Coast Highway, and five minutes after that he was home.

Half a dozen cars were parked outside the house, a couple of them completely blocking his garage. It was just after seven P.M. Obviously the girls' party had started early.

James didn't want to go to the party. Knowing the girls' inclinations he guessed the guests would be of similar persuasion. He had nothing against gays. On a one-to-one basis, he enjoyed their company. It was when they flocked that he got depressed. They had a faculty for enjoying themselves rarely found among the straight people he knew. But not being inclined that way himself, he invariably felt like an outsider, on the edge of some conspiracy to enjoy every moment, and the hell with the nonmembers.

He parked the car fifty yards down from the house and let himself in through the front gate hoping he wouldn't be seen from the main house. There was one call on his answering machine. Jaclyn Amway. He dialed her number and she answered the phone herself.

"I can do you half-a-day on Wednesdays providing you're a single gentleman. I don't do for no women," she said.

"I don't need a cleaning lady," said James. In fact, he had needed a cleaning lady for longer than he could remember, but he had never got around to deciding he could afford one.

"Well I figure you ain't after my black ass, so what d'y'all want?" she said.

"I just wanted to ask you some questions," said James.

"You ain't from the welfare is you?" she asked.

The deep brown voice had asked the same question. Obviously the two of them had some scam going with the welfare department that was giving them cause for concern.

James assured her that he wasn't anything to do with the welfare.

"So what y'all wanna ask me?"

"You worked for Mr. Everly in Malibu?"

"So?"

"That's what I want to talk to you about," said James.

"I didn't steal nothing," she said.

"Why did you quit?"

"I told you. I don' do for no women. Womens move in, Jaclyn moves out."

"Charlotee Fisher?"

"I don' know what her name was. Blond, built like a thin stick."

"What can you tell me about her?" asked James.

"Nothin' anybody'd want to hear. She was a mean one, that one was."

"Mean how?"

There was a pause on the other end of the line. James could hear a low rumble of voices. Obviously she was communicating with her live-in. She came back on the line a couple of moments later.

"What's in it for me?" she asked.

"That depends on what you can tell me," said James.

She thought about this for a short time. "Y'all live in Malibu?" she asked finally.

James told her where he lived.

"I'm workin' out there tomorrow. I'll come by 'n visit when I finish. Four o'clock."

James thanked her and hung up. The phone rang immediately. He picked it up. It was Carlotta from the main house.

"I saw your light on," she said. "When are you coming over?"

Because he couldn't immediately come up with a reason not to, James said he'd be over in twenty minutes.

He showered and shaved, put on a clean pair of jeans and a shirt he'd only worn twice, and went to join the party.

His first instincts had been right. He shouldn't have gone. Not because the dozen or so guests were all gay, but because they all came from New York and spent the whole evening agreeing with each other what a terrible place Los Angeles was. While James didn't particularly disagree with any of their statements, he didn't need to hear them again from a bunch of East Coasters. After his fifth drink, he got into an argument with a beautifully groomed middle-aged man with iron-gray hair and large teeth who wondered how anyone who had been brought up in London could possibly settle for living in LA. James pointed out that London, right now, was probably one of the most depressing cities in the world to live in. The man exposed his teeth and brayed his disbelief. How could James say such a thing. Why, he'd been in London only last week... the theater, the ballet, the restaurants, the Connaught, the Ritz, Fortnums and Aspreys... my dear, the whole place is just one big honey jar of sensual delights.

James started to point out that ninety-nine percent of Londoners had never even heard of most of the places just mentioned, let alone used them, but he saw the man's eyes start to glaze with boredom, so he gave up and satisfied himself by telling the man that only a prize asshole would choose London over Los Angeles, and the biggest assholes of them all were the ones who chose New York. He didn't actually believe anything he had said, but he had drunk himself into a mood where he was prepared to disagree with everything.

Carlotta headed him off from another confrontation with an intense young woman who was in Los Angeles trying to raise money to shoot a movie in New York. She'd been to three of the major studios already. They had listened to her politely for a few minutes and then, not quite so politely, pleaded other engagements. James was just about to retort to her phrase "pearls before swine," when Carlotta grabbed him. She eased him over to the bar.

"Enjoying yourself?" she asked.

"I'm having a ball," said James, helping himself to another drink.

"Speaking of which…" said Carlotta.

James was suddenly aware of how close she was standing. Unlike her guests, she was dressed Malibu style, jeans which looked like they'd been sprayed on and a T-shirt that allowed her nipples full prominence. She smelled of fresh lavender, and her full mouth, without benefit of lipstick, looked good enough to be eaten by. James glanced back toward the other guests, looking for Amy. Carlotta read his mind.

"Amy won't mind," she said.

"Sure she will," said James, who wasn't yet sufficiently drunk to risk seeing his lease go out the window.

"She knows I swing both ways," said Carlotta. "Just so long as I come home to roost, she's amenable."

She slipped her hand down between them and pressed it against his crotch. James nearly dropped the bottle he was holding.

"What do you say?" she said.

He glanced back toward Amy once more. As he did so, she turned from the guy she was talking to and caught his eye across the room. She saw the two of them standing close together and gave James a small grin and a fractional tilt of her head. Permission granted. Carlotta saw this interchange. She placed her mouth close to James's ear and whispered that she would join him in the guest house as soon as the last of the guests had gone. Then she flicked the tip of her tongue into his ear before moving away toward a group on the terrace.

James downed his drink, poured himself another, then set about bringing the party to a close as soon as possible. He talked to a couple of fashion designers who announced they were only in LA en route to the Far East, and couldn't wait to get out of the place. He offered to drive them to the airport there and then.

The lady who was trying to raise money for her movie rejoined him and said he should seek professional help to exorcise his "festering aggressions which were obviously caused by his inability to come to terms with his true sexuality." James told her that what she needed was a good fuck, and if she'd care to step outside, he would oblige her.

He made an extremely obscene suggestion to a gentle-faced middle-aged gay who had been calling him "darling boy" whenever they spoke, and finally he told Amy that the neighbors were complaining about all the cars parked outside. She didn't believe him, but she'd had enough of the party herself by then, and she started to bring things to a close.

James left with the other guests, all of whom ignored his over-enthusiastic "Good night, nice to have met you." As he let himself into the guest house, his answering machine was blinking at him. He ignored it and went straight through to the bedroom to change the sheets on the bed. He figured he'd allow Carlotta ten minutes, which would give him time for a quick shower.

He was wrong. He was just soaping himself when the shower door was opened from the outside and Carlotta slipped in beside him. She had dropped her clothes on the bathroom floor. Now she slid straight into his soapy arms, pressing the full length of her body against his. She opened her mouth to kiss him. James dropped the soap and grabbed her.

Her skin felt like wet silk. After a breathless few seconds, he disengaged himself and pushed her to arm's length. He wanted to see if her red hair was natural. He wasn't able to tell. Carlotta, it seemed, was one of those ladies who didn't like body hair. She was as smooth and clean as a newborn babe.

James had always preferred the veiled delights, but right now he couldn't have cared less. He pulled her back into his arms, and without bothering to turn off the shower the two of them slipped to the tiled floor with her straddling him.

It was all over for him embarrassingly quickly. He'd never been what could be called a great lover, one of those supermen who, if one believed what they said, could keep a girl dangling four or five hours, but this was ridiculous.

"Sorry about that," he said. They were still sprawled at the bottom of the shower.

"It'll be better next time," said Carlotta, who didn't seem to mind.

James wondered whether he should mention that, at his time of life, "next time" didn't usually come round for a good few hours. Then she went down on him and he was glad he hadn't said anything, because she started to work miracles.

Eventually they found their way to the bed, where, an hour later, feeling like a ten-foot reincarnation of Casanova, James dropped into an exhausted sleep.

When he woke up a couple of hours later, Carlotta opened her smoky blue eyes at precisely the same moment and went to work on him again. This time she didn't have quite so much success. James started to go down on her but she stopped him. She told him he couldn't possibly be as good at it as Amy and, anyway, if she allowed it she would feel she was being unfaithful. Not unhappy to be let off the hook, James went to sleep again.

When he woke up a couple of hours later all that remained of Carlotta was the faint smell of lavender and sex. She had gone. Feeling inordinately pleased with himself, he rolled over and went back to sleep. He didn't wake up until nine thirty the following morning, and then only because the phone was ringing.

It was Wally from the E-Bar-E.

"You find anything out yet?" he asked, when he had identified himself.

"They've disappeared," said James.

"You're still working on it?"

"Sure I am." He was still half asleep.

"You wanna call me from time-to-time?"

James said that he would, if, and when he had anything to call about. Then he asked if Everly had gotten back from Las Vegas in one piece.

"No problem," said Wally. "The boys picked him up and brought him right on home."

"Tell him I'll send him an accounting of my expenses."

"I'll tell him," said Wally. "But don't lose no sleep over it. He won't."

"Is he really worth two hundred million dollars?" said James.

"That was last time he counted. Three, four years back."

"Meaning it could be less?"

"You work it out son. Make believe he's got his money invested at a nice steady ten percent. I'll talk to you later." He hung up.

James rolled out of bed and into the bathroom. He was cleaning his teeth when it hit him. Two hundred million at ten percent would bring in an income of two million dollars a year, forty thousand a week or, based on a normal forty-hour working week, a thousand dollars per hour. Even Everly couldn't spend that kind of money, he was too drunk most of the time. Assuming a twenty-five-percent expenditure, or half a million dollars a year, his capital would be increasing at a rate of a million and a half a year. Climbing into the shower, James resolved to start padding his expenses.

The shower brought back pleasant memories of Carlotta. When he emerged, he picked up the phone and dialed the main house. Amy answered. He asked to speak to Carlotta.

"She's still sleeping," said Amy. "Did you two have a good time last night?"

James admitted to having a good time. "That's what I wanted to talk to her about."

"Don't bother," said Amy. "She won't be interested. Not for a couple of weeks, anyway."

"You're not pissed off are you?" asked James, beginning to worry about his lease again.

"Darling James, of course I'm not. It's a fact of life I've grown to live with. Once every two or three weeks, our baby girl feels the need of a good old-fashioned fuck. It's purely medicinal. She always comes back to Momma."

"I see," said James.

Amy laughed on the other end of the line. "Now you're sulking," she said. "Your masculinity has been impugned."

"I guess I just don't like being used," said James, realizing, as he said it, how pompous it sounded.

"Come on! I know Carlotta. I'll bet you liked it a whole lot."

"That's not what I meant," said James.

"I know what you meant, honey," said Amy. "But don't take it to heart. It happens to all of us."

"Tell her I called anyway," said James.

"Of course," said Amy. "We have no secrets."

The telephone call depressed him more than it should have. So much so that he didn't even bother to take his morning run on the beach. Instead, as soon as he'd had some juice and coffee, he sat down at his desk, pushed his word processor to one side, lined up a pencil and some paper and started to make some phone calls. He needn't have bothered with the pencil and paper. Forty-five minutes and a dozen calls later, he still hadn't written anything down.

He called the Department of Motor Vehicles and told them he was calling from the Malibu police department and did they have any record of a Charlotee or Charlie Fisher? They didn't.

He told the Malibu station cop he called next that he was from the Department of Motor Vehicles and asked the same question. Again nothing.

He called the property tax offices that dealt with Glendale and asked who was the owner of the house he had visited yesterday? After some clever verbal footwork, he was eventually given a name that meant nothing to him. The only address for that name was the same house. It was useless information.

He called the downtown police department to see if they had any information on the lady who had brought a charge of rape against one James Reed, charge later dropped. They didn't have, and even if they had, they told him, they wouldn't give it to him.

He called the Glendale post office and asked if there was a mail forwarding address for the Fishers. There wasn't.

He called the telephone company and asked where they sent their bills for the house in Glendale now that the tenants were no longer in residence. They said the bill had been settled two or three weeks earlier and there were no further charges. Same with the electric company, whom he called next.

Finally, he called the offices of Banks, Balkin and Simms and asked to speak to Charles Simms. He was out of town, and if this was the James Reed who had recently called on the services of Mr. Simms to defend him against a charge of rape, when was he going to send them his check?

He hung up and made himself another pot of coffee. As far as he could see, his last hope was Jaclyn Amway, who "didn't like doing for womens," but who might have been nosy enough to poke around in Charlotee's personal things. She wasn't due until four P.M. Right now it was half past ten. What was he going to do with the rest of the day?

He played chess with his computer for a couple of hours. He cheated during the third game, which enabled him to come out the winner. That was the only way he ever beat the computer at chess. By then it was lunchtime. He jogged along the beach as far as Malibu Village and went into a bar where, if you bought enough drinks, they'd give you a hard-boiled egg for free. He managed to drink enough to get two eggs, then he jogged home again.

It was just after two and the beach had been taken over by the day trippers. Even in the middle of a working week, with schools in, there seemed to be enough people playing hooky to clutter up the place. He stopped for a time to watch a volleyball game being enthusiastically played by a gaggle of young girls any one of whom would have been a beauty contest winner anywhere else in the world. In Southern California they seemed to clone them. Long-legged, fair-haired, blue-eyed nymphs with café-au-lait-colored bodies and energy enough to make James tired just watching them. After puberty, they disappeared into instant middle age. But there was always the next generation to take their places. They waited tables, they parked cars, they worked in boutiques, some of them even attended school. James watched them, quietly lusting, until the ball was thrown out of the game area landing at his feet. A magnificent-looking nineteen-year-old ran toward him. James sucked in his gut, a reflex action he had developed over the past few years, and prepared to make small talk. He picked up the ball and handed it to her. She flashed him a dazzling smile.

"Thank you, sir," she said. A remark that immediately put James in a bad mood.

He jogged the rest of the way home, vowing to lose some weight and maybe go back on the wagon. There was nothing better guaranteed to make a guy take stock of himself than a girl who he was prepared to chat up calling him "sir." His mood wasn't improved by the sight of Carlotta oiling her body on the terrace. "Hi!" he called up to her.

She looked down toward him. "Hi!" she said, and immediately went on about her business.

Amy's warning notwithstanding, James wasn't prepared to let go that easily. "How about dinner tonight?"

"Sounds good," said Carlotta.

Great, thought James, Amy had been full of shit. "What time?" he asked.

"I'll ask Amy," said Carlotta.

"I wasn't inviting Amy," said James.

"Oh," she said. "Maybe some other time then?"

"Sure," said James. He let himself in through the gate that led from the beach. "Over my rotting carcass," he mumbled to himself as he walked up toward the guest house.

There was a call on his machine from one of his poker school. Was he going to be playing this week because his dropping out at the last minute last week had really screwed up the evening. James called the guy back. He didn't know whether he was going to be able to make it so, rather than leave them in the lurch, he'd cancel.

"Fuck you," said the guy and hung up. James had won over a hundred bucks from him over the past month and he desperately wanted to get even. The fact that he was a Beverly Hills plastic surgeon and pulled down half a million dollars a year made no difference. The hundred that James had won from him was the most important money in the world right now.

James showered and dressed and was just pouring himself a drink when there was a knock on the door. It was Jaclyn Amway. She was as black as night, five foot two inches tall, and skinny as a beanpole.

"You the man wants to see me?" she asked.

"James Reed," he said, holding the door open for her.

She peered inside before crossing the threshold. Having satisfied herself that it was safe, she came in.

"I only got fifteen minutes," she said. "I gotta get home'n get ma man's supper."

She peered into the bedroom, and then moved into the kitchen area. There were some dirty glasses in the sink. Instinctively, she started to wash and dry them. "What y'all wanna talk to me about?"

"Charlotee Fisher."

"You gonna pay me?"

"Depends on what you've got to tell me," said James.

"No, sir," she said. "No sir, no way. I could tell you everything I know 'n you could turn right around and show me the door. Ma man says I gotta make a deal up front."

"Fifty dollars," said James.

"Hundred."

"It's a deal," said James.

"No it ain't. Ma man said if you came back at me that fast you was prepared to pay more."

"How much do you want?" asked James.

"Two hundred and fifty," she said, without change of expression.

What the hell, thought James. It's Everly's money. "Okay," he said.

She looked surprised. Obviously "her man" had told her to ask for more than she expected and be prepared to come down.

"Two hundred and fifty dollars?" she said, in case James had misunderstood her.

"You want it now?" asked James.

"Ah sure do," she said. She came out of the kitchen and watched James as he produced his billfold and extracted two hundreds and a fifty. He held it toward her. She was still holding the dish towel. She dried her hands carefully, took the money and, after checking the bills, she put it in the pocket of her dress. "What d'y'all wanna know?"

"Everything you can tell me," said James.

"Can I sit?"

"Sure, you can sit," said James. He watched as she perched herself on the only straight back chair in the room.

"Charlotee Fisher. Is that what she was called?" she said.

"Skinny blonde," said James.

"Ain't they all, honey," she said. "But that's the one. She was around 'bout two weeks. See, he'd had girls there before, that Mr. Everly, but they only stayed two, three days, so they didn't bother me overmuch. I don't do for womens, but most of them was gone before I knew they was there. After she'd been around for 'bout ten days I told him. Fair and square, I told him. Either she goes or I go."

"What did he say?"

"Man, he was so drunk he hardly said nothing. He was like that most of the time. So I gave it a couple more days until she started takin' over, like she owned the place, you know what I mean. Clean this, scrub that. Then I met that crazy husband of hers, and that was enough for me. I quit there and then."

"What husband?" asked James.

"He gave me the frights, honey. All twisted and crippled, like a great huge spider."

"That's her brother," said James. "Charlie."

"That was his name all right. But he weren't no brother." She paused a moment, considering something. "If he was her brother then that's a family that's got problems of the worst kind."

"Tell me," said James.

"This ain't gonna get me in no trouble is it?"

"No trouble."

"I caught them doin' it," said Jaclyn.

"Doing what?"

"It. Doin' it."

"Doing what, for Pete's sake?"

She looked at him as though he were simpleminded. "They was fucking," she said.

Score one for the good guys, thought James. "What else?" he asked.

"Nothin' else. That's when I quit. Like, I'm broad-minded 'n all but when a girl's livin' with a man 'n then invites her own husband in for a quicky in the afternoon, honey, that's too much even for Jaclyn." She paused for a moment. "Even moreso when it ain't her husband at all. You sure you know what you're talkin' about? I mean, 'bout it being her brother?"

"That's what I heard," said James. "But maybe not."

"Honey. I been doin' for white folk most of ma life. I could tell you stories that would curl your hair tighter than ma man's. There ain't nothin' white folks can get up to that's gonna surprise me no more. 'N that's a fact."

"Would you like a drink, Ms. Amway?" asked James.

"Yes, sir, I surely would. I got me a forty-five-minute drive back home, clear in the middle of rush hour. A drink inside me will improve ma disposition no end."

"Scotch?"

"Scotch would be just fine."

James fetched some ice and poured a small Scotch for her and a larger one for himself. He brought her the drink but she ignored it and took his instead.

"Allah be praised," she said, downing the drink in one swallow. She held the glass toward him. "That's a real smooth Scotch," she said. "Another wouldn't offend."

"You going to be all right to drive?" asked James.

"Honey, I'm a terrible driver, drunk or sober. So, the way I see it, I might just as well be drunk."

He fetched her another drink and sat down across from her.

"What else can you tell me?" he asked.

"You look like that honky actor."

"I already know that."

"He always wears glasses."

"I don't. Tell me more about the Fishers."

"Like what?"

"They've disappeared. I need to find them."

"I was you, I'd let sleeping dogs lie," said Jaclyn. "They're a no-good pair. Real trouble."

"I still need to find them," said James. "Did you ever see or hear anything that might suggest where they might have gone?"

"Maybe they just went home," said Jaclyn.

"Glendale?"

"Needles."

"Needles, California?"

"If there's another Needles, I ain't heard tell of it," said Jaclyn.

"What makes you think Needles is home?" asked James.

"Heard her callin' her momma one day. She called collect, that's how I know it was Needles. Said somethin' 'bout her and Charlie missin' her 'n all, 'n they'd be seein' her real soon."

Score two for the good guys, thought James.

"Anything else?" he asked.

"What do you expect for two hundred and fifty bucks?" said Jaclyn. She was beginning to enjoy herself as the Scotch took hold. One more drink, thought James, and "ma man" ain't gonna get fed tonight.

She looked around the room from where she was sitting. "Any womens live here?" she asked.

"Not on a regular basis," said James.

"I could give you three hours on Wednesday mornings," she said.

"I don't need a cleaner, thank you," said James.

"That's what you think, honey." She downed the last of her drink and stood up. She gave a little lurch as she found her balance.

"Gotta go," she said.

James walked her to her car. It was a new Mustang. Either a cleaning lady in Malibu got paid a hell of a lot more than James had thought, or Jaclyn had something going for her on the side. Whichever it was, good luck to her.

She rummaged in her purse for her keys, at the same time transferring the $250 from pocket to purse.

"Been a real pleasure doin' business with you," she said.

She started to get into the car, then she turned back to him.

"Mebbee you might be talkin' to ma man again. If you do, I'd consider it a real favor you not lettin' on 'bout the money. If he should ask, tell him you gave me twenty dollars."

James agreed to do as she asked. He helped her into the car, closed the door for her and stepped back just in time to avoid having his feet run over as she took off in a shower of loose gravel.

He called Los Angeles Information and asked for the number to call for Needles Information. He dialed it.

Yes, sir, they had a number for Fisher. In fact, they had quite a few. Carl Fisher, Harold Fisher, D. C. Fisher and Jonathan Fisher, M.D. They also had a W. Fischer, spelled with a *c*, and a Fissure who ran a local gas station. Which particular Fisher did James want to speak to? James told them to forget it and he hung up.

He went out to the garage and rooted around in the car until he found a road map of Southern California. He took it back to the guest house. He'd heard of Needles, it was the place where Snoopy's degenerate old Uncle Spike came from. But, apart from a vague memory of seeing it on a road sign when he'd been driving some place with Katherine, he couldn't place it geographically.

He found it on the map easily enough. Due east out of LA to San Bernardino, to Barstow, then, instead of continuing on toward Las Vegas, hang a right and drive as far as the Arizona State line. There was Needles. Four hour's drive at best. In his car, say six. Maybe he shouldn't even take his car. The chance of a breakdown in the middle of the desert was too intimidating to contemplate. He called the main house. Amy answered the phone.

"Either of you girls going out this evening?" he asked.

"I told you, James. You're wasting your time," said Amy.

"I don't want to get laid," said James. "I want to borrow your car."

He went over to the main house to collect the keys. Carlotta answered the door and handed them to him.

"Last night was great," he said. "Can we do it again?"

Carlotta smiled at him. It was a genuine smile, full of warmth, the kind of smile usually reserved for very good friends or very old relatives.

"I don't think so," she said.

James was an old hand at flogging dead horses. "In case you change your mind, you know where to find me," he said.

"Drive carefully," said Carlotta and closed the door.

Heading out of town, James's mood improved. The air conditioner was working fine, the radio was putting out some cool jazz, and, once the road started to climb into the San Bernardino mountains, even the scenery became pleasant to look at. Then the gradient leveled out and, once past Victorville, he hit the edges of the desert. Trees gave way to scrub, green to brown, and, if it hadn't been getting dark, he would have been able to see the road stretching out in a dead straight line for fifteen miles in front of him.

It was eight thirty when he reached Barstow. There he gassed the car and grabbed himself a bite in a coffee shop. Half an hour later he was on the road again heading for Needles. That's when the doubts started to creep in.

Maybe he had been too impulsive. He should have waited until tomorrow. He wasn't going to arrive until eleven at the earliest. From what he knew of places like Needles, they rolled up the sidewalks at dusk. And what the hell did he expect to find there in the middle of the night anyway? He could hardly bang on every Fisher front door and ask if they had a crippled son named Charlie and a daughter or daughter-in-law who was a natural blonde with the unlikely name of Charlotee. Trying something like that in the after-dark in a place like Needles could get him shot or arrested. He was going to have to wait until morning when he could cloak his actions in the respectability of daylight.

This decision raised problems of its own. One, he wasn't going to be able to return the girls' car and, two, he was going to have to find a place to stay. Problem one wasn't really much of a problem at all. All of a sudden he didn't much care about his tenants. So what if they did get pissed off at him and decide to break their lease. He'd hit Everly for any money he might lose on the deal. The second problem didn't turn out to be a problem either. It seemed that Needles was a tourist spot. As such, there were half a dozen places to stay. What tourists actually got up to in Needles, he couldn't imagine. Maybe it was their halfway stop between Los Angeles and the Grand Canyon. Maybe some people just liked the desert. Whatever it was, he gave thanks for it as he checked into a sterile but comfortable motel room on the edge of town.

There was a local phone book in the nightstand. He turned to the page containing half a dozen Fishers and looked down the list of names and addresses. Nothing rang any bells. He tore the page out of the book for use tomorrow. He called the front desk and they told him that it would be very difficult to obtain a bottle of Scotch at this time of night.

"Difficult or expensive?" he asked.

"Both."

A weary-looking black guy brought him his bottle ten minutes later.

"That'll be twenty-five dollars," he said.

James didn't even bother arguing. He paid the man and gave him another five bucks to buy him a toothbrush. The guy reappeared five minutes later with a new toothbrush.

"I bought you some toothpaste too," he said.

James tipped him another five to fetch some ice. Then, breaking the seal on the bottle, he poured himself a stiff shot and added everything to the list of expenses he was keeping for Everly. He got undressed, cleaned his teeth and climbed into bed with his bottle of Scotch. He flipped the television channels until he came to an old movie of Katherine's playing the late late show. He knew the movie well. When they were first married, and she was at the studio working, he used to run her movies during the day, filling time until the breadwinner came home. Fifteen minutes into the film he fell asleep. He woke up some time in the night. It was snowing on the TV. He didn't even get out of bed to switch it off.

CHAPTER FIVE

At seven thirty in the morning, the coffee shop next door to the motel was empty. James sat down in one of the booths and waited for something to happen. After a few minutes, he went over to the counter.

"Anyone home?" he called toward the back.

The waitress who eventually came to take his order looked as though she hadn't been to bed for a week. She was about nineteen years old with mud-colored smudges under her eyes and fingernails bitten close to extinction. Her uniform was grubby with yesterday's spilled food and she moved like she was sleepwalking. James ordered orange juice and coffee and when she returned with them, he asked her if she had lived in Needles long.

She looked at him for a long moment as if she wasn't quite sure that he was speaking to her at all.

"I'm passing through," she said with as much enthusiasm as if she was passing through Death Valley in midsummer.

"How long have you been passing through?"

"Too long."

Then James thought he detected a flicker of hope in her eyes.

"Where are you heading?" she asked.

"Back to LA eventually," he said.

"That your Cadillac out there?"

James said that it was.

"You wouldn't give me a ride, would you?"

"To Los Angeles?"

"Anyplace you're going," she said. A quiet desperation had edged into her voice.

"I've got business here in Needles," said James. "Let's talk about it when I'm through."

She moved closer to the table, leaning her hip against the edge. She smelled of cheap perfume and bacon fat.

"Listen. I've got to get out of here."

They were no more than 250 miles from LA. Buses ran all the time and there must have been fifty people a day coming through who could have given her a ride. The need or the desire to get out right now had to be something new. Maybe she'd had a row with her boyfriend or her husband or her parents. Maybe her pusher had gone out of business. Maybe her pimp was pissed off at her. Whichever way he looked at it, James could only see trouble.

"I'll check back with you when I'm through," he said.

"When will that be?"

"I'm trying to locate some people who live here. I don't know how long it'll take."

"Maybe I know them."

"Fisher?" said James.

"Bob Fisher?"

"Charlie Fisher. Charlie and Charlotee."

She looked disappointed. "I don't know no Charlie nor Charlotte Fisher," she said.

"It's Charlotee," said James.

She didn't know Charlotee either. But right now she wanted to help badly. She figured James as a way out of whatever bind she was in and she desperately wanted to please him.

"Everyone comes in here," she said. "I'll ask around for you."

Not a good idea, thought James. If Charlie got wind of him too soon, he'd probably disappear again.

"I'd prefer you didn't," said James. "They're old friends. I want to surprise them."

"You don't want them to know you're looking for them, right?"

"Right." He realized straightaway he'd made a tactical error. It showed in her expression. She leaned closer to him.

"You ride me on out of here when you're through and I won't say a word," she said.

"You've got a deal," said James, resolving to come nowhere near the coffee shop again.

She disappeared in the direction of the kitchen. James finished his coffee and orange juice, which was canned. When he called for his check, the girl reappeared and told him it was on the house.

"Daphne's my name," she said. "Daphne Spruce. I'll see you later."

James agreed that he would see her later and went out to the car. On the back seat was a battered old suitcase, tied with a length of cord. He was still looking at it when he heard someone calling to him. Daphne was standing in the door of the coffee shop.

"That's my stuff," she said. "Just so's you don't forget me."

"I won't forget you," said James.

"What time you gonna be callin' for me?"

"I'll let you know," said James.

"You take care of my stuff," said Daphne. "I sure would hate for anything to happen to it."

She had him over a barrel. If he took off with her case she'd report it stolen. Same if he just dumped it. He was going to have to come back for her, and she knew it. She smiled at him from the door of the coffee shop.

"Have a nice day," she said. She disappeared back inside.

He returned to his motel room and started to call all the Fishers in the local phone book.

"I'd like to speak to Charlie," he said, whenever the phone was answered. Third time, he got lucky.

"He's out back, I'll go get him," said a female voice on the other end of the line. A minute later a male voice came on.

"Charlie Fisher, what can I do for you?" It wasn't the voice he was looking for. He hung up, and dialed the next number on the list.

"I'd like to speak to Charlie," he said to the woman who answered the phone.

"He ain't here."

"Do you know where I can reach him?" said James.

"Him and Charlotee are up at the ranch," said the woman.

Bingo! Score three for the good guys.

"Which ranch would that be?" said James, wondering perhaps if they'd already left for E-Bar-E.

"Charlie's ranch."

"Any idea when they'll be back?" he asked.

"What d'you want with him?"

"I'm an old buddy of his from Nam," said James. "He told me any time I was in town to look him up."

"They been up there a coupla days now," said the woman. "They didn't tell me."

"Maybe I'll drive up there and surprise them," said James. "Where's the ranch located?"

"East out of town ten miles. Hang a left at Indian Wells. Five or six miles on, there's a sign."

"Thank you very much, ma'am," said James. "It'll be good to see old Charlie again."

"A buddy of his, did you say?" asked the woman.

"That's right," said James.

"Didn't know the son of a bitch had any," she said before hanging up.

James made a note of the woman's address from the phone book. The black guy who had brought his Scotch the night before was still on duty, dozing in a chair by the check-in desk. James shook him awake, and handed him the balance of the bottle of Scotch.

"What's the matter with it?" the guy asked.

"Nothing. It's for you," said James.

Immediately the guy was suspicious. "What y'all want?" he asked.

"Two things," said James. "First, you can tell me where this address is located."

The guy looked at the slip of paper James showed him. "Hang a left outside. Third turning on the right, then second left. What's the other thing?"

"There's a suitcase in back of my car. I want you to look after it for me. Later today I want you to go to the coffee shop next door and give it to the girl who works there."

He became even more suspicious. "What's in it?"

"Nothing. It belongs to her."

"So give it to her yourself."

"I can't do that," said James.

The guy thought about it for a moment. He looked at the bottle of Scotch, still three-quarters full, then back to James.

"When should I give it her?"

"Sometime this afternoon will be good."

"Okay, mister," said the guy. "You want I should get it from your car?"

"I'll get it," said James quickly.

He walked to his car. As he got in, he could see Daphne waiting on a table in the coffee shop. She saw him and waved. He waved back before driving off.

He drove to the back of the motel. He took Daphne's suitcase from the back seat and carried it through to the lobby where the black guy had gone to sleep again. James had only been gone a couple of minutes, but already there was a sizable dent in the amount of Scotch left in the bottle. James woke him up again and turned over the suitcase.

"Her name is Daphne," he said. "Daphne Spruce."

"I know her," said the guy. "I know her husband too," he added. "I don't reckon you'd want him to know nothing 'bout this."

James agreed he didn't want Daphne's husband to know nothing 'bout this and handed over twenty dollars to douse the gleam that had suddenly appeared in the old guy's eyes.

He followed the directions he had been given, hanging a left, then a third right followed by another left. He found himself driving down a street of tidy little single-story houses with neat front yards. Number 2147 was halfway down the street. James drove past it to the end of the road, a quarter of a mile further on. There he made a U-turn and drove half the distance back toward the house. He parked the car, locked it, and started to walk the rest of the way back to number 2147.

A kid who should have been at school nearly ran him down with his skateboard, and a mongrel barked halfheartedly at him from one of the neighboring yards. Apart from that, nobody took any notice of him. He walked past the house, noting that there was an old Pinto parked in the car port. There were net drapes over the windows, and the door behind the screen on the front porch was wide open.

A hundred and fifty yards further down the road, where it intersected with the cross street, there was a small general store. James asked the woman behind the counter if he might use the telephone. She wanted to listen to his conversation, but James timed it so he was dialing the number just as a couple of customers came into the store, needing her attention.

"Mrs. Fisher?" he said, when the woman came on the line. "We've located your automobile."

"I don't know what you're talking about," she said.

"This is the police, ma'am. We've found your car."

"My car's right outside," she said.

"You reported it stolen, ma'am."

"I did no such thing."

"Nineteen seventy-five Pinto, green," said James. He quoted the registration number of the car parked outside her house.

"Sure, that's my car. But it's parked outside. And I never reported it stolen."

"I guess somebody's fouled up," said James. "I wonder if you'd care to drive on down to the department and help me straighten it out."

"This got anything to do with Charlie?" she asked.

"Who's Charlie, ma'am?"

"My son. Is this something to do with him?"

"I don't know, ma'am. But you come on down here and I'm sure we can straighten it out."

Reluctantly, she agreed to drive down to the police department. She'd be there in fifteen minutes. James thanked the store owner for the use of the phone and started back up the street toward 2147.

As he passed the house, on the opposite side of the street, a woman came out. She slammed the front door and headed for the Pinto. She was in her early sixties, wearing a brightly colored flower-print dress. Her hair was stuffed with rollers and she had a transparent scarf tied around her head. She walked like her feet were giving her trouble. She got into the car, backed out and drove off down the road toward the center of town.

James crossed the street, walked up the short driveway and through the car port to the back door that he just knew was going to be unlocked. It was. A moment later he was in the house.

There were two bedrooms. The first that he looked into obviously belonged to the lady of the house. The bed hadn't yet been made. At the foot was a twenty-inch color TV, and the vanity looked as though it hadn't been tidied for a month. The second bedroom was the guest room. If, as and when Charlie and/or Charlotee visited Momma, this is where they would sleep. The room held a double bed, a dresser with four long drawers and a matching wardrobe. At the foot of the bed was a large tea chest draped with an Indian shawl. There was a photograph on the nightstand. Charlie and Charlotee, she smiling and he snarling at the camera. The photo had been taken in the front of the house. James undid the frame and, slipping the photograph out, looked at the back. The date of the processing was printed there. Two years ago. He made a note of the date and put the photo back. Then he started to search the room properly. Ten minutes later he let himself out of the house the same way he had come in.

He didn't want to use the phone at the general store again so he drove to the nearest gas station. He collected some change and put in a call to E-Bar-E. The phone was answered by a man who didn't identify himself. James asked to speak to Wally.

"He ain't here right now."

"Is Mr. Everly available?"

"Who wants to know?"

"James Reed," said James.

Everly came to the phone fifty cents later.

"Hey, James. How's everything with you? Did you get back to LA all right?"

"I'm not in LA," said James. "I'm in Needles."

"Whatever turns you on," said Everly. "What did you want to talk to me about?"

"Business," said James.

"Do we have business between us?"

"No, we don't. But if we did, I'd tell you to forget your upcoming nuptials. They won't be taking place."

"Is that right! Why?"

"Your intended already has a husband."

"Are you sure?"

"I've got the marriage license right here," said James. "Charlie Fisher married one Charlotee Edwards two years ago in Las Vegas."

"That's good news," said Everly. He didn't sound as though it was good news at all.

"If they're going to put the bite on you, it'll have to be some other way," said James.

"If they're going to put the bite on me, they'll figure something," said Everly.

There was a long pause on the other end of the line and James reached for more change. "Do you know where they are?" Everly asked finally.

"They're holed up a few miles from here. I'm going out there soon as we get through talking."

"What are you going to do?"

"Talk to them. Explain to Charlie that it'll be in his best interests to forget he and Charlotee ever met you."

"How are you going to do that?"

"Do you really want to know?" asked James.

"Not really," said Everly.

"I'll be in touch," said James.

He gassed up the car. This reminded him that he'd better call Amy. There was no answer from the house. He assumed they must both be out on the beach. They sure as hell couldn't have driven anywhere. He climbed back into the car and headed for the ranch. A mile out of town, he was in the middle of the desert once more, the highway a long, flat ribbon marking the shortest distance between two points. Ten miles from Needles, he came to Indian Wells. There had to be a hundred places called Indian Wells in this part of America. Some of them had flourished, growing into prosperous little communities. Most hadn't. This particular Indian Wells consisted of the inevitable gas station, a small general store, and a roadside line of stalls selling genuine Indian artifacts most of which had been made in Taiwan. The stalls were manned by families of weary-looking Indians.

Following the directions he had been given, James turned left off the main highway. He found himself on a single-track road which, after four miles, gave way to packed dirt. The impression of emptiness was overwhelming. If the Fisher ranch was located on land like this it was no wonder Charlie indulged in extracurricular activities. Right now, James knew pretty much what those activities were.

He'd found what he was looking for in the chest at the end of the bed. He'd saved it until last, going through the wardrobe and the drawers first. All he had found there were clothes, Charlie's and Charlotee's. The chest had made the whole thing worthwhile.

There he discovered Charlie's army discharge papers. Sure, he had been blown up in Vietnam, as he had told James. He and a buddy had been looting an ammo store, having made a deal with a local entrepreneur who was, no doubt, selling the stuff to the Cong who in turn were probably using it to blow up Charlie's fellow GIs. Either Charlie or his buddy had been careless and one of the land mines they had been stealing had blown up. The buddy had been killed outright and Charlie had wound up nearly losing his leg. There was too much bad publicity going on back home at that time for a full-blown trial, so they had given Charlie a nice quiet court-martial, three years in the stockade, and a dishonorable discharge. In fact, Charlie had come out of it fairly well. They'd fixed his leg for free. It would have cost him thousands of dollars had he been a civilian. So much for his army record. James had found it interesting, but it hadn't contained any real surprises and certainly nothing he could use against Charlie. And that was what he was looking for.

He had found at the bottom of the chest a slim, leatherbound notebook. It had taken him two minutes to realize what it contained. Score four for the good guys. By then he had started to worry that Mrs. Fisher might be returning from the police department, so he had slipped the notebook in his pocket along with the other papers he thought might be useful. They had included the discharge papers and the marriage license. Now, armed with what he considered ample ammunition, he was heading for the showdown.

Five miles from Indian Wells, where the road had become little more than an extension of the desert that surrounded it, there was a board nailed to a post stuck in the ground. Painted crudely on the board was the name FISHER. An arrow pointed toward a low line of hills about four miles away. James pulled off in the direction of the arrow.

The only sign of a track across the desert were tire marks, looping and curving around those cacti that were too large to bulldoze down. A mile in, there was a fork in the track. Over to the left James could just make out a small, partially demolished shack. Guessing it once belonged to one of the Indian families whose reservation he was now on, he took the right fork. For the second time in less than a week he was driving toward a ranch in an unsuitable vehicle. The Cadillac handled the flats okay, but it scraped bottom as it passed over a couple of washouts caused by flash floods. At least the ground was dry, so the car didn't bog down like last time.

James wasn't sure what he expected to find on the other side of the hills. He'd been surprised by the E-Bar-E, so he was prepared for anything. In fact, as he crested the rise, all he saw was more desert, seemingly stretching forever. So where was the ranch?

He stopped the car and got out. There was another rise in the land barely visible from where he was standing. He estimated it at about six miles, maybe seven. Between here and there, nothing. Over to the left was a slash of white, an old salt flat. To the right, just more desert.

He didn't fancy the next part of the drive without confirmation that he was heading in the right direction. He decided to drive back to the shack he had spotted. Maybe one of the local Indians still lived there and would be able to give him some information. He was about to get back into the car when he heard the gunshots.

There were four evenly spaced booms overlapped by their own echoes. It was impossible to fix their direction; they could have come from anywhere. James's first instinct was to duck. But it was a reflex action. The sound was coming from too far away for him to be the target.

Okay, he decided, someone's out shooting gophers or coyotes or whatever guys shoot at in the desert. Maybe they were just shooting at targets. You could conduct a full-scale war out here without getting in anyone's way. He climbed back into the car, turned around and headed back the way he had come.

He reached the fork in the track and turned off toward the shack, half a mile away. The closer he got, the more desolate it appeared. If anyone lived here they were either destitute or crazy. Maybe a little of both. There was just the one building, which looked as though it had been constructed from materials that nobody could possibly have had any further use for. It also looked in urgent need of demolition. If there was an Indian family living here and they could give him the information he wanted, James resolved to buy all the junk they wanted to sell him.

The track led straight to the front of the shack and then ended. It wasn't until James had stopped the car and got out that he saw the other vehicle. It was parked at the back, close to the shack. An old jeep that had seen far better days. James leaned back into the Cadillac and sounded the horn. He might be a big-city boy, but he knew better than to knock on a door like this unannounced. He'd seen *Deliverance* twice, and while this might be a different part of the country, it was just another form of wilderness. People who lived in such isolation were often known to have pretty unsociable tendencies.

Nobody reacted to the sound of his horn. The silence was almost deafening. Without going too close to the building, James walked around back. There was a five-hundred-gallon water tank tight up against the back wall, galvanized iron with a couple of sheets of corrugated iron serving as a lid. A single pipe led from the tank into the shack. The jeep was dirty, but not as dilapidated as James had first thought. He walked around front again and stopped five feet away from the door.

"Anyone home?" he called.

The answer was more silence. Obviously nobody was home. Either that, or they were crouched behind the kitchen table ready to blow the head off anyone foolish enough to invade their privacy. Whichever it was, James wasn't going to get any information here. He was going to have to go clear back to Indian Wells. He started back toward the car. That's when the snake bit him.

He heard the sound first, like the rattle of dry twigs. He'd seen enough Western movies to recognize it immediately, except he didn't. He stopped, turning back toward the shack, looking for the source of the sound. The snake in question took this as a sign of aggression and struck at him just above his ankle. Somehow it got its fangs entangled with the fabric of James's pants and was unable to pull free right away. James kicked out with involuntary horror. The fangs came free and the snake flew six feet away and then slithered off, back under the shack where it had come from.

James flopped to the ground. He dragged up his trouser leg and pulled down his sock. There were two tiny punctures just above his left ankle.

Shit, he'd been bitten by a rattlesnake. People died from rattlesnake bites. On the other hand, maybe it wasn't as bad as it could have been. After all, the snake had to penetrate through pants and sock. But it had been a big son of a bitch, four feet long at least. A snake like that probably carried enough venom to kill a horse. Except a horse would have recognized the sound immediately and have got the hell away.

That makes me dumber than a horse, which is pretty fucking dumb, but I've still been bitten by a snake and I've got to do something about it unless I want to croak out here in the desert a million miles from anyplace, where the buzzards will start to gather and they'll come down and start to pick my bones clean—with luck not before I'm dead.

Steady on, thought James. Panic's not going to get you anyplace. All it's going to do is get the blood pumping faster which means that the poison will spread quicker. He counted to ten very slowly. Then, because he couldn't think of anything else to do, he opened his mouth and yelled.

"Help!"

Nothing happened. Nobody appeared from the shack. Nobody answered his call. He was on his own. Or, if he wasn't, and there was some retarded desert dweller lurking inside the shack waiting to blow his head off, so be it. He climbed to his feet and hobbled over to the door. He experienced another moment of panic as he reached the shack and mounted the stoop. Maybe the snake would appear from under the building to finish the job. Then he was banging on the door. Receiving no reply he tried the handle and the door swung open.

"I'm coming in," he said superfluously as he stepped inside.

The place was empty. There was a single bed in the far corner, still unmade. There was a table and a couple of hardback chairs. There was a dresser against the wall to the left. The back wall held a sink next to a small gas cooker.

James made straight for the sink. Somewhere in the back of his mind he remembered reading that the best way to treat a snakebite was to incise the actual bite with a sharp instrument and then suck out the venom.

Okay, first things first. He needed a sharp instrument. Right away he got lucky. Whoever lived in the shack used an open razor, the kind of razor the English called a cutthroat. Let's see how it cut ankles. Opening the razor, he wiped it on a grubby towel and then made a crosswise incision on his ankle over the twin puncture marks. He didn't mean to cut quite so deep and he was momentarily startled by the amount of blood that began to flow. Sucking the wound proved more of a problem. He sat on the floor, his back against the sink and tried to get his ankle up to his mouth. He was off by a good six inches. He nearly dislocated his leg before he realized he wasn't going to make it. So he did what he considered was the next best thing and applied pressure to the edges of the incisions, trying to squeeze out as much venom as he could. He had no idea whether he was doing any good, but it was better than sitting there and waiting to die. The only visible result of his efforts was a great deal of blood.

After a few minutes, he gave up and decided to employ the next item of folklore that was lurking at the back of his mind. A tourniquet to stop the venom flowing up the veins to his heart.

Still sitting on the floor, he tore the towel into strips and tied one of them around his leg above his knee. He groped around the draining board behind him and came up with a wooden spoon which he used to tighten the tourniquet. Must remember to loosen it from time to time, he remembered, or his foot would turn black and his toes would drop off. The blood stopped flowing and the panic started to fade. He was still scared shitless, but he was more or less together.

He stood up and put his foot to the ground experimentally. Then he took a couple of steps. He wasn't even limping. What's more, he wasn't feeling any pain. A slight giddiness perhaps, but that could be due to the amount of blood he'd managed to squeeze out of himself. It was everywhere. A pool on the floor. A puddle in the bottom of his shoe, and his hands were scarlet up to his wrists. He turned to the sink and stuck his hands under the single faucet connected directly to the water tank out back. The water ran down over his hands and wrists, washing away the blood, turning pink before it disappeared down the drain.

After a while, he started to feel like Lady Macbeth. As hard as he scrubbed his hands, the water remained the same shade of pink. It took him a full minute of hand-wringing before he realized that it was no longer his blood that was staining the water.

The corrugated iron sheets covering the water tank slid aside easily. The top of the tank was too high to see down into and James had to go back into the shack and fetch one of the chairs. He stood on it and looked over the edge down into the tank. There were two bodies, face down in the water. He didn't have to turn them over to know who they were, but he turned them over anyway.

Charlie had been shot in the face and in the stomach. It looked like it had been done at close range with a heavy-caliber gun. The side of the face that had taken the full impact no longer existed, and there was a hole in his stomach large enough for his insides to drop out, most of which had. Charlotee had been shot once in the chest. As James replaced the corrugated iron sheets, he wondered peripherally what had happened to the fourth shot he had heard.

He carried the chair back indoors and looked around the place for the first time, taking in the generalities before starting in on the specifics. In ten minutes, he had turned the place upside-down and discovered absolutely nothing. He sat on the edge of the unmade bed and looked around again. No bloodstains, apart from his own, so they must have been shot outside. Maybe they'd been about to leave when it happened. In which case there would have been a suitcase or something in the jeep. Maybe they came out to welcome whoever had chopped them down. Or maybe they had just been dragged outside before being shot.

James stood up and suddenly became aware that his ankle had started to throb. Shit, he'd been bitten by a snake. He'd forgotten all about it. Nothing like finding a couple of dead bodies floating in the water tank to make a guy forget his own problems. Charlotee and Charlie were going to have to wait. James needed to see a doctor. He went back out to the car treading softly so's not to annoy the snake again.

The pain hadn't gotten any worse by the time he hit the highway heading into Indian Wells. Neither had it gotten any better. He pulled into the gas station and asked the attendant where he could locate the nearest doctor.

"What's your problem, mister?" he was asked.

Normally James would have told the guy to mind his own business. But it wasn't every day one could say he'd been bitten by a rattlesnake.

"Snakebite," he said, trying not to sound like Gary Cooper.

"How long ago?"

"Thirty minutes."

"Rattler?"

"Yep."

"How big?"

" 'Bout four feet big?"

"Forget it," said the garage man. "Time you get to the doctor you'll be dead."

"I'm not dead yet," said James. "Where's the nearest doctor?"

The garage man wasn't impressed. "If you was bitten by a four-foot rattler thirty minutes ago and you ain't dead, you weren't bitten by a four-foot rattler, friend."

He told James his best bet would be to go straight to the hospital in Needles. They had an emergency room which handled stuff like snakebites and rabies and scorpion stings, all those ailments that went hand-in-hand with living on the edge of the desert. James limped out to the car again.

"You want I should check under your hood?" the garage man called after him.

James was prevented from pulling straight out onto the highway by the sound of sirens. He sat behind the wheel of the Cadillac and watched two police cars speeding up the road from Needles. They hung a left at the junction without slowing, barreling into the dust of the dirt road that James had just driven down. James got out of the car and limped over to the garage man who had emerged from his office to watch the police cars.

"Where does that road lead to?" he asked.

"No place," said the garage man.

"No place?"

"Couple of folk got small places out there. Otherwise it's just Indians."

"What do you suppose the trouble is?"

"It sure ain't the Indians," said the garage man. "They wouldn't be in such a hurry."

James reached the hospital at Needles fifteen minutes later. He was kept waiting for ten minutes while they checked that the information he'd given them about his medical insurance was accurate. Then he was shown into the office of a bored middle-aged doctor who, it seemed, handled rattlesnake bites on a day-to-day basis. He examined James's ankle, wincing slightly when he saw the amount of damage James had inflicted on himself.

"What did you use? A bayonet?"

"Can I take the tourniquet off?" asked James.

"How long have you had it on?"

"About forty-five minutes?"

"Take it off," said the doctor, with a quick look at James's toenails. He asked James to describe the snake that bit him. He didn't seem particularly impressed to hear that it was four feet long.

"There's more than twenty types of rattler round these parts, any of them can be four feet or more. Be a help if we knew what we were dealing with. Couldn't have been a diamondback or you'd be dead by now. Same with a sidewinder. Very nasty, both of them. You'd be swollen up twice your normal size. Bit you through your pants and sock, you said?"

James admitted that is what he'd said.

"Probably accounts for it," said the doctor. "Didn't get his fangs all the way in. Squirted most of his venom down your leg. Your main problem's going to be infection from all that cutting and chopping you did on yourself."

He looked at James's ankle again and shook his head. "Boy oh boy."

He gave James an injection of antibiotics to prevent infection and another injection designed to take care of the snakebite. Both were extremely painful. They made him feel light-headed. He told the doctor.

"Lie down for a couple of hours."

He turned James over to a nurse who led him to one of the curtained cubicles off the emergency department. James asked her for a telephone.

"This isn't a hotel," she said. She closed the curtains like she was slamming a door.

James was about to go looking for a phone when he suffered a wave of giddiness so severe that he nearly lost his balance. He climbed onto the gurney and lay back. So he'd wait ten minutes before calling the police. After all, he didn't think he'd be telling them anything they didn't already know. Those two police cars had to be heading somewhere, and he was willing to take money that it was the Fisher place. He lay back, waiting for his head to stop spinning. Then he sat up again quickly. He may have been feeling light-headed, but he hadn't completely lost his marbles. If the police cars were heading for the Fisher place, somebody must have given them cause. Apart from James, the only other person who could know about the bodies in the water tank was the one who had put them there. Assuming the shots he'd heard were the ones that blew away Charlie and Charlotee, there wouldn't have been time for anyone to discover the bodies before James arrived at the shack. Okay, so maybe he was wrong. Maybe the police were heading someplace else. Maybe there was trouble on the reservation, an Indian uprising, another Little Big Horn. He'd rest up here until his head stopped going around in circles, then he'd drive to the police department and tell them about the bodies. He closed his eyes for a moment. It helped slightly, but not much.

The next thing he knew he was being shaken awake by the nurse who had slammed the curtains on him.

"How are we feeling?" she asked disinterestedly.

James reported he was feeling much better, thank you, and he'd like to leave now. He had been asleep for just over an hour.

He signed a release form at the hospital desk. He flatly refused to be escorted from the premises in a wheelchair, whatever it said in their rules. Outside, the heat hit him like a hammer and he started to feel giddy again. Maybe he should have stayed where he was for another hour or two. Then he spotted his car. He was right, he should have stayed in the hospital. Daphne Spruce was sitting on her suitcase, waiting for him to turn up.

It was too late to take evasive action. She had spotted him as he had come out of the main doors. She waved toward him, getting to her feet. She started talking while he was still ten feet away. "I honestly thought you'd forgotten all about me or changed your mind or something. Then the guy from the motel, the black guy who brought me my bag, he told me he'd seen your car parked here at the hospital. I thought maybe you'd had an accident or something so I asked at the desk. They didn't want to tell me anything at first so I told them I was your daughter. They told me it was just a little old snakebite, and you'd be out in no time, so I waited. Are we going to LA now?"

James wasn't feeling well enough to argue with her.

"I've got to go to the police department," he said.

"That's cool," she said. "I'll wait in the car."

"I may be there some time."

"I don't care," she said. "I'm not going no place." Then she giggled. "Except LA."

She didn't look half as bad as James remembered. She'd tidied herself and made up her face so the shadows under her eyes weren't so obvious. The shirt and jeans which she had changed into were clean and freshly pressed.

"What's your husband going to say?" asked James.

"That's my problem," said Daphne. She didn't ask how he knew she'd got a husband.

"Just so long as it stays your problem," said James.

He carried her suitcase around to the back of the car and started to unlock the trunk.

"You know where the police department is?" he asked, throwing back the lid of the trunk.

"It's about four blocks from here," she said. "Take a left out of the parking lot. I'll show you where."

But he wasn't listening to her. He slammed the lid of the trunk quickly.

"You forgot my bag," she said. Then she looked at him curiously.

"Are you okay?"

James wasn't okay. He'd started to feel light-headed again. This time it was nothing to do with the antibiotics or the snake-bite. It was the rifle he'd just seen, lying at the bottom of the trunk.

⚜ ⚜ ⚜

"So how come you changed your mind about going to the police department?" said Daphne.

They were fifteen minutes outside Needles, heading for Barstow.

"Plans change," said James.

They sure as hell did. He'd thrown Daphne's suitcase onto the back seat and told her to wait for him. He'd gone back into the hospital to the nearest pay phone where he'd called Amy. Before she could even start to yell at him about the car he asked her whether she just happened to have a rifle which she kept in the trunk. Needless to say, she didn't.

"I'll talk to you later," he'd said and then hung up before she could say anything more.

He'd come back to the car and got in beside Daphne.

"Which way did you say was the police department?" he'd asked.

"Left out of the parking lot."

He'd turned right. He'd skirted the town, picked up the highway on the far side and put his foot down.

"You're driving awful fast," said Daphne.

He looked at the speedometer. He was doing eighty-five. He slowed down to the sixty-five that everyone drove since the limit had been set at fifty-five.

"What time are we going to be in LA?" she asked.

"Do me a favor, Daphne," he said. "Just stop talking for a few minutes. I need to think."

She shrugged. "Suit yourself."

She reached forward and tried to tune in some music on the radio. The noise set his teeth on edge but it was preferable to the sound of Daphne's voice, so he let it go.

Somebody had put him into deep shit. He was quite sure that the gun in the trunk was the murder weapon. It couldn't have been any other way. How it had got there wasn't too difficult to work out either. Whoever had killed Charlie and Charlotee had seen him arrive at the shack then followed him when he left. They could have stashed the gun any time during the hour and a half he was in the hospital. That took care of the "how." As for the "why," that wasn't too much of a problem either. He was the patsy. And what a patsy. There must have been a dozen people who knew he was looking for the Fishers. Daphne for one. The guy at the motel. Charlie's mother, who might not have seen him, but had given him directions over the phone. Then there was the garage man who'd probably noticed that he'd come from the direction of the Fisher place. That was four in Needles alone. Back in LA there was Jaclyn Amway. Then there was Amy and Carlotta who'd both seen Charlie when he'd come to the beach house originally. He could see them all, traipsing into the witness box one after the other. Hell, the way the case against him would shape up he might just as well turn himself in with a full confession.

Shit, why hadn't he gone straight to the police when he discovered the bodies? Because he thought he might die from snakebite was why. Then again, if he hadn't been bitten by the snake in the first place, he wouldn't have hung around the shack long enough to use the faucet. And if he hadn't used the faucet, he'd never have discovered the bodies. The ifs and the buts and the maybes started to give him a headache. He reached forward and switched off the radio.

"You all right?" asked Daphne.

"I'm okay," said James.

"You wanna pull over and we'll mess around?"

"No," said James.

"I could show you a couple of things I bet you've never even heard of."

He looked at her. She was nineteen, for Christ's sake, but he believed every word. He took pity on her. After all, she was only trying to cheer him up.

"Maybe some other time," he said. "Right now I've got an awful lot on my mind."

She shrugged. She obviously didn't care either way. But she stopped talking and she didn't switch the radio back on.

Okay, thought James, now we come to the sixty-four-dollar question. The "who." He thought back on the contents of the notebook he had found at Charlie's house. There had been twenty names in it. If the book contained what James thought it did, then any one of the twenty would have stood in line to pull the trigger. He was going to have to find out which one it was before the law nailed him. Because one thing was for sure. When the police *did* catch up with him, and there was no doubt in his mind that they would, he was going to be in for the high jump.

They reached Barstow just after three P.M. James drove straight to the bus station where he gave Daphne the money for a bus ticket the rest of the way to Los Angeles. He told her he had business to take care of in Barstow and he didn't know how long it would take him. She offered to wait for him, even if it meant spending the night. But she didn't seem too disappointed when he turned her down. He gave her an extra fifty dollars and told her to take care of herself. She thanked him, promising to pay him back as soon as she got settled. He escorted her to the bus and even stood and waved as the bus pulled out.

At the newsstand he bought a copy of the *Los Angeles Times*. He asked the guy behind the counter if he had any twine. The man gave him a couple of lengths and he took them, with the newspaper, back to the Cadillac. He reparked the car, backing it against the wall of the bus depot so that when he opened the trunk there was no chance of anybody seeing what he was up to. It is difficult to wrap a rifle in newspaper and have it look like anything else but what it is, namely a rifle wrapped in newspaper. James managed. But first he checked the magazine. It was designed to hold eight shells. It held four, which, all things considered, figured.

He wrapped the gun in part of the newspaper and tied it up. Then he crumpled up more of the newspaper and, bunching it around the gun loosely, he tied the whole lot together in a shapeless bundle, half as broad as it was long. He carried the bundle back into the bus depot over to a bank of luggage lockers. He thought for a moment he'd made the package too large. But he finally managed to force it into the locker. He bought a roll of sticky tape from the newsstand and went into the men's washroom. In a cubicle, he taped the locker key to the top of the partition that separated that cubicle from the next one. He figured the only person who would see it would be someone who was peering from one cubicle into the other and he'd have too many other things on his mind to worry about a key.

He came out of the cubicle, washed his hands, and headed out to the parking lot once more. Getting rid of the gun had made him feel better. Not a lot better, but better. His ankle had stopped throbbing and his headache was gone. It came back fast when he found Daphne's husband waiting for him by his car.

Hank Spruce was about twenty-six years old, six feet four and two hundred pounds, a large proportion of them in his arms and chest.

"Where is she?" was the first question he asked.

"Where's who?" asked James, who had no idea what he was talking about.

"Daphne." Then, in case James hadn't worked it out yet. "My wife."

"She's on the bus to LA," said James.

"I ought to break your neck," said Hank.

James relaxed slightly. He had long ago learned that any guy who prefaced a threat with "ought to" wasn't going to do anything physical. At least, not in the immediate future.

"You hurry, you could catch up," he said.

"I'm gonna bust you one first," said Hank.

"I've got a better idea," said James. "Let me buy you a drink. You've got plenty of time. She only left fifteen minutes ago."

"I'm not sure I even want her back no more," said Hank.

"Sure you do or you wouldn't have come this far. Come on. A quick drink, and I'll tell you something that'll help you hang onto her next time."

Hank shrugged. "Why not," he said.

They started toward a bar at the far side of the parking lot.

"You got here real fast," said James. "What are you driving?"

Hank nodded toward a pickup truck parked close to the Cadillac. "That's my pickup. Mine and Daphne's. I went to pick her up at work 'n they told me the guy from the motel had brung her bags over so's I went to talk to him. He told me 'bout you and that Cadillac of yours. I knew I'd catch up with you if I traveled fast."

"You certainly did," said James, holding the bar door open for Hank.

He ordered a Scotch for himself and a beer for Hank. Then he excused himself.

"Got to take a pee," he said.

He went out through the back of the bar into the parking lot. Thirty seconds to reach Hank's pickup, thirty seconds under the hood and thirty seconds to get back to the bar. He came back in zipping up his fly. At the bar he picked up his Scotch.

"Mud in your eye," he said. They both drank.

"Okay," said James. "This is what you do. You head for Los Angeles. You'll pass the bus easily. Soon as you get there, you check into some nice little motel. Then you go out and buy some flowers and a bottle of wine. Then you go to the bus terminal and wait for her. Soon as she gets off, you give her a big kiss, drag her back to the motel, open the wine and show her a good time. She'll love you for it."

James could see Hank liked the idea. Maybe it was just the thought of a night in a Los Angeles motel that appealed to him. But whatever it was, he went for it.

He was almost embarrassing in his thanks. He wanted to buy James another drink but James pointed out that he'd better get on his way, he was going to have a lot to do in LA before meeting the bus. Hank thanked him again and left. Three minutes later he was back in the bar looking like a whipped moose.

"The pickup won't start," he said.

James gave the matter some thought. "Tell you what," he said finally. "I'm partly to blame for all this. I mean, if I hadn't given her a ride, none of this would have happened. Look, I've got business here in Barstow that's going to keep me overnight. Take my car. I'm not going to need it."

"I can't do that," said Hank.

"Sure you can. I'll call a garage to fix your pickup. You drop my car back here on your way home to Needles tomorrow."

Hank was adamant. He couldn't. Then he softened it to wouldn't and, finally, he allowed James to talk him around. James suspected that the idea of getting to drive the Cadillac had as much to do with his acceptance as the chance of getting his wife back. But whichever it was, Hank was pathetically grateful. As James handed over the keys, he could see the tears in Hank's eyes. They walked out to the car together. Hank handed James the keys of the pickup for him to pass on to the garage. Two minutes later, he was on his way.

James went back to the bar and ordered another drink. Sure, he felt guilty but, as was invariably the case, his sense of survival came first. If the police had put out an APB on him already, they'd be looking for the Cadillac without, as yet, any idea who was driving. So let them pull Hank over and take him in.

They'd most likely jump him halfway to Los Angeles. Highway patrol or the sheriff's department whose territory he was driving through. San Bernardino, most likely. They'd call Needles to say they'd got their man. The police at Needles would need to get some kind of warrant to have him transferred back to their jurisdiction. He would have to be collected and signed for. Once back in Needles, the questioning would start. They wouldn't believe his story first time around, they never did.

"Sure, buddy. A complete stranger lends you his automobile just like that!"

They'd keep on at him for four or five hours. Meantime, they'd start checking. They'd interview the witnesses. The guy at the motel, the doctor, the garage man. They'd get a search warrant and go through Hank's home. They'd check out Hank's alibi, assuming he had one. Eventually they'd realize that Hank was telling the truth and they'd let him go. Only then would they come looking for James. But all that would take time. Forty-eight hours at least. He'd have preferred a couple of weeks. Months even. Then again, perhaps nobody was looking for him, and he'd hung Hank out to dry for no reason at all. He downed his drink, paid his tab and went to find a phone.

"This is the *Los Angeles Times*," he said on the phone. "Understand you've got yourself a double homicide out there?"

The woman on the other end of the line asked him to hang on. A minute later a man came on the phone.

"Lieutenant Peters here. Who am I talking to?"

"Marvin Compact, *Los Angeles Times*," said James. "What can you tell me about this homicide of yours?"

"I don't know what you're talking about," said the lieutenant.

"Sure you do. Out near Indian Wells."

James could hear the lieutenant speak to someone else. Then, back to the phone. "How did you hear about this, Mr. Compact?"

"We've got our sources," said James.

"You want to tell me about them?" said the lieutenant.

"You've got to be kidding. Any suspects?"

"I haven't told you there's been a crime yet."

"You haven't told me there hasn't been one either," said James.

"If you know anything about it, I strongly suggest you tell me," said the lieutenant.

"Double homicide. Gunshot. Victims in a water tank, and you're looking for a guy who drives a Lincoln."

"It's a Cadillac," said the lieutenant, as though he had scored a point. James hung up.

He replaced the engine part he'd removed from Hank's pickup, started the engine and headed for Los Angeles.

He was half expecting to see some roadside activity on his drive. Maybe the Cadillac pulled over to the side of the highway surrounded by cops brandishing guns. Perhaps he had overestimated the efficiency of the Needles police department and they hadn't yet put out an APB. In which case, Hank would meet his Daphne off her bus, they would spend a night of connubial bliss, and tomorrow, Hank would be wandering around the parking lot at the Barstow bus station looking to return James's car. And James would have gained another twelve hours to accomplish whatever the hell he thought he was going to.

In fact, he gained considerably more than twelve hours, and Daphne never did get her flowers or her bottle of wine. It seemed that on the long descent from the high desert plateau down toward the city of San Bernardino the brakes of the Cadillac had failed. Various estimates put the speed of the vehicle somewhere between eighty-five and one hundred miles per hour when it hit the guard rail. These rails were designed to deflect an automobile back onto the road, only this time it hadn't worked that way. Due possibly to the size and weight of the car, coupled with its excessive speed, combined with the angle of contact, the guard rail had collapsed and the car had gone over the edge. It had rolled and bounced down a two-hundred-foot slope, collecting a couple of substantial trees en route. By the time it had come to a stop at the bottom, it was smashed beyond recognition. Then the gas tank had exploded. Twenty minutes later, when the first people managed to get down to it, there was nothing left that in any way resembled an automobile. And certainly nothing inside that resembled a human being.

All this James discovered after he was pulled to the side of the road half an hour after leaving Barstow. At first, when he saw the road flares and the blinking lights of authority, he thought he'd run into a police roadblock set up specifically to catch him. He debated for a second whether he should make a run for it, but that would have involved making a U-turn and heading the wrong way back up the freeway. So he pulled over and joined the line of vehicles that were being funneled down to a single lane. He saw the police cars and the ambulance and the tow truck grouped around the break in the guard rail, and realizing that this was just another accident scene, he spared a moment to feel sorry for the poor schmuck who'd gone over the edge.

He slowed to a crawl going past the roadside activity. Along with every other motorist, he tried to see down the hill toward the wreck. A portable spotlight mounted on a tow truck had its beam directed downward. There wasn't much to see. Just a group of people working over a charred, shapeless lump of metal. Maybe it was a flash of color from the wreckage, the last trace of unscorched paint. But whatever it was, something made him pull over once he had got through the congestion. He walked back to where a group of men both uniformed and otherwise were standing around the break in the guard rail. In the background, a police radio crackled loudly, passing routine messages. The men standing around didn't seem to be taking much notice of anything. Somebody said something, someone else laughed. James moved to the edge of the guard rail and looked down.

"You wanna move along, sir." It was a highway patrolman, bulky in his fur-lined jacket.

"What happened?" asked James.

"Just move it along, buddy," said the patrolman.

"Listen. My wife and kids were driving ahead of me. Maybe twenty minutes. I want to know what happened."

"Car went through the guard rail," said the patrolman. "A guy saw it. Said he was doing close to a hundred. Fighting the wheel like a maniac. No skid marks. Guess his brakes failed. What kind of a car was your wife driving, sir?"

"A white Chevy," said James.

"Then you don't have to worry. This was a Cadillac. A blue Caddy. At least, they think it was a Caddy. There's not much of it left."

"What about the driver?"

"Barbecued," said the cop.

James returned to the pickup. He rejoined the flow of traffic heading down toward the lights of San Bernardino.

James was a guy who made up scenarios in his head. He did it all the time. Right now there was someone else out there who'd made up a scenario. Not only was it made up, it had become, in movie parlance, a "go project." It was in full production, and James was the star performer. He'd been cast as the villain.

Scene one, place the villain at the scene of the crime.

Scene two, make sure the villain is apprehended still in possession of the murder weapon.

Scene three, clean up the loose ends by having the villain die in the penultimate reel.

Scene four would be the inquest. Yes, your honor, the villain had a motive for the slaying. He was reputed to have raped one of the victims. The charge had been dropped, but as your honor is fully aware, there's no smoke without fire. If the villain were able to stand up in court, no doubt he would plead not guilty and attempt to cloud the issue with a mass of conflicting testimony. But, unfortunately, the villain is deceased, killed while speeding from the scene of his dastardly crime. Yes, your honor, the murder weapon was still in the trunk of the car. I submit, your honor, what we have here is an open-and-shut case.

It was a nice straightforward script, thought James, as he turned onto the San Bernardino Freeway, heading toward LA. But as was often the case in the movie business, the script that the author had worked out so carefully was changed during the actual production. This was going to be the case here.

First, the police would not find the murder weapon at the scene of the accident and, second, the deceased, the so-called villain, wasn't deceased at all. He was running around loose. And, right now, he was as pissed off as he could ever remember being. It didn't take a Hercule Poirot to work out who had set him up, but it sure was going to take one to rewrite the scenario so it all came out right in the end.

CHAPTER SIX

He reached downtown Los Angeles just after ten P.M. He switched onto the Hollywood Freeway. The Hollywood Bowl was letting out, and for a moment he was stuck in traffic. Then it eased and he started to make time again.

He came off the freeway onto Ventura Boulevard and drove until he spotted a sign advertising an adult motel. The place was discreet. It would take a major earthquake to fetch the manager from his office to knock on anyone's door.

James signed the registration form. The night clerk glanced at it. "How long you want the room Mr. Weatherspoon?"

"Does it make any difference?" asked James.

"Just give me a shout when you leave so's I know it's free again."

"I'll be staying a couple of nights," said James.

The night clerk peered past James, out of the office, trying to see who was waiting in the front of the pickup. He was accustomed to clients staying a couple of hours, three or four at most. Obviously, James had something very special going for him. He couldn't see anyone.

"She's shy," said James.

"She's over fourteen I hope," said the clerk.

"I thought sixteen was the legal age," said James.

"You want to bang jailbait, that's your business," said the clerk. "It's me who draws the line when they're under fourteen."

"You're a solid citizen," said James.

He collected his key and drove the pickup to his assigned parking slot. Before he went into the room, he walked out to the street and checked that the pickup couldn't be seen by any pedestrians. Fifty yards along the boulevard was a 7-Eleven. There he spent close to thirty dollars on a bottle of Scotch, some packaged cold cuts, a loaf of bread, some milk, a can of orange juice, some instant coffee and a couple of bars of chocolate. He also bought a toothbrush, razor and shaving cream. The guy at the checkout stand hinted that if he wanted anything else...something to smoke...to sniff maybe...just say the word. James decided that he must look a lot more disreputable than he'd thought.

Back in his motel room, he poured a very large drink, which he kept topped up while he put together a sandwich which tasted like reconstituted sawdust. But it was the first food he'd had since breakfast that morning, over fifteen hours ago.

That was when he had met Daphne, who at this moment was probably wandering around the Los Angeles bus terminal wondering where she was going to spend the night, blissfully unaware that she was no longer a runaway wife, but a widow.

Two sandwiches and a quarter of a bottle of Scotch later, James climbed onto the waterbed, took out the leather-covered notebook he had found in Charlie's hope chest and started to decipher its contents.

There were twenty names in all, a fresh page for each. Beneath every name, an address, and beneath that columns of dates and figures. First the date, and next to it an amount of money varying from $350 up as high as $750. The dates were approximately a month apart. Some of the names in the book had been paying out for over three years.

James went through them again. One of them was ringing a bell. Not loudly, but enough for James to know he'd heard it before. He tried to dredge it up from the back of his mind. Maybe if he relaxed and thought about nothing for a moment, it would pop to the surface. He should have known better. During the past sixteen hours he'd driven close to six hundred miles, he'd been framed for a double murder, he'd nearly been assassinated, and he'd been bitten by a rattlesnake. Not a day's activities conducive to a fresh, clear state of mind. Sleep hit him like an eighteen-wheel truck. When he woke up it was nine o'clock and there was somebody banging on his door.

It took him a full minute to work out where he was, and another minute to get to his feet and hobble to the door. By then, the knocking had stopped. Peering through the window he saw an old cleaning woman heading across the small compound to try another room. He hobbled into the bathroom and sat down on the toilet. That's when he realized why he was hobbling.

His ankle was swollen. Also it hurt. Without getting up he pulled down his sock, still encrusted with his own dried blood, and pulled off the dressing the doctor had stuck over the wound. It didn't look too healthy. In fact it looked revolting.

The site of the place where he had slashed himself with the razor had turned a sickly shade of yellow, and the whole surrounding area was angrily red. Great! That's all he needed. A nice dose of blood poisoning aggravated by snakebite. But there wasn't much he could do about it right now. He stuck the dressing back on, finished on the toilet and started to clean his teeth.

He discovered that he didn't smell too good, so he stripped off all his clothes and stepped into the shower. The soap was one of those ridiculously small bars that hotels give to their guests. He kept on dropping it as he was showering.

It was while he was fishing around for it a third time that he remembered the name that had been eluding him last night. He climbed out of the shower, and without bothering to dry off, he went into the bedroom and checked the name in Charlie's notebook.

Mossman, Harvey P.

That had been the name given to him by the Glendale tax office. The owner of the house where Charlie and Charlotee had been living for a time.

According to the figures under Mossman's name he had been a pretty regular payee up to about a year ago. It averaged out at about $450 per month. Then suddenly the payments stopped.

Okay, thought James. Let's assume this is Charlie's list of "clients," men and women he was blackmailing. Maybe what had happened was that Mossman told Charlie and Charlotee they could use the house in lieu of the monthly payout. Charlie had been no fool. The fact he was only hitting his victims for around $500 per month proved that. It was an affordable figure, an amount that wasn't going to drive anybody to bankruptcy or to the law. He'd probably figured the use of the house was just as good as Mossman's $450 a month. So he and Charlotee had moved in and Mossman had stopped paying cash money to cover up his indiscretion, whatever that might have been.

James added up the payments in the book. They came to around $10,000 per month. A pretty healthy income considering it was tax-free. Charlie and Charlotee could have lived very comfortably on that amount of bread. But then had come the big strike, Harold J. Everly, who had $200 million in the bank. Screw all the little guys, we've hit the jackpot.

The names in the book didn't know it, but even if Charlie was still alive, they would probably have been let off the hook. Who'd bother to screw around with a few grand a month when with a quick "I do" Charlie and Charlotee could lay their hands on a large part of $200 million. Sure, they would have had to get a divorce first. That's why they'd gone to ground, disappeared for a couple of weeks. They'd been waiting for the divorce papers to be filed.

James flipped through the names again. None of them meant anything to him. But of one thing he was now sure. None of them had pulled the trigger on Charlie and Charlotee. One, they had been paying up too long to suddenly decide to take that course of action and two, who's going to risk a murder rap for comparative peanuts? Half of $200 million, that was different. Also, none of the names in the book knew James. Everly did. So did Wally.

He must have appeared to them like a gift from the gods. He started to work out how the scenario must have developed.

They'd probably known where Charlie and Charlotee were all along, but James had to be allowed to find them himself. That way there'd be plenty of witnesses to testify that he'd been looking for them.

When they thought he was getting close, a fact James had confirmed when he had called Everly from Needles, they'd moved in, killed Charlie and Charlotee and left James to face the consequences.

He hadn't been meant to discover the bodies in the water tank. It had been assumed that he would leave the shack in the desert and go on back to Needles to continue his search for the Fishers. Meanwhile, an anonymous call to the police to notify them of the bodies, a moment to slip the gun into the trunk of James's car and another moment to screw around with his brakes. A fatal accident, murder weapon discovered in the wreckage, case closed. And the dead James would never even have known he was being sought for murder.

But nobody had figured on an angry rattlesnake that had allowed James to discover the bodies for himself and, thereafter, stay one jump ahead of the part that had been written for him. Nobody likes an actor who doesn't stick to the script, least of all the guy who wrote it. One way or another, Everly and Wally were going to discover that. Everly had called him a vindictive bastard. Given enough time, James was going to show him just how right he had been.

He picked up a copy of the *Los Angeles Times* at a drugstore a few yards from the motel and brought it back to his room. He ignored the motel manager who waved to him from his office, just as he ignored his room phone which was ringing as he came back in. Nobody knew he was here except the manager, and if having a straight client on the premises upset him, that was tough.

There was nothing in the paper about the murder. There was an inside story about a fatal accident just outside San Bernardino. At the time of going to press the victim, who had been burned beyond immediate recognition, remained unidentified.

He figured the police would already have traced the car from the engine or registration number or whatever other identification might have survived the wreck. They would run it through the Department of Motor Vehicles who would give them the name of the registered owners, in this case, the rental company. They, in turn, would give them the name of Amy. She would tell them that the car had been borrowed by her landlord, one James Reed. Until something or someone told them otherwise, they would assume that said James Reed had been the driver.

Somewhere down the line Hank Spruce would be reported missing and the police might start looking for his pickup. Later on, when Daphne surfaced, as she probably would, some cop might start putting two and two together. Maybe there was sufficient skin left on Hank to fingerprint the corpse. Maybe they'd go for dental records. But whatever was going to happen was going to take time, and time, right now, was what James needed.

He also needed another form of transport. He may have miscalculated somewhere along the line and the police could be looking for Hank's pickup right now. This was going to be a problem. He could hardly use one of his credit cards because any moment now the police were going to pronounce him dead. It's highly illegal to use a dead person's credit card, especially if it's your own. He had some of Everly's cash left. A couple of thousand dollars. But he was going to need that for eating and drinking money. He could hardly go down to Malibu and pick up his own car. So how was he going to get himself some wheels? He had always been a believer in killing as many birds as possible with a single stone, so he went back to Charlie's notebook.

Harvey P. Mossman's address was in Westwood. James rang the number that Charlie had written beneath the address.

"Mossman and Company," said a voice on the other end of the line.

"I'd like to buy some stocks," said James.

"I'm sorry, you must have the wrong number. This is Mossman and Company."

"You don't sell stocks?"

"No sir, we sell jewelry."

James apologized and hung up. Okay, so Harvey Mossman was a jeweler. Hopefully he was a successful one who had more than one automobile.

James climbed into the pickup and drove out of the motel, ignoring the manager for what he hoped would be the last time. He headed over Coldwater Canyon and through Beverly Hills toward Westwood. He wondered briefly what Katherine would feel when she read of his death. Very little, he imagined. Come to think of it there were very few people who were going to mourn his recent demise. Sure, there were a few acquaintances who might feel a pang of regret, but there was nobody to shed any tears. Well, he was dead, so what did he care.

He left the pickup on the far side of the city parking lot on the western edge of Westwood Village. He locked it and put the key on the top of the front wheel. There were a couple of other keys on the ring. Hank's home probably, the one he had shared with Daphne and which was going to stay empty for a long time to come. James hoped he hadn't left any pets locked indoors.

Mossman and Company was a small shop just off Westwood Boulevard. Important jewelry-buying takes place in Beverly Hills, at Van Cleef's or Harry Winston's. Harvey Mossman catered to the people who wanted a lot of bang for their buck. Make it big and make it flashy, providing it doesn't cost more than five hundred dollars. So the gold chains in the window were nine-karat, the stones were artificial, and there wasn't a solid gold Rolex to be seen. Nevertheless, there was an iron grille inside the door that permitted vetting of the customer before he was actually buzzed in to the premises.

It seemed that James passed the test. The iron grille buzzed discreetly, James pushed it open and went into the shop. A predatory-looking woman came from behind the counter to greet him.

She was tall, broad, dark-haired and had a small mustache that she had tried to bleach out but hadn't quite succeeded. She wore a diamond clip on the lapel of her dark suit which, if it had been genuine, would have cost fifty thousand dollars. James seriously doubted it was genuine. She was about forty-five years old.

"Good morning, sir," she said in a deep voice, dripping with servility. "How can I help you?"

"I'd like to see Mr. Mossman please," said James.

"On what business, may I ask?"

"I'm an old friend," said James.

"Really. I'm Mrs. Mossman." The servility had gone from her tone.

"More an acquaintance," said James. "A friend of a friend."

She looked at him suspiciously. James noticed that she had a slight cast in one eye. Then without taking her good eye off him she called her husband's name.

"Harvey. Someone to see you."

Mossman didn't immediately appear, and Mrs. Mossman remained staring at James as though she was just begging for him to try something.

If Harvey Mossman had been paying Charlie Fisher to prevent his wife learning of some indiscretion, then he'd been getting value for his money. Mrs. Mossman had a face you could break stones with, and the physique to match.

"What friend?" she said suddenly.

James didn't understand her, and said so.

"You said you were a friend of a friend of my husband."

"Right," said James.

"Which friend are you a friend of?"

The conversation was saved from degenerating further by the arrival of Mossman, who appeared from an office at the back of the shop. He was older than his wife, about sixty. He was shorter too, and rounder, and he had lost most of his hair. He had a jeweler's eyeglass clipped to one lens of his spectacles, pushed up out of the way.

"Yes?" he said.

"He says he's a friend of a friend," said Mrs. Mossman.

"I see. Who is our mutual acquaintance?"

"Charlie," said James.

"Charlie? I don't think I know any Charlie."

"Charlie Fisher."

James watched the color drain from his face. His wife, who was standing behind him, didn't notice.

"Who's Charlie Fisher?" she asked her husband.

He pulled himself together remarkably quickly. "He's the man I met at the convention," he said. "I told you about him."

"No you didn't," said Mrs. Mossman. But she had lost interest and she moved away behind the counter and started to rearrange a tray of rings.

"How is Charlie?" said Mossman, his eyes beseeching James.

"Not well," said James. "Not well at all."

"I'm sorry to hear that," said Mossman.

"Maybe we could go for a cup of coffee," said James, allowing his eyes to flick toward Mrs. Mossman.

"Yes. Of course. What a good idea. I'm going out for ten minutes, dear."

Mrs. Mossman looked up from her tray of rings. For one moment, James thought she was going to forbid her husband to do any such thing. Then she nodded. "Bring me back a bagel. Cream cheese and lox, no onions," she said.

Mossman bundled James out of the shop quickly as if he was scared she'd change her mind.

The only coffee shop in the immediate vicinity was crowded with UCLA students and young executives in shiny track suits.

"We can't talk in there," said James.

Mossman started to have trouble with his priorities. "I've got to get her bagel," he said.

"Do it after," said James. "This isn't going to take long."

James led him around back of the coffee shop to the parking lot. There they sat side-by-side on a low wall, surrounded by the neighborhood garbage cans which hadn't yet been emptied from the previous day. A group of kids were throwing a football at the far side of the lot. The guy in charge was yelling at them to fuck off. But they were big kids so he wasn't yelling very hard.

"I thought it was all finished," said Mossman.

"Why would you have thought that?"

"When they moved out of the house, then he didn't call me like he always did... I thought it was all finished."

"Maybe it is," said James. "Then again, maybe it isn't."

Mossman looked sideways at him. James noticed for the first time that he had forgotten to remove the jeweler's eyeglass from his spectacles.

"How much this time?" Mossman asked.

"No money," said James. "Just information."

"About what?"

His voice was flat, without emotion. He wasn't even listening. All he knew was that a nightmare he'd thought was over had returned.

"Charlie Fisher," said James.

"You're his friend. That's what you said."

"He's no friend of mine," said James. "Neither is his wife."

"He hasn't got a wife."

"Charlotee."

"She's his sister."

"She's his wife."

Mossman straightened up from his slouched position. He started to ask a question, then changed his mind.

"I've got to get back to the store," he said.

"What does he have on you?" asked James.

"I don't know what you're talking about."

"Sure you do. You were paying him four fifty a month. Then you let him move into that house you own in Glendale. You're not going to tell me it was because you felt sorry for him."

For one moment, James thought Mossman was going to grin. He didn't quite make it.

"No, I didn't feel sorry for him," he said. Then he had a sudden thought. "You're from the police."

"I'm not from the police," said James. "I'm just another sucker on Charlie's list."

"I didn't..." Mossman started to say, then he lapsed into silence again.

"What's the matter?" said James. "Did you think you're the only guy he's hitting on?"

"I didn't think about it at all," said Mossman. He was looking at James differently, seeing a fellow victim. "How much are you paying him?"

"That doesn't matter right now," said James. "What's important is I think I can stick it to Charlie, but I'm going to need some help."

"How are you going to stick it to him?"

"What do you care, so long as you're off the hook?"

"His hook. What about yours?"

"I'm not in that line of business," said James.

"What line of business are you in?"

"Look. I don't care what you did. For a lousy four hundred and fifty bucks a month payout, it couldn't have been all that spectacular."

"It wasn't," said Mossman.

"See, I figure Charlie as pretty bright, but strictly small time. Only squeeze the customer for what he can afford without too much sweat. Set too high a price, and the guy's going to overreact and do something stupid. Like go to the police or beat Charlie to death with his crutch."

"I thought about it," said Mossman.

"Which one?"

"What's the difference? I didn't do either."

"What was he going to do? Tell your wife on you?"

"Yes," said Mossman.

"That would do it," said James. "I've met her."

This time when Mossman tried to grin, he made it.

"Apart from anything else, the business is in her name," he said.

"Let me guess," said James. "Your wife was out of town. You were lonely. You met Charlotee. A quick one-night stand, where's the harm. Only she wouldn't move out until Charlie had negotiated a deal."

"More or less," said Mossman.

"I figure that was their racket in a nutshell."

Mossman picked up quickly. "Was?"

James covered his slip. "I'm going to close them down," he said. "But I'm going to need some help from you."

"What kind of help?"

"First, tell me everything you know about Charlie Fisher. How he contacted you. Where he contacted you. How you paid over the money. Everything you can remember."

"What else?"

"You don't happen to have a spare car I could borrow?"

Mossman didn't have a spare car. But after he and James had talked for a few more minutes, he went with James to a hire company and rented one in his own name. James tried to give him some cash to cover the cost. Mossman wouldn't take it. If James was truly going to get Charlie off his back at last, then the car was on him.

"One more thing," said James just before he drove off. "Do you trust me?"

"I suppose I must," said Mossman. "Although I don't know why."

"I'm only asking," said James. "Because you might be seeing my picture in the paper sometime in the next few days. Don't let it worry you. And don't believe a word it says."

He drove off before Mossman could ask any questions, leaving the little jeweler clutching a bagel with cream cheese and lox and no onions.

James didn't doubt that his picture would be in the newspapers. As soon as news of his death was released by the police, some enterprising newspaperman would remember that he had once been married to Katherine Long, superstar. He could see the story heading already:

MOVIE STAR'S EX BURNED TO DEATH IN FATAL CRASH

That would be followed by a lot of information about Katherine and practically none about him. He'd never made good copy, even when they'd been married.

All that would change when the police finally decided to release their main bombshell:

KATHERINE LONG'S EX-HUSBAND TIED TO DOUBLE SLAYING

Maybe by then he would be able to come out in the open. That would involve even more media coverage. Then again, maybe by then he'd be dead for real.

Mossman hadn't been able to tell him as much as he had hoped. "Mostly he'd call me on the phone," he'd said. "He'd arrange to meet me someplace where I'd hand over the money in cash."

"Mostly?" asked James.

"There was this one time. He told me to take the money to this place on the beach. A restaurant, a bar actually. I was to give it to the man who owned the place."

"Why the change in plan?"

"He was out of town. He told me he was calling from San Diego and he owed the man. To tell you the truth, I wasn't really interested. As far as I was concerned, it was just another payment."

Mossman had finally relaxed enough for James to delve a little deeper.

"What hard evidence did he have on you?" he'd asked.

"Photographs," said Mossman.

"How did he take photographs without you knowing?"

Mossman didn't answer right away. Finally, he'd decided that he was too deep in to back out now.

"I took them," he said.

"How did you manage that?"

"Delayed-action shutter."

"When you and Charlotee were actually...?"

Mossman had cut in on him quickly. "It was her idea. She had this instant camera. It seemed... I don't know... I must have been mad."

"Crazier things have happened," said James, who couldn't think of any right off.

The restaurant-cum-bar that Mossman had told him about was on the Venice beachfront. James tried to park in the city lot next to the paddle tennis courts, but it was full. So too were the other lots within half a mile of the beach.

After cruising around for fifteen minutes, he spotted a car vacating a curbside parking spot. He executed a U-turn which set up a cacophony of hooters and just managed to beat a Mustang loaded with teenagers into the space. Ignoring the abuse being heaped on him by the teenagers, he locked his car, and walked back the half mile to the beach.

Venice beach in the summer always looked, to James, like an Occidental version of a Moroccan bazaar. There were the street peddlers selling cheap jewelry and cheaper clothing; there were the entertainers with their guitars and bongo drums and their ghetto blasters; there were mimes, and fortune tellers; there were stalls selling couscous or orange juice or hamburgers or hot dogs or tacos or falafel; there were roller skaters and cyclists and skateboarders; there was the roped-off enclosure where exhibitionists could display their pectorals and dorsals while they wrestled with barbells; there were the areas monopolized by cool-looking blacks skating to a disco beat and the stretch being used by kids showing off their prowess by slalom roller-skating. Finally there were the tourists, who were just having a good time.

James found the place Mossman had told him about. The place where Charlie had once told him to deliver the money. It was tucked between a roller-skate rental store and an untidy building with a sign tacked to the wall: ROOMS TO RENT. There were two tables set up outside, but nobody was using them, probably due to the crush of people moving backward and forward like a herd of good-natured bison.

Inside, the place was hot and dark and narrow. No air conditioning here, probably because there was very little air to condition. Half a dozen tables down one side, a long bar down the other. The tables were empty and the bar was full.

The smell coming from the kitchen at the back had to be the reason for the empty tables. A starving man only needed one whiff to turn right around and walk out again. In case he'd been having trouble with his nose, the group of guys seated at the bar would have done the trick. James hadn't seen so much leather in one place since he'd got rid of his charge account at Gucci. The place looked like it was holding a Nazi party rally and all the little stormtroopers were looking straight at him.

He came up to the end of the bar and was greeted by the bartender—a mean-looking guy with blond hair and pale blue eyes. The ultimate Aryan. Himmler would have been proud of him, except he was gay.

"We're closing," he said.

"I'd like to talk to the owner," said James. Everyone at the bar was still looking at him.

"I just told you, we're closing."

"I don't give a fuck if you're closing or not. I want to talk to the owner."

The bartender flashed a look at his customers, then back to James.

"You're not a cop." It was a statement, not a question, but James answered anyway.

"I'm not a cop."

"Health department?"

"You've got to be kidding. I'd have closed you down while I was still outside."

One of the guys at the bar giggled. He was silenced by a look from the bartender.

"So who are you?"

"I'm a guy who wants to talk to the owner," said James. Then, in case he hadn't got his point across, he added, "You asshole."

This time there was a definite laugh from a couple of the customers. "He's cute," someone said.

The bartender was confused now. He was used to strangers bolting from the place, if not when they first came in, then when he started talking to them. Also he was used to a hundred-percent backup from "the boys in the band." Still, he had a reputation to maintain.

"Beat it, buddy," he said. To add weight, he dropped his hands below the level of the bar as if he might be reaching for something, like an iron bar or a baseball bat.

James was in a hurry. As soon as he had walked into the place, he had decided the best way to handle things was by coming on as a hard case. It had worked so far.

"If you're reaching down there for anything other than your cock, I'm going to break both your wrists," he said.

"He's mean, too," said another voice from the bar.

The bartender gave up. Both his hands came up to bar level, empty.

"I'm the owner," he said. "What do you want?"

"To talk," said James.

"I'm listening."

"So's everyone else," said James. "So why don't you go ahead and do what you said you were going to?"

"What's that?"

"Close."

"Shit, man. I can't close. I got customers."

"They'll understand. Won't you, girls?"

They loved it. One of them wanted to know how long James was going to be.

"You won't die of thirst," said James.

They straggled out of the bar with a "Ciao Bubba, see you later." It was James who closed and locked the door behind them. When he turned back to the bar, Bubba was pouring himself a drink.

James took a stool at the bar. "You wanna pour me one of those?"

"No," said Bubba. But he poured it just the same. "So what do you want to talk about?"

"Charlie Fisher," said James.

"Never heard of him."

"Sure you have."

"Listen, ducky. You ask me if I've heard of Charlie Fisher. I tell you I haven't. End of conversation."

"He's dead," said James.

There was a flicker of something in the pale blue eyes, gone almost before James could see it.

"So. A guy named Charlie Fisher is dead. If I knew him, maybe I'd feel sorry for him. But I don't."

"You would if you'd seen him," said James. "He had a hole in him big enough to put your hand inside. Half his face was missing too."

Definite reaction this time. As Bubba poured himself another drink, the neck of the bottle rattled against the edge of the glass.

"I still don't know any Charlie Fisher."

"Is that what you're going to tell the cops?"

"What cops? What are you talking about?"

"The cops who are gonna be asking you questions."

"You're crazy," said Bubba. He'd started to sweat. "Why should the cops want to talk to me?"

"Because I'm going to tell them," said James.

"Tell them what?"

"How you used to pick up his hush money for him."

"Come on! Three times in as many years." He realized what he had said. "Anyway, who said anything about blackmail? Some guys handed me envelopes, I passed them on to Charlie."

"Who you don't know."

"Okay, so I know him. Is he really dead?"

"Oh, yes," said James. "He's dead."

"How?"

"Somebody blew him away," said James. "Charlotee too."

"Oh, shit," said Bubba.

He downed his drink and poured himself another. "Why are you laying this on me?" he asked.

"Somebody's got to take the rap," said James. "You're my best bet at the moment."

"Where do you fit in?"

"I'm the guy the cops think did it," said James.

Bubba looked at him for a moment.

"Did you?" he asked finally.

"No. But I know who did."

"Don't tell me," said Bubba. "I don't want to know."

"I wasn't going to," said James.

There was banging on the front door. Bubba looked out. His group had obviously grown tired of frightening the tourists and wanted back in.

"Fuck off," he yelled at them. Then he turned back to James.

"Okay. What do I have to do to get you off my back?"

"Tell me about Charlie."

"What's to tell? I met him in vet's hospital when he got shipped back from Nam."

"What were you doing in hospital?"

"I was a nurse," said Bubba.

"Cute," said James. "Charlie was in for his legs. Right?"

"Yeah. He'd stepped on a land mine. He was a mess."

"He still is," said James.

Bubba thought about it for a moment. Then he nodded. "You're right. Charlie isn't one of nature's best efforts. Anyway, while he was in hospital, he and I, we got friendly."

"How friendly?"

"About as friendly as you can," said Bubba. He nearly batted his eyelids as he said it. "Then I mustered out and he disappeared for a couple of years. One day, he just turned up here out of the blue. Boy, he looked terrible. He'd lost an eye since I last saw him. He told me it was in a bar fight."

"Not unless they've got bars in army prisons," said James.

"I figured something like that. Still, it was none of my business. He hadn't changed much though. He could scare people just being in the same room with them. But I'd always got on with him okay and I was willing to start up where we'd left off. Then he produced this skinny little chick, said she was his wife."

"Charlotee," said James.

"Would you believe a name like that! I was a bit pissed off at first. Then I thought, what the hell, so he's gone straight, it happens."

"Had he?" asked James.

"Not as far as I was concerned. Charlotee didn't seem to mind which way he swung. They needed a place to shack for a time so I rented them an upstairs room I don't use. They moved in."

"For how long?"

"It's still theirs. At least, the rent's paid up till the end of the month."

"But they weren't using it much, right?"

"Hardly ever these past few months. I'd not see him for weeks on end. I'd hear from him from time to time. He'd tell me some dude owed him money and was going to drop it off here. I'd hang onto it for him and he'd drop by later to pick it up."

"Those were his payoffs."

"As far as I was concerned, it was just money."

"Sure," said James drily.

"That's the honest truth."

"You didn't know what he did for a living?"

"No."

"Bullshit," said James.

"Okay. Maybe I guessed. But I didn't have any part in it."

"Did he get any mail?" asked James.

"Not here. He's got ... he had ... a box down at the post office."

"Anyone been up to his room recently?"

"Not since he was last here. He dropped by a couple of weeks ago."

"Did he say anything about what he was doing?"

"Charlotee was staying someplace in Malibu, he said. I kidded him about it. He's got a crummy room above a bar in Venice while his old lady's swanning it in Malibu."

"What did he say?"

"'It's a living,' he said. Just like that. 'It's a living.'"

"What did that mean to you?"

"He was laying for another sucker."

"A special sucker? Something big?"

Bubba thought about it for a moment, then he shook his head. "Nothing special. I mean, he didn't act over the moon about it."

"What then?"

"I haven't seen him or heard from him since. He was here though. I didn't see him because it was the night of the big storm. I was with some friends down on the peninsula helping them sandbag their underground garage. Christ, you should have seen the mess. Ten automobiles up to their roofs in ocean. Anyway, when I got back the next day he'd left me a note along with a month's rent. Seems he was going to be out of circulation for a time."

"That's all the note said?"

"There was something else. Didn't make much sense to me. Something about winning the big one. He couldn't have been talking about the lottery 'cause Charlie never gambled."

He'd gambled, thought James, and he'd lost.

"That's it?" he asked.

"That's it. And if you think that ties me into anything, you're crazy."

"It's not what I think," said James. "It's what the cops will want to make of it."

"Come on, man. I've been straight with you. Now get off my back."

"Have you got a key to his room?"

"No," said Bubba.

"Pity," said James. "The only way I'm going to pin this killing where it belongs is by finding out everything I can about your friend Charlie. There might be something I could use up there."

"If you find what you're looking for, am I off the hook?"

"We're both off the hook," said James.

"I've got a key," said Bubba.

James told him it would be okay to let the circus back in the bar. He took the key Bubba had given him and followed directions up the stairs at the back, along a narrow passage from which Bubba's living quarters led, up another short flight of stairs to a door at the top. He unlocked the door and let himself in.

Bubba had described it correctly when he called it a crummy room. There was one window, overlooking the next-door neighbor's garbage cans. There was a tiny alcove holding a cracked washbasin and an electric burner. There was a single bed, a wardrobe, a chest of drawers, a table with two wooden chairs. There was also a makeshift desk against the far wall holding a word processor.

"I've got one of them. The same make," Charlie had said that night in the guest house. Pity he hadn't gone on to tell James what he used it for. There were half a dozen floppy discs on the desktop next to the keyboard. James looked at them. One was the standard word processing program that he'd never quite mastered, two others held video games of the nonintellectual variety, the other three were still in their original wrappings, unopened.

James covered the rest of the room quickly. There were a few items of clothing, male and female, some dirty dishes in the washbasin, some dirty sheets on the bed and very little else. The chest of drawers yielded some more clothing and a reminder from the post office that if Charlie didn't pay the back rent on his mailbox he was going to lose it. The box number was printed clearly on the reminder notice.

James came back downstairs and handed the key back to Bubba, behind the bar. The gang had returned. James had no idea what Bubba had told them about him, but it had to have been something pretty heavy because nobody made any cracks when he came in. They sat on their stools, peering into their drinks with complete concentration. James beckoned for Bubba to come to the door with him. Bubba came out from behind the bar, reluctantly, and walked with James to the door.

"Did you find what you were looking for?" asked Bubba.

"I'll let you know," said James. "One more thing. I walk quietly, but I carry a very big stick, so don't believe what you read in the papers."

"What's that supposed to mean?"

"Dead ain't necessarily so," said James as he walked out into the fresh air.

He knew he was taking a chance, but there were a couple of things he needed to pick up at home. Assuming the girls were sunning themselves on the terrace, he reckoned he could get in and out without being spotted. He parked the car a quarter of a mile from the house and walked the rest of the way. He let himself in through the front gate, and into the guest house. His answering machine was blinking at him like crazy. James checked the number of calls he'd had. There were twelve. But dead men can't pick up their messages, so he ignored the machine, going straight through into the bedroom. At the back of his closet was a carryall. He dragged it out and checked the contents. One short-barreled shotgun. One box of shells for same. He'd bought the gun years ago when he was still married to Katherine. Everybody had been buying guns in those days, especially if they were rich and lived in Beverly Hills. As far as James knew, they were still buying them. He hadn't wanted the gun, but it had made Katherine feel better. It had never been fired, and after exposure to the sea air for three years, there was a strong probability that the only damage it would inflict would be on the guy who pulled the trigger. But it was the only gun he owned, and he figured that he might have urgent need of it sometime during the next few days. He threw a couple more things into the carryall, and left as quietly and as unobtrusively as he had arrived. He walked back to his car, climbed in and headed back toward town.

He booked into a thirty-five-dollar-a-day motel on Washington Boulevard, two miles from the beach. It was clean and impersonal and the guy who checked him in didn't even look at him. Checking himself in his bathroom mirror, James figured that even if he had, he'd not be able to finger him when his picture hit the media. He had a two-day stubble on his face, dark hollows under his eyes, and looked like he hadn't slept for a week. Let someone tell him now that he looked like Michael Caine and the actor would be entitled to sue for defamation of character.

He walked to the nearest drugstore and bought a packet of disposable razors, toothbrush, shaving cream, toothpaste and a bottle of hair dye. He also bought some fresh dressings and antiseptic for his ankle, which continued to throb, but not quite as badly as it had when he had woken up this morning. There was a men's clothing store next door where he picked up a couple of shirts, some fresh socks and shorts and a pair of jeans. Then he walked back to the motel, picking up a bottle of Scotch on the way.

Back in his room, he poured himself a drink and then he stripped off everything he was wearing and stuffed it into a laundry bag supplied by the motel. He examined his ankle. Some of the swelling had gone down, and it didn't look quite as bad as he remembered. He washed it, drowned it with antiseptic and put on a clean dressing. Then he started to dye his hair.

Fifteen minutes later he was wishing he'd left well enough alone. He had meant to change the color from its natural lightish brown to black. What he came out with was piebald. He tried to wash out the dye. But, true to the wording on the label, it was colorfast. It was going to take a Vidal Sassoon to repair the damage. What the hell, he decided finally. The object was to escape chance recognition. The way he looked right now, nobody would even look at his face, they'd be too fascinated by the strange growth on his head. He topped up his drink, climbed onto the bed and waited to see himself on television.

He made the six-o'clock news. The victim of the fatal automobile accident in San Bernardino County last night was James Reed, former husband of movie star Katherine Long. There was a photo of James, taken four years earlier, and half a dozen of Katherine, taken from some of her most successful movie roles. Miss Long, who was not available for comment, is currently appearing in a remake of…

James switched off the television and poured himself another drink.

He went out to get himself something to eat around seven. He chose a small Mexican restaurant not far from the motel where he ate well, in spite of the sidelong glances he was getting from some of the other diners. The odd looks were all toward the top of his head, and not for his face.

On the way back to the motel, he stopped off at a sporting-goods store and bought himself a wool ski hat and a lightweight parka. Back in the motel room, he put together some of the things he had collected from the guest house and then sat down to wait until he considered the time was right for him to set out to commit a federal crime.

Robbing a United States Post Office is not a matter to be taken lightly. The investigation falls within the jurisdiction of the FBI. They may be slow and ponderous, but they're thorough, and even if they're not like the Mounties, who claim to always get their man, their batting average is still pretty impressive. James had considered this before making his decision and, if he could have thought of another way, he would have taken it. He wanted badly to get a look at the contents of Charlie's mailbox. Not having the key to the box meant he was going to have to break it open. He could hardly do that when the post office was open for business and full of people. He was risking a five-year stretch, at least. But the alternative, if he didn't come up with some answers pretty soon, was the murder charge that was going to be laid on him as soon as the authorities realized they'd wrongly identified the body in the San Bernardino auto crash.

He waited until close to eleven thirty before leaving the motel. He guessed there would be heavy traffic in and out of the Venice bars around this time. Wandering cop cars would be concentrating their efforts along the main drag, looking to bust rowdy drunks, enterprising hookers or overworked pushers. He drove to a spot a couple hundred yards from the post office and parked, switching off the lights. He didn't get out of the car right away. He sat watching the foot traffic.

Unlike Beverly Hills or Bel Air, where walking the streets is almost considered a felony in itself, down here, close to the beach, everyone walks. This is often due to the fact that in the summer it's almost impossible to find a parking place anywhere close to where you want to go.

James had timed it well. There was just the right number of people on the street. Most of them were on their way home after a long, late supper. Some had left one bar and were in search of another. They were sufficiently wrapped up in themselves not to take any notice of a man wearing a woolen ski hat and a parka, heading toward the post office.

The building was fronted by a small forecourt planted with some extremely tired-looking shrubbery. What could have been an effective screen from the sidewalk, wasn't. So an all-out assault on the front doors of the building was out of the question.

Perhaps ten years ago James would have relied on speed and picked the lock in as short a time as it took to turn a key. But he was woefully out of practice. He hadn't picked a lock in years. It was an art he had learned as a plainclothes cop in London. Later he had added to his knowledge when he had left the police force and gone to work for a private security company. One of their employees was a reformed old lag who went by the name of Ernie Scruggs. Ernie's boast was that the lock hadn't been made that he couldn't open given the right amount of time and the right equipment. He'd shown James some of his simpler methods of illegal entry and had even given him half a dozen twisted pieces of metal which he swore were more use than a bunch of keys. Subsequently James had used them a couple of times, once to get into the house when he'd locked himself out, and once to get into an ex-girlfriend's apartment to collect his things because she had threatened to burn them all if he didn't move back in. He hoped it was going to be like riding a bicycle. Once learned, never forgotten. It wasn't.

The gate set into the wire fence at the back of the post office proved no problem, but this was because somebody had forgotten to snap the padlock closed. James slipped through and pulled the gate shut behind him. He crossed the yard to the back of the main building. As post offices go, this one wasn't up to much. The place was as dark as the night that enveloped it. Darker, in fact, because outside in the street there was light spilling from a hundred signs. Very little of that light leaked back here.

Using the small flashlight he'd brought from home, James selected a promising-looking picklock from Ernie Scruggs's small canvas wallet and went to work on the door. It took him twenty minutes and three more picklocks before he heard the tumblers click back. Old Ernie would have died laughing.

He held his breath, counted to three and then pulled the door open. Not a sound. If the place was alarmed, it was of the silent variety. Maybe right now there was a light blinking frantically at the local police station. James doubted it. Maybe the safe or the vault or whatever they had here was wired, but all James wanted was to pick up Charlie Fisher's mail, and nobody was going to spend taxpayer's money to protect a group of private mailboxes.

He came through the door, pulling it shut behind him. He was in the sorting area, three or four trestle tables with bins beside them. There was a partition separating it from the counter where there were stations for two clerks. James crossed the sorting room to the back of the individual mailboxes. Out front it required a key to get into them; here, at back, they were wide open. The individual numbers were stuck on each box. He located Charlie Fisher's box. It was bulging with uncollected mail. He went through it quickly, replacing the junk and tucking the remainder in his pocket. Two minutes later, he let himself out of the rear door, re-crossed the small yard and went out through the rear gate.

As he reached the street in front of the post office, a police car was prowling past. The occupants didn't even look toward him. He crossed toward his car, climbed in and started to look through the mail by the light of the street lamp. It was too dark. He started the engine, and driving very carefully, obeying all the rules, he pointed the car back toward his motel. Fifteen minutes later he was back in his room pouring himself a drink. Then he started to examine his haul.

It was interesting, but nothing more. There were a couple of checks from people whose names James had seen in Charlie's notebook. Poor schmucks still paying for a moment of indiscretion which, if it hadn't been for Charlie, would no doubt have been long forgotten. There was a note from one guy saying he couldn't afford this month's installment, would Charlie wait until next month? There was a letter from another saying his wife had just divorced him so he was no longer vulnerable. If he ever heard from Charlie again, he'd go straight to the police, something he might do anyway. There was one envelope containing three one-hundred-dollar bills. There was no note with this one and no return address on the envelope. There were a couple of bills, one from a finance company that was helping Charlie buy his auto, the other from Sears for $58.27. And there was Charlie's monthly Visa statement with a note at the bottom saying he had exceeded his one-thousand-dollar credit limit. There was nothing else.

James poured himself another Scotch and tried to figure out where the hell he could go next. Somewhere, Charlie had a place where he kept his important papers, the material that he had built up over the years and which he used to extort regular payments from his victims. That was what James needed badly to locate. And he had to do it quickly because, before long, a lot of other people would be looking too.

The bodies of Charlie and Charlotee would have been identified almost as soon as they were discovered. Obviously, the police were keeping this information to themselves while they tried to get a jump on the killer or killers. He figured he had maybe one or two more days before they identified the James Reed killed in San Bernardino as the same guy who had been chasing all over Needles looking for the Fishers. When they did they would release the names of the murder victims. Everybody on Charlie's list would breathe a sigh of relief. This would be followed very quickly by the realization that somewhere out there the material that Charlie had been holding over them for so long was still in existence and maybe they were just out of a frying pan into a much hotter fire. James doubted any of them would have the ability to go quite as far as he had, but they could sure get in the way. And it would only take one of them putting a foot wrong to have the police join the hunt also.

He poured himself another drink and went through the mail again. The Sears bill was for auto parts, purchased at the midtown Los Angeles branch. The Visa statement was unremarkable providing one discounted the total balance due. One thousand three hundred twenty eight dollars and some odd cents. There was no carry-forward figure from the previous statement, so the full cost had been incurred during that one billing period, a matter of thirty-odd days. James ran his eye down the list of charges. He fetched a notepad from next to the phone on his nightstand and, sitting down at the table, he started to go through the individual charges again, this time making notes.

The first two entries were for restaurants in the Los Angeles area. Then came a restaurant charge for a meal at Ventura. The following day, two meals and a bill for gas in Santa Barbara. Three days later another gas bill in Santa Barbara, a large one this time, close to seventy-five dollars.

James knew Santa Barbara fairly well. He stood up and went to pour himself another drink. Suddenly he was feeling pleased with himself. He had recognized the name of the station which had sold Charlie all that gas. It was located in the Santa Barbara Marina. It looked like Charlie owned a boat.

CHAPTER SEVEN

The morning papers contained follow-ups to the story that had been on last night's TV news. There was mention of Katherine Long's ex-husband's fatal freeway accident, complete with photographs. Not that James expected to be recognized with his three-day stubble and his piebald hair, which looked even more bizarre in the light of day.

He had decided this morning, when he had looked in the mirror, that he looked like an over-age punk. Anywhere else in America, he would be viewed with considerable suspicion. Here in Southern California, he would hardly warrant a second glance except from the tourists.

He did not check out of the motel, deciding it would be as good a base to work from as any other. He'd hung a *Do Not Disturb* notice on the door, and by eight thirty he was on the way to Santa Barbara. For one moment, last night, he had considered leaving there and then. But he'd decided to wait. A lone auto on Pacific Coast Highway at two thirty A.M. was liable to be stopped if for no other reason than that the cops had nothing better to do at that hour of the night. His car papers were in order, but they were in Mossman's name. Apart from that, the only ID that James carried was his own. He couldn't risk having to show it to a highway cop who might have caught the TV news. Now, on a bright, sunny morning the coast highway north was busy with regular traffic.

Ninety minutes after leaving Santa Monica, he reached Montecito, where he left the freeway and swung down toward the sea. He drove past the Biltmore Hotel and onto the main Santa Barbara beach road. He drove past the pier and turned left into the marina. The place had changed since he was last here. The city fathers had decided to upgrade the facility. That costs money, so one of the first things they'd done was to erect a pay booth at the entrance to the marina parking lot, which used to be free. James collected his parking ticket and a "Have a nice day" from the kid who was manning the booth, and parked his car. From a pay phone, he called Information and asked for the number of Charles Fisher, a boat owner in the marina. They didn't have it. He wasn't surprised, it would have been too easy.

He could have gone to the harbor office and found an excuse to look through the list of registered boat owners but, he decided, that wasn't a good idea. Clerks or secretaries might remember him later. He was going to have to do it the hard way. He stood outside the locked gates that led down to one of the slip areas. Only boat owners possessed the plastic cards which opened these gates. Within a couple of minutes somebody came up from the slips and let themselves out. James caught the gate before it could close behind them and walked through. Halfway down the first set of slips, a man was working on his yacht. James stopped beside the slip.

"Nice boat," he said.

The man looked up from where he was scraping paint. "Thanks."

"What is she?"

That was all that was needed. First, it gave the man an excuse to stop working and, second, it gave him the opportunity to extol the virtues of his pride and joy.

James listened politely for a few minutes, interspersing a couple of grunts of admiration as the man explained the area of sail in ratio to the depth of the keel as opposed to the amount of water she drew providing the spinnaker wasn't being used in conjunction with the restanger which, if the droft wasn't properly set, would cause the boat to breach or broach or both. At least, that's how it sounded to James, whose ignorance of boats was only exceeded by his dislike. Finally, when he considered his man was securely hooked, he risked an interruption.

"Friend of mine's got a boat here," he said. "Not as good as yours, though. Maybe you know him. Charlie Fisher?"

The man didn't know Charlie Fisher. Even when James described him, he still didn't know. Once seen, never forgotten, thought James. If this guy didn't remember Charlie, then Charlie's boat wasn't berthed in this part of the marina.

He gained access to the next group of slips the same way, by waiting until somebody let themselves out. This time, he hit on a pretty girl in her early twenties dressed in a bikini top and cutoff jeans. She was sitting in the stem of a cabin cruiser gutting some fish. He opened with the same line.

"Nice boat," he said.

She looked up from her work. "What's it to you?" she said.

Youth used to have charm, thought James. What happened to it? "Friend of mine's got a boat here. Maybe you know him. Charlie Fisher?"

"Never heard of him," she said.

"I keep telling him it's crazy a guy like him having a boat. With that crutch of his, he's going to fall overboard one of these days."

"Oh, him!" she said. "I've seen him around." She was interested suddenly. "What happened to him?"

"Nothing that I know of," said James, misunderstanding.

"I mean. How did he get like that?"

"Oh. Vietnam."

"Serves him right," said the girl. "He shouldn't have been there."

James estimated she could only have been about twelve years old at the end of the war. Some attitudes are perpetuated from one generation to the next.

"I'm visiting him right now, as a matter of fact," he said.

"You're wasting your time," said the girl. "There's nobody on board."

"He was expecting me," said James.

"Nobody's used that boat for a couple of weeks now," she said. "I live right here. I'd know, wouldn't I."

"Would you?" asked James.

"I'd have to be blind and deaf not to," she said, nodding toward the boat that was moored directly opposite.

"I guess you would," said James. "Nice talking to you."

He started toward the boat she'd indicated.

"I told you, there's nobody aboard. She's locked up," said the girl.

"Charlie gave me a key," said James.

It was a boat that suited Charlie. It was scruffy and a little lopsided. A twenty-five-foot cabin cruiser held together, it seemed, by peeling paint. James walked along the access slip and climbed aboard. There was the aft deck with engines below. The cabin space was forward. To the right of the hatch that led down to the cabin were the controls, a single wheel and dual throttles. The superstructure was between him and the girl so that, even if she had been interested, she wouldn't have been able to see what he was doing. He selected a pick-lock from the canvas wallet and in two minutes he had the hatch open. He stepped down into the cabin.

It was small and, if one liked boats and was prepared to ignore the mess, comparatively cozy. There was a table to seat four on the right and a cooker and sink on the left. Moving forward, there was a narrow closet on one side and a tiny toilet compartment opposite. The whole of the prow was taken up by a double berth. Like on most boats, there was a multitude of concealed storage places. James went through them all, starting on the left and working his way around methodically. He found some navigation charts for various places along the Southern California coast down as far as San Diego. He found an instruction manual for the radio, which Charlie didn't have. He found a couple of swimsuits, some unopened cans of food, some paperback novels of the *Scruples* variety, a Walkman with the earphones missing, some dirty bed linen, a half-consumed bottle of vodka, three cans of Coke, and two unsmoked joints.

He was about to start again when the deck beneath him rocked slightly. Somebody had come aboard. He turned to the hatch just as the girl from across the way stuck her head in.

"I told you there was nobody here," she said.

"You were right," said James.

"Do you like swordfish?"

"Personally?"

"Barbecued."

James admitted to liking swordfish.

"So come next door and eat," she said, and disappeared. A moment later she reappeared. "I'm Missy," she said.

"Henry," said James.

"Okay, Henry. Five minutes." She disappeared again.

He spent the next five minutes covering territory he'd already been over. He found a drawer under the main berth which he had missed first time around. Again, there was nothing of interest unless you were into pornographic books, which James wasn't. He stood in the center of the cabin and looked around. Maybe a break would do him good. Have some food and then start again. He went back up on deck, climbed ashore and walked across the main slip to join Missy.

She'd made a salad to accompany two of the largest swordfish steaks James had ever seen. She even had a bottle of California Chardonnay which she said she'd open if James was willing to pay for it. James was willing.

"It's not that I'm stingy," said Missy. "But my old man'll kill me if he comes back and finds we've drunk his wine. I'll go out later and buy another bottle."

"Where is he?" asked James.

"Urchin fishing." She nodded vaguely toward the shadowy bulk of one of the Channel Islands, six or seven miles out. "He goes out every day he can."

"You don't go with him?"

"I get seasick," she said. She poured the wine he had opened. "Cheers," she said.

"Cheers yourself," said James, as he started to eat.

"How's your fish?"

"Delicious," said James.

She watched him for a time in silence. Finally she spoke again. "You're not a bad-looking guy for your age. What do you want to bother dyeing your hair?"

James realized that his wool ski hat had ridden to the back of his head, exposing most of the black and brown disaster beneath. He pulled it forward again.

"It was a mistake," he said.

"It sure was." She held out her glass for a top up. "Did you find what you were looking for?"

There didn't seem much point in denying it. "Not yet," said James.

"You're not a friend of his, are you," she said. It was a statement, not a question.

"Charlie? Why do you say that?"

"He's not the type to have any friends for one. And for two, you're not the type who'd hang around with a creep like that."

"Being a cripple doesn't make you a creep," said James.

"Making a pass at another guy's old lady when your wife's only ten feet away makes him a creep."

"You?"

Missy nodded. "I told my old man when he got back that night. He wanted to go over and beat his brains out. He would have done too if Bobby hadn't been aboard."

"Aboard here or aboard there?" asked James.

"Aboard there. Bobby's always hanging around that boat."

"Who's Bobby?"

"I just told you. A guy who's always hanging around. Does odd jobs around the boat for your nonfriend Charlie." She glanced across toward Charlie's boat. "Not that you'd notice," she added.

"Any idea where I might find this Bobby?"

"I figured that would be the next thing you asked," she said. She was looking at him steadily through her dark brown eyes. James got the impression that she hadn't believed a word he'd said since he arrived.

"Are you going to tell me?" he asked.

"That depends. Is it good news or bad news... for Charlie, I mean?"

James decided to take a chance. "Bad news," he said.

"He rents a room in town," she said. "I'll write down the address."

She declined his offer to help with the dishes so he went back to Charlie's boat to have one more look around. He found a couple of things he had missed last time, but nothing that was going to do him any good. He didn't bother tidying up. After all, Charlie wasn't going to come back and complain. He relocked the hatch and climbed off the boat.

Missy was on deck patching a wet suit.

"Thanks for lunch," he said.

"You're welcome."

"Don't forget to buy the wine."

"There's plenty of time. He never gets back till after dark."

"And thanks for this." He held up the slip of paper on which she'd written Bobby's address.

"Watch out for Bobby," she said. "He's flaky."

"Flaky, how?"

"He hangs around Charlie, doesn't he?"

For one moment, James debated whether he should offer her some explanation for what she would shortly be learning from the newspapers. He decided to leave well enough alone. Maybe by the time she read about Charlie, Charlotee and the late James Reed, everything would have been cleared up. There was no harm in indulging in a little wishful thinking from time to time. He said good-bye and headed back to his car.

The address that Missy had given him was on the north edge of town, in an area of small, untidy houses, most of them sadly in need of repair. Twenty years ago, this could have been a pleasant real-estate development, the kind of place where retired couples might have planned to spend their remaining years, or newly-weds bring up their families. Somehow it had all gone wrong. Blame it on the recession or on population shift or town planning, whatever, but the neighborhood had definitely slid downhill to the very bottom.

Bobby's address was the last house on the street. In fact, James had begun to think Missy had given him a wrong steer. The house itself was invisible from the road, screened by a yard overgrown with shrubbery and littered with the stripped and rusting wrecks of half a dozen automobiles. It looked like a junkyard for the use of the whole street. He was about to turn the car and head back when he spotted a mailbox.

He parked the car and, getting out, walked over to it. He was just able to read the house number painted on the flag. He looked past it and, for the first time, he saw the house. It was thirty feet back from the road and looked like an urban version of Charlie's desert shack.

He headed toward it, picking his way through the stripped autos. Close up, it looked even more dilapidated, as though a good gust of wind could bring the whole place down. If Bobby was paying more than a couple of bucks to rent a room here, he was being taken. There was a screen full of holes over the front door. James pulled it back and knocked. For a long moment nothing happened. He was about to knock again when he heard some movement from inside the house, followed by a male voice.

"Fuck off!"

James knocked again. More movement from inside and the sound of something being knocked over. A couple of seconds later the door was pulled half open from inside and a woman peered out.

"What do you want?" she said.

James couldn't see her too well; the inside of the house was dark and she stayed behind the door with just her head poking around the edge. She was black and looked about thirty years old with sixty years of hard life behind her.

"I'd like to talk to Bobby," he said.

She continued to look at him without change of expression. Maybe she was deaf, thought James.

"I'd like to talk to Bobby," he said again, louder this time.

"Out back," she said and closed the door in his face.

As he walked around the side of the house, he could hear a mumble of voices from inside then the sound of a door slamming. He doubled back quickly to the front of the house just in time to see a tall, skinny black guy come out of the front door and take off toward the road.

"Bobby!" he yelled.

The guy broke into a run and James went after him.

By the time he reached the street, Bobby was thirty yards away. James climbed into his car, made a U-turn and took off. It was no contest. He overtook the running Bobby fifty yards down the street. He pulled ahead and slammed on the brakes. He jumped out of the car and braced himself for physical combat. He needn't have bothered. Bobby was way out of condition. His hundred-yard dash had finished him. He slowed to a walk, and finally, as he reached James, he just stopped.

"Okay, man!" he managed to say as he gasped for breath. "Okay!"

"You want to get in the car," said James.

"What for, man?"

"So I can drive you back home."

He looked at James, then to the car, then back to James.

"Which one are you?" he asked.

"Get in the car," said James.

"I knew I shouldn't have messed with that stuff. Barney told me."

"What did Barney tell you?" asked James.

"He told me not to mess with that stuff."

"I don't know who you think I am," said James. "But whoever it is, you're wrong. I want to talk to you. We can do it here in the street or we can go back to your house."

Bobby shrugged his narrow shoulders and, walking over to the car, he got into the front passenger seat. James walked around the car and got in behind the wheel. Bobby didn't smell too good, and his recent physical activity hadn't improved matters. He was sweating hard. He was tall, at least six-two, and couldn't have weighed more than 150 pounds. He was in his late thirties and looked like a skeleton wrapped in dark brown paper.

He didn't say anything as James U-turned the car and headed back toward the house. James parked the car curbside and switched off the engine.

"Let's go," he said.

Bobby made no move. "What d'you want, man?" he asked.

"I told you," said James. "I want to talk."

"Sure," said Bobby.

James reached across him and opened the passenger door. Bobby remained where he was for a moment, then he seemed to make up his mind. He uncoiled himself from the car and stood waiting for James to join him.

They walked back to the house, Bobby leading the way. He pulled the screen aside, opened the front door and walked in. James followed him. The first thing he saw, when his eyes had accustomed themselves to the change of light, was a large black guy holding a sawed-off shotgun.

"It's cool, Barney," said Bobby.

"Who is he?" asked the formidable-looking Barney, without letting go of the shotgun.

"Shit, man. I dunno."

"So why you saying it's cool?" said Barney, who hadn't taken his eyes off James.

"If I says it's cool, it's cool. So put down the heater and get lost," said Bobby.

"I told you not to mess with that stuff," said Barney.

"I know what you told me," said Bobby.

The woman who had originally answered the door appeared from out of the shadows.

"He told you, Bobby," she said.

"Will you two shut the fuck up," said Bobby.

"I only want to talk to him," said James.

Barney still hadn't relinquished the gun. "Is he one of them?" he asked Bobby.

"I don't know," said Bobby wearily.

"Sure he is," said the woman. She moved across toward James, looking up at him.

"Which one is you, mister?"

"I don't know what you're talking about," said James.

The whole situation was becoming Kafkaesque. He decided he would ignore the gun.

"I'm going to have some conversation with Bobby here. You two can stay or you can leave, it makes no difference either way."

There was a long pause. Finally, Barney glanced toward Bobby. "Bobby?"

"Suit yourself," said Bobby. "I got nothing to hide."

"Ha!" said the woman, explosively.

Barney finally relaxed sufficiently to lower the gun. He didn't put it down, but at least it wasn't pointing at James any longer.

"Say what you gotta, mister," said Bobby.

"Charlie Fisher..." started James. Immediately the gun came up again.

"I told you," said the woman. "Didn't I tell you?"

She confronted James once more, thrusting her face close to his. "Which one is you?"

James felt the whole thing slipping out of control once more. Coming on like a heavy had worked yesterday, maybe it would again.

"Sit down, you old crone," he said to the woman. He turned toward Barney. "You don't put that gun down, I'm gonna ram it up your black ass and pull both triggers." Then, to Bobby, "Where can we talk?"

Bobby was looking as surprised as the other two. He nodded toward a door. "My room," he said.

"Let's go," said James.

"Y'all watch yourself, Bobby," said the woman.

"Beat it," said James.

The woman backed away from him, then turned and fled into the kitchen. Barney was still holding the gun, but it was no longer a threat. James took half a step toward him and he quickly put it on the table. James picked it up and broke it open. There were no shells in it. He shook his head, dropped it back on the table and followed Bobby into his room.

The room was no more than ten by eight feet. It held a bed, a nightstand, a rail for hanging clothes and a small table and chair. Unlike the rest of the house, it was immaculately tidy. Not particularly clean, but with everything neatly folded or hanging or stacked. Even the bed had been made up with military precision, with knife-edge corners smoothed into the slightly grubby covers.

As James came in, Bobby moved over to the window overlooking the yard and stood with his back to it. James closed the door behind him and looked around the room. It didn't take an Einstein to figure Bobby's background.

"What branch of the service were you in?" asked James.

"Army," said Bobby.

"Where?"

"Around."

"Vietnam?"

"I was there."

"That's where you met Charlie Fisher. Right?"

Bobby nodded.

"Were you part of his racket out there?"

"Not me, man. Time he startin' pullin' all that shit, I'd been sent home."

"Why?" asked James.

"Ulcers," said Bobby.

"You still got ulcers?"

"I still got 'em. Look, mister. I don't know which one of them you are. But you tell me 'n I'll let you have the stuff. If you want to slip me a few dollars, cool. If you don't, that's okay too. I got to figure, this blackmail shit just ain't my style."

James finally understood what everyone had been getting at.

"I'm Mossman," he said.

"Dirty pictures, right?" said Bobby.

"Right," said James.

He watched as Bobby bent down and reached under the bed. He pulled out a military-type rucksack and threw it onto the bed. He undid the clips and opened it up. Inside were about twenty envelopes, some larger than others. Bobby looked through them and found what he was looking for. He started to hold it out toward James, then he changed his mind.

"Wait a minute. You're not the dude in the photos." Just to be sure his memory was accurate, he opened the envelope and pulled out a photograph. He looked at it, then back up to James.

"I dig. You want to take over Charlie's racket."

"I'll tell you what I want when I'm good and ready," said James. "Now sit down and let's talk."

Bobby put the photograph back in the envelope and moving aside the rucksack he sat on the edge of the bed.

"How did you get hold of that stuff?" asked James.

"Charlie gave it to me."

"When?"

"He brung it up here a couple of weeks ago. He said him and Charlotee was going out of town for a spell and he didn't want it just layin' round the boat."

"You're lying," said James.

Bobby thought about this for a moment.

"Okay. So I found it. I went down to check out the boat last week. Charlie likes me to turn the engines over. I found this wedged down in the bilges."

"Charlie's not going to like that."

"He don't need this stuff no more. He told me. He's hit it big."

"So you figured you'd make a few bucks on your own."

"Where's the harm, man? These dudes have been paying up regular for a long time now. They ain't hurtin' or they'd've done somethin' about it." He had a sudden idea. "Look, like I said, this ain't my kind of racket. How'd it be if I turn the stuff over to you? You can handle the business end 'n cut me in for fifty percent."

"What business end are you talking about?"

"These dudes pay out to Charlie, right? So they gotta be told that from now on there's a new banker … you 'n me. I don' know, you write 'em or call 'em, pay a visit even. Handle it your way. How does it sound?"

"Sounds cool," said James.

Bobby even managed a grin. "Great, man. It's gonna be easy street from now on." Then he got down to business. "We're gonna have to copy all this stuff first."

"Why?" asked James.

"Shit, man, I don't know you from a hole in the ground. You could walk on out of here 'n just never get back to old Bobby. Way

I see it if we've both got copies of the stuff neither of us can get hurt."

"You're right," said James. "Let me have it and I'll get copies run off right away."

It couldn't be that easy, thought James. But it was. Bobby refastened the rucksack and handed it over. James promised he'd be back within a couple of hours with the copies. Bobby even walked him out to his car. Like he'd said, he wasn't cut out for this racket.

James managed to resist going through the rucksack until he got back to Los Angeles. It wasn't easy. Half a dozen times during the drive he had to fight the impulse to pull over and empty everything onto the front seat and go through it. He parked the car in his slot at the motel and carried the rucksack into his room. The maid had taken note of his *Do Not Disturb* sign. The room hadn't been made up.

He poured himself a large drink, pushed everything off the table and emptied out the contents of the rucksack. Each envelope had a name on it corresponding to the names in Charlie's notebook. There was no envelope marked "EVERLY."

He piled the envelopes to one side of the table and started to go through them, starting with Mossman. There were three photographs taken one after the other. Mossman and Charlotee were clearly identifiable. What they were actually doing wasn't quite so clear.

Charlotee, wearing an unfastened plastic raincoat and nothing else, was brandishing a leather strap over a naked Mossman who was spread-eagled on a bed. His hands and feet were tied to the four corners with what looked like towels. Both of them were grinning at the camera, evidence that a good time was being had by all. At the foot of the bed, as though discarded, was a copy of the *Los Angeles Times*. But whoever had discarded it had made sure the front page was clearly visible. It was difficult to read without a magnifying glass, but James managed.

A front-page story announced that the search for the wreckage of the *Challenger* was still going on. This effectively pegged the date of the photograph to the last few days of January 1986, fixing it in time. James tried to visualize Mrs. Mossman's reaction to such a photograph. It didn't bear thinking about.

The next envelope concerned a man named McMahan who had been indiscreet enough to write a love letter to Charlotee both thanking her for their night of enchantment together and asking for a repeat performance next time he was in town. There was a copy of a motel bill from San Diego made out to Mr. and Mrs. McMahan and a newspaper cutting from a small Eastern newspaper announcing that the Reverend McMahan was going to San Diego to attend a religious convention; his wife would not be going with him due to her workload for the PTA.

After the fifth envelope, James started to weary of this catalogue of minor infidelities. They were all so boringly similar. A husband on his own, a pretty girl, what's the harm? The harm was Charlie. He'd picked his clients well. Upright, solid citizens or, in one case, a guy whose wife had all the money, and who, if the newspaper photo of the two of them celebrating their twenty-fifth wedding anniversary was anything to go by, was going to hang onto it come hell or high water.

He poured himself another drink and then emptied the contents of the sixth envelope onto the table. A schoolteacher from Idaho or Iowa, James wasn't even interested any longer. He started to shove the material back into the envelope when he stopped. Among the motel receipts and newspaper cuttings and incriminating letters from the unfortunate schoolteacher, was another envelope. About four inches square, heavy, and sealed. There was nothing written on the outside, but James knew what it was before he opened it. He slit the flap and tipped out a flat, clear plastic case holding a floppy disc.

There was nothing written on the outside of the disc or the case. The only way he was going to be able to check the contents was by using a computer. And if it was just backup material on the schoolteacher, he didn't need to bother. He started to slip the disc back in its envelope when he saw the photograph.

It had remained in the envelope when James had extracted the disc. James pulled it out and looked at it. He turned it over to check the back, then he looked at the front again.

"Shit!" he said out loud.

He stood up and poured himself another drink. He came back to the table and looked at the photo some more, without picking it up.

"Shit!" he said again.

It was a Polaroid picture, in color, of a boy and a girl. They looked about thirteen or fourteen years old. Both were naked and lying side-by-side, face down on a double bed. Their hands were tied behind their backs. Both of their heads were turned inward, looking up toward the camera. Beneath the fear that was etched on their faces was pain and confusion. There was extensive bruising on their buttocks and upper thighs and some small marks around their shoulder blades which could have been cigarette burns.

James tried to see beyond their terrified faces, examining the background details of the photo. Behind the bed was a plain stone wall with what looked like an Indian tapestry draped over a brass rod. The bed itself had a dark wood headboard. There was a matching nightstand on one side of the bed. On the nightstand was a digital radio alarm, a lamp, and a framed picture. James carried the photo to the window where the light was better. He tried to make something out of the picture on the nightstand. He couldn't. He checked the name on the larger envelope, the teacher from Idaho. He fetched Charlie's notebook and turned to the page that listed the teacher's payments. Three hundred fifty dollars per month. If that's all he was paying to keep Charlie quiet about his activities in the photo, he was getting a hell of a bargain.

James went through the catalogue of the teacher's indiscretions. It was the same as the others, a two-day bash with Charlotee while in Anaheim on some kind of a convention. There was even a picture of Charlotee with a mild-looking middle-aged man, taken at Disneyland. The man had his hand on Charlotee's backside and was grinning at her with possessive delight. There was a hotel bill, and two letters from the guy mailed to Charlotee after he had returned to Idaho. It was the mixture as before. The photo of the two terrified kids just didn't belong.

James stuffed everything back into the rucksack and fastened it shut. He looked around the room for somewhere to hide it and decided, eventually, that there wasn't any place. He took it with him, slinging it over his shoulder like a backpack.

The drugstore, two blocks down the street, was open. He tried to buy a magnifying glass but they didn't have one. He settled for a woman's makeup mirror, normal on one side, and magnifying on the other. He also bought two dozen large manila envelopes.

It was beginning to get dark by the time he got back to his motel room. He took the photo and the makeup mirror into the bathroom and switched on the light over the washbasin. He held the photo up to the magnifying mirror, angling it for the maximum effect. Close up, the two kids looked even more scared and he could see, for the first time, that they were slightly dark-skinned, Mexican or Central American. But his main concentration was on the framed picture on the nightstand. He wasn't quite sure what he had been expecting, but he was disappointed. It was an eight-by-ten studio portrait of an extremely attractive blond woman. James couldn't be sure, but it looked as if something had been written on the photograph. Of one thing he was sure, however, he had never seen the woman before.

He spent the next two hours carefully going through every envelope in the rucksack. His first impression had been correct. They were all depressingly similar. Some contained photographs, some contained motel receipts and newspaper clippings, fixing a time frame. Some consisted just of letters to Charlotee which somehow managed to be both lurid and pathetic at the same time. He was impressed by the way Charlie had operated his business. It was neat and methodical, and if he hadn't got greedy all of a sudden, he'd still be alive today.

Using Charlie's notebook, James addressed twenty of the envelopes he had just bought. Into each he put the material relevant to the addressee. He sealed the envelopes and put them all back into the rucksack. All he kept out was the floppy disc and the photograph of the two kids. These he slipped into an inside pocket of his parka.

He threw the rest of his stuff into the carryall he had fetched from the guest house yesterday evening, alongside the shotgun and Ernie Scruggs's bag of tricks. He left the *Do Not Disturb* notice on his door and, taking everything with him, he walked out to the car. Fifteen minutes later, he walked into Bubba's bar on Venice beach.

"Shit," said Bubba, when he saw James.

"I need Charlie's key," he said to Bubba.

Bubba came out from behind the bar and nodded for James to move to the back of the place, out of earshot of the other customers.

"What the fuck do you want now?" hissed Bubba.

"I just told you. The key to Charlie's room."

"What for, for Christ's sake?"

"Just give it to me," said James.

"I'm getting pretty fed up with you, buddy," said Bubba. "I been thinking things over since you were here yesterday. You know what I think?"

"What?"

"I think you're full of shit. I don't think Charlie's dead. I think either you're one of those poor suckers he's got his hooks into and you're trying to get out from under or you're aiming to muscle in on his racket."

"You could be right on either score," said James. "On the other hand, you could be wrong on both. It's your choice."

Bubba looked at him for a long moment. "What do you want the key for?"

"I want to use his computer," said James.

Bubba laughed explosively. "Jesus, man, you're something else."

"Do I get it?"

"Yeah, you get it."

He went back behind the bar and fetched he key. He brought it back to where James was waiting.

"Listen," he said, as he handed it over. "What did you mean yesterday when you said dead ain't necessarily so?"

"I guess you don't watch television."

"Are you kidding?"

"Read your newspaper tomorrow," said James. He took the key and headed upstairs.

He closed and bolted the door to Charlie's room and switched on the overhead light. He was still carrying the rucksack, not wanting to leave it in his car. He dumped it on the bed, pulled up a chair to the small desk and took the floppy disc from his pocket. He switched on the computer and, with the screen glowing green, he put in one of Charlie's utility discs. He listened to the familiar buzz of the disc drive and watched as the program came up on the screen.

It was a familiar program, the same one he had fought with so long on his own machine. He removed the utility disc and replaced it with the one he had brought with him. He hit the "change disc" key and watched the screen change. There was one file on the disc labeled EVERLY. He punched it up onto the screen, keeping his fingers crossed he was hitting the right keys and wouldn't lose the lot.

He'd hit the right keys. Up onto the screen came Charlie's story as it related to Harold J. Everly. It was only a couple of pages.

There were places and dates. There were some cross-references and there was a stream of suppositions which James knew he was going to have to check out.

He ran a printout from the disc. Then he replaced the disc in its envelope and addressed it to Charlie's post office mailbox. It would be safe there. The printout he folded neatly and put in his pocket along with the photograph of the two children, about whom he now knew a hell of a lot more.

Bubba's customers were gone when James came downstairs. He looked up from where he was polishing the top of the bar. He didn't say a word as James crossed to him and dropped the key on the bar in front of him.

"Thanks," said James.

"Go fuck yourself," said Bubba.

The drive to Bishop took him four and a half hours. It was just after five A.M. when he arrived. The town hadn't started to stir yet. He found a coffee shop with a sign that announced it opened at seven thirty A.M. He parked the car toward the rear of the lot and tried to grab a couple of hours' sleep in the back seat.

He was awakened at eight as an eighteen-wheeler pulled into the parking lot with its air brakes hissing like a crate full of angry snakes. The sound reminded him of the problem with his ankle. Before getting out of the car he pulled off a corner of the dressing and took a quick look. The swelling had disappeared and, apart from the self-inflicted scar, the ankle looked perfectly normal.

The drivers of the eighteen-wheeler were a husband-and-wife team. They were arguing quietly and vehemently when James came into the coffee shop. They didn't even look up as he slipped onto a stool at the opposite end of the counter. He ordered orange juice, bacon, eggs, hotcakes and coffee from a dispirited-looking waitress who reminded him of Daphne. Perhaps, after a lonely weekend in Los Angeles, she might decide to return to Needles. She'd find Hank missing and would ask around, maybe even talk to the cops. Eventually, they would find the pickup where James had left it in Westwood and somewhere down the line somebody would eventually put two and two together and not come up with five. By then James hoped he would be out of the woods. Either that or buried in them.

He finished his breakfast and paid his tab. The truck driver and his wife were still arguing as he left the coffee shop.

The public library didn't open until ten, so he drove straight to the post office. There he mailed nineteen of the twenty envelopes he'd recently addressed. Mossman's he kept. Having seen Mrs. Mossman, he didn't put it past her to open her husband's mail. Maybe some of Charlie's other ex-clients would be in the same boat, but that was going to be their problem. He was returning to them the pathetic evidence that Charlie had been using against them over the years. Their first reactions on opening the envelopes would, no doubt, be fear. They'd wonder what the hell Charlie was planning now. Eventually they'd learn of Charlie's death and they might start to hope everything was going to be okay. Then, when no demands for payment turned up after two or three months, they'd really feel in the clear. Good luck to them, thought James, poor little schmucks.

After the post office, he drove to a drugstore and bought himself a Polaroid camera, flashbulbs and three packs of film. He was waiting outside the library when it opened.

The information on Charlie's computer hadn't been specific about the dates. Sometime in July, three years ago. James asked the librarian for copies of the local newspaper covering the whole of that month. She disappeared for a few minutes and returned with a box of microfilm files. He assured her that he knew how to operate the viewer and settled himself down in front of it. He found what he was looking for in the July 15 edition. It was a small story, a single paragraph on an inside page. Mr. and Mrs. Juan

Garcías had reported to the local police that their two children, Pepe, age fourteen, and Maria, age twelve and a half, were missing. The Garcías lived and worked on a farm just outside Bishop where Mr. Garcías was the foreman. The next item was two days later. It had moved to the front page, but still didn't occupy much space. There was still no trace of the Garcías children. Anyone with information should contact the local police. Two days after that there was a photograph of the two missing children on the front page. "Have you seen these children?" James had seen them, in a different photograph.

He went through the files for the rest of the month. There was no follow-up story. He went to fetch the librarian. She was a forty-year-old woman, not unattractive, and rather bored with her job. She was only too happy to return with James to the viewer to see if she could help him out. He explained to her that he was a writer researching a series of "missing children" stories throughout Southern California. What could she tell him about the Garcías case?

Oh yes, she remembered it well. "Mrs. Selwyn, she's married to Pete Selwyn. He's the farmer who employed the Garcías. She comes in here all the time. She takes out books, but mostly she just likes to talk. It's lonely out there on the farm. I remember when those kids first disappeared, we talked about it a lot."

"Did they ever find them?" asked James.

"Not that I remember." She thought about it for a moment. "No, they didn't. After about six months, she came in one day and was she ever mad. The Garcías had quit, she said. They were going back to Mexico. After all she'd done for them. She told me they'd given up on finding their children. I think the police had told them there wasn't a chance any longer."

James thanked her for her help and went back out to the car. Maybe he should ask some questions at the police station. Then he caught sight of a pile of *Los Angeles Times* that were just being put into a vending machine. His photograph was on the front page.

He waited until the newspaper vendor had moved on, then bought himself a copy. He carried it back to the car, climbed in, and started to read. It was a follow-up story to the TV newscast. James Reed, formerly married to movie star Katherine Long, was killed in an auto accident outside San Bernardino late Friday night. The car he had been driving had been borrowed from friend and neighbor Amy Darwin of New York, who, it is reported, had rented it. It was only through this connection that the authorities had been able to identify the victim due to the seriousness of the accident and the subsequent fire. A coroner's inquest would be held in San Bernardino, date and time to be announced.

There was a story on an inside page, dateline Needles, California. The police were investigating the deaths of Charles and Charlotte (they spelled it wrong) Fisher, husband and wife, victims of a double homicide. The police are interviewing a number of witnesses and shortly expect to be able to announce that a suspect has been detained.

If there was any connection between the two stories, James couldn't find it in the paper. Not that that meant anything. For all he knew, the police could have already fingered him as the killer and were keeping quiet about it for reasons known only to themselves. Still, as of now, he was officially and finally dead. The *Los Angeles Times* said as much.

Before leaving Bishop, James checked the printout he'd taken from Charlie's computer. Charlie was batting a hundred up to now. Let's see how he made out in the next innings. He tucked the printout back in his pocket and headed north out of Bishop toward Mammoth Lakes.

According to what Charlie had put into his computer, he had known he was onto something big the moment he saw the photograph that Charlotee took from Everly's safe. He wasn't sure of any of the details, but he had started to ferret around. It seemed he had connections with the kid-porno circuit and one of these connections had recognized the Garcías children (he'd also offered Charlie five hundred dollars for the photograph). Charlie had then dug into Everly's background and come up with the information that Everly owned a house in Mammoth Lakes, only thirty miles from Bishop. It was one coincidence piled on top of another, but it had been enough for Charlie to confront Everly. The worst that could have happened would have been for Everly to say he'd bought the photograph, or he'd never seen it before, or it didn't belong to him. But he hadn't said any of these things. All he'd said was "How much do you want?" Charlie knew he was home and dry. What he hadn't realized was that he was no longer dealing with just another guy who had cheated on his wife. He was trying to put the screws on a multimillionaire who, according to Bee Kendrick, liked to shoot things. He had moved way out of his league. The moment Charlotee found the photograph, she and Charlie were as good as dead.

In the winter, Mammoth is like any other popular ski resort. The main street is solid with traffic. Every hotel, motel and condominium is booked solid and the place bristles with bars and restaurants. The whole town is lively, noisy and exuberant. In the summer it is completely different. There are very few tourists and the town starts to resemble what it originally was, a small village built on the edge of a magnificent wilderness.

James parked outside the first real estate office that was open and went inside. There were eight desks in the main part of the office. Only two were occupied. The property boom of a few years back had fizzled out through overbuilding and the constant threat of earthquake. The whole area was perched on top of a giant land fault which refused to remain dormant for more than a couple of days at a time. Minor tremors were a biweekly occurrence. But such was the attitude of Southern Californians toward earthquakes that ninety percent of them went unnoticed by everybody other than those who might be tempted to invest their hard-earned cash in real estate.

A slightly precious young man looked up from his desk as James came in.

"Can I help you?"

"I certainly hope so," said James, shading his accent back to its origins as he frequently did when he was about to ask a favor from a stranger.

"You're English, aren't you?" asked the young man.

"How did you know?"

"It's the accent. Say something for Vera." He turned to speak to the girl sitting at the desk furthest away from the door. "Listen to the way he talks, darling."

Vera looked up from the crossword she was doing. It was the *Los Angeles Times* crossword. James hoped it was yesterday's.

"Go on," prompted the young man. "Say something for Vera."

"What would Vera like me to say?" asked James.

"Anything. Say anything."

"The rain in Spain falls mainly on the plain," said James.

The young man squealed with delight. James looked toward Vera who was grinning at him sympathetically. She was about twenty-eight years old with a healthy outdoor complexion and a shock of very light blond hair.

"That's very cute," she said.

"It's divine is what it is," said the young man. Then back to business. "How can we help you?"

"I'm here on holiday," said James. "Driving around this wonderful country of yours. An American I met in London told me he had a place up here. I thought I might drop in on him. Unfortunately, I don't have his address."

"Oh dear," said the man. "What's his name?"

"Everly. Harold J. Everly."

"Never heard of him. Vera?"

Vera had never heard of Everly either. "I might be able to find out for you," she said.

"I'd be extremely grateful," said James.

"I'll do it," said the young man.

"You can't," said Vera. "You've got the Youngmans arriving from LA any minute."

As if on cue, a Mercedes 450 SL pulled up outside the office and a man and a woman got out. They breathed deeply for a couple of moments. Where they had come from, fresh air was a commodity in short supply. Here, eight thousand feet up in the Sierras, it was potent enough to deliver a minor high.

After stretching their legs, they came in. They were Los Angeles chic. They looked as though they'd come straight from Rodeo Drive. They were in the market for a condominium and they didn't expect to be kept waiting. The young real estate man turned James over to Vera reluctantly. He gathered up various sets of keys and set out with the Young-mans to show them what was on the market. Just before he left, he had one more word with James.

"Is everyone coloring their hair like that in London this year?"

"It's all the rage," said James.

"What's your friend's name again?" asked Vera when they were finally alone in the office.

"Everly. Harold J.," said James.

"I'll see if Bobo knows him. She knows everyone."

She dialed a number and asked for Bobo. No, Bobo didn't know Everly. Why didn't she try Charles, he knew absolutely everyone. Charles didn't know either.

James had moved to the back of the office during these telephone conversations. He was now seated at Vera's desk, across from her. She was even prettier close up. She smelled of fresh air and cologne.

"What now?" she said to James after hanging up from Charles.

James didn't know "what now," and said so. He was about to thank her and try some other place, when she had an idea.

"What kind of a place does your friend have? I mean, is it a condo or a house?"

"A house," said James, guessing that a man like Everly wouldn't be satisfied with just a condominium.

"Big house? Little house?" asked Vera.

"Big. He's disgustingly rich."

"Young? Old? Married?"

"Fortyish. Single," said James.

"I'm surprised I don't know him," said Vera, obviously wondering how she could have overlooked a disgustingly rich forty-year-old bachelor on her own stomping ground.

"He doesn't socialize much." It was the only thing James could think of to say.

She tried looking him up in the local phone book, without any luck. She called Information and they had nothing on him either.

"It doesn't look as though I'm going to be able to help you," said Vera, finally.

She didn't look too happy about it. James almost felt sorry for her, so he allowed her to make the move that he had been prepared to make himself if he'd been forced to.

"I don't know how things work here," he said. "But in England one can always telephone the local tax offices."

It wasn't true, but he didn't figure she'd know that. She thought it was a brilliant idea. She made the call and told them who she was. She said she'd had a call from a Mr. Harold J. Everly asking if she would be interested in selling a house that he owned at Mammoth Lakes. Mr. Everly had said he would be in to sign the agency papers the next time he was in town. Now, all of a sudden, she thought she had a buyer, and silly old me, I haven't even got the address of Mr. Everly's house. She'd been going to take all those details when Mr. Everly signed the papers. She's tried to call Mr. Everly in Los Angeles but he's out of town. I know it's a terrible drag, but could you have a quick look through your property tax rolls for Mr. Everly, Harold J., and let me know the address of the property on which he pays his taxes? They put her on hold.

"What are you doing for lunch?" she asked James while she was waiting.

"I'm a stranger here," said James. "You tell me."

They came back on the phone. Vera wrote something down, thanked them and hung up. She tore off what she had written, and standing up, she walked over to a large-scale map pinned on the wall. She checked the map against the information she'd received from the tax office.

"How rich did you say he was?" she asked James.

"Very."

"He must be," said Vera. "According to this, he owns a whole mountain."

They lunched at Whiskey Creek, one of the few restaurants that stayed open all year. The food was adequate and the ambience convivial. James had a couple more drinks than he'd intended, and Vera two or three more than that. Halfway through lunch, she offered to drive him to the Everly house. He declined politely. She sulked for a few minutes and then came up with a better idea. She didn't have to go back to the office this afternoon. If James wasn't in a hurry to see his old friend Everly, maybe he'd like to come back to her place for a coffee. Later, much later, they could drive out to the Everly place together. Once more, James declined politely. Vera wasn't used to being turned down and started to sulk again. It took two cognacs to bring her out of it. That, and a promise to come back to town this evening to take her out to dinner. Would he also please move hell and high water to bring Everly with him because she was just dying to meet him. James agreed to both requests.

He said good-bye to her in the parking lot of the restaurant. She kissed him in a manner designed to make him regret turning down her matinee offer, at the same time providing a preview of forthcoming attractions. He watched her drive away before getting back in his own car and heading out of town.

He followed the rough directions she had given him back down the hill from Mammoth village onto the main highway. There he turned north. He drove about four miles before he came to the turnoff. It wasn't even signposted. It was little more than a dirt track leading from the main highway, heading into nowhere. James took it.

In the winter it would be impassable unless one had one's own snowplow. Knowing Everly, he probably did. The track headed back up into the high ground north of Mammoth. According to the information from the tax office, Everly owned all the land as far as the top of the mountain and halfway down the other side. It wasn't as big as the E-Bar-E but it didn't need to be. No cattle grazed, no crops grew, nobody worked it. It was virgin land, untouched, its only function to provide a great deal of privacy for the owner.

James caught sight of the house half a mile before he reached it. The track had been ascending the side of the mountain in a series of long, lazy loops. As he turned at the end of one of these loops, he saw the building nestling in a slight hollow close to the summit.

Four more loops in the road and he had arrived. It was a large A-frame. The apex of the roof was at least fifty feet high. The ground-floor walls were of local stone. They looked solid enough to withstand a major siege. Let into the front were a couple of small windows on either side of the front door. There was also a garage, which looked wide enough from the outside to hold at least four cars. On the second floor there were twelve-foot-high windows. They were screened glass, and faced out onto a terrace running the entire width of the house. Above that was another series of windows denoting a third story.

James parked the car and rang the front doorbell. As expected, there was no answer. He walked around the outside of the house. There was a lean-to at back holding enough wood to last for ten winters. There was also a T-bar ski lift that led up out of sight over the next rim of the mountain. The drive mechanism for the T-bar was down here, close to the house. You had to hand it to the guy, thought James. Not only does he own the mountain, but he put in his own ski lift.

In amongst the huge pile of logs, James found an axe. He returned to the front of the house and collected his newly bought Polaroid and that day's copy of the *Los Angeles Times* from the car. Then he proceeded to let himself into the house with the aid of the axe. Half-a-dozen blows and the front door splintered open. Maybe he could have picked the lock. But this took less time and he didn't think anybody was going to file a complaint for property damage.

The ground floor consisted of the garage which held a couple of snow scooters and a small snowplow. On the opposite side of the front door was a room for storing ski equipment. Stairs led up to the main floor.

Upstairs was reminiscent of Everly's quarters at the E-Bar-E, comfortable, functional and masculine. The main room contained twelve-foot-high windows which overlooked a view that seemed to go on forever. It was a large room with a huge open fireplace. The otherwise bare stone walls were hung with Western art, about which James knew very little, but enough to realize that a couple of the pictures hanging there had to be worth a great deal of money. The furniture looked as though it had come from Hearst Castle, oversized and overstuffed. The only other room on this floor was the kitchen, which was divided into two areas. One held a table large enough to seat a dozen people, the other contained enough equipment to service an average-sized restaurant. At the back of the main room, stairs led up to the next floor.

The master bedroom was at the front of the house, sharing the spectacular view James had seen from downstairs. But James wasn't interested in the view. He was looking at the bed, the Indian tapestry behind it, the dark wood headboard and the matching nightstand with its digital clock, lamp, and the framed photograph of an attractive blond woman.

He had been right, there was something written across the bottom of the photograph. *To my darling Hal, for always, Glenda.* And he had been wrong when he'd decided he hadn't seen the woman before. He remembered a photograph of her with Everly hanging in the study at the E-Bar-E.

He replaced the photo on the nightstand. He loaded the Polaroid and stuck on a rack of flashbulbs. He placed the copy of the LA *Times* on the bed with the front page uppermost, his own picture looking back at him. He moved to the end of the bed and started to take photographs. First, the long shots, from the same angle as the photographs of the children. Then in closer, to get the details on the nightstand. He used up one pack of film and bulbs and reloaded. Now he moved further away, out of the door of the bedroom, composing his pictures so that each one led into the other. The bedroom, as it related to the passageway, as it related to the staircase, as it related to the main room below.

He took a couple of shots of the view from the tall windows, then went outside and took a couple more of the outside of the house. He came back inside and spread the Polaroids out on the kitchen table, checking that he had everything he needed. Ten minutes later, he drove back down the hill toward the main highway. Back in Bishop, he hung a left, heading in the direction of Tonopah.

Three hours later he reached Las Vegas. He checked into a motel on the Strip. It was small, it was cheap and it was slightly grubby. There was an icemaker right outside his room which kept regurgitating ice cubes with a clatter. The air conditioner only worked when it was on high, at which time it made a noise like a buzz saw. As soon as he had checked into his room, he went out again. He found a store with a copying machine and, collecting a pile of change, he copied every photograph he had taken at the house. They weren't good copies by any means, but good enough.

Back in his motel room, he put the original Polaroids along with the picture of the two children into an envelope and sealed it. He addressed the envelope and took it down to the front desk. There, he asked the clerk to put it in the hotel safe for him. If he didn't claim it back within twenty-four hours, the clerk should mail it as addressed. He gave the clerk twenty-five dollars. Later, he went out for a Chinese meal, which he ate in an otherwise empty restaurant while the owner and two waiters played some obscure Oriental card game at a back table. On the way back to the motel, he stopped at a liquor store and bought himself a bottle of Scotch. By the time he got back to his room, it was eleven P.M. He set his bedside alarm for three A.M. and went to bed.

The alarm pulled him back from the dead. It took him a full minute before he remembered where he was. He switched it off and climbed out of bed and staggered into the bathroom. He cleaned his teeth and, taking the bathroom glass back into the room, he broke the seal on the bottle of Scotch and poured himself a stiff drink. Then he pulled on his clothes and twenty minutes later he was heading out of Las Vegas toward the E-Bar-E.

In the old days, as a cop in London, James had learned that the best time to catch a person off balance was at the crack of dawn. It was then that reactions, both physical and mental, were at their lowest ebb.

He made good time and pulled off the road onto E-Bar-E property just after four thirty A.M. The washout that had bogged him down last time had dried out, and five minutes later he crested the rise and started down toward the valley. There was a thin light beginning to appear in the west, sufficient to enable him to turn off his car lights. He reached the valley floor and drove half of the three-quarters of a mile toward the ranch complex. There he pulled his car off the track, turning it first so that it faced back the way he had come. He left the keys under the front seat and set out to walk the remaining quarter of a mile.

There was no sign of life around the complex. No lights in the bunkhouse or mess hall or the main ranch house. Even the Chinese cook hadn't started his day. He crossed past the stables on his way toward the main house. He could hear the horses moving about in their stalls. In the distance, a cow lowed mournfully and somewhere at the back of the bunkhouse a dog started to bark without much excitement.

He ignored the front door, heading straight for the back of the building and the windows he knew led into Everly's study. Obviously, they weren't bothered about intruders out here. One of the windows was halfway open. James reached in and opened it the rest of the way and climbed in.

The far corners of the room were still dark. But there was enough early dawn light outside to allow James not to bang into the furniture. There was also sufficient light for him to be able to go through the contents of Everly's desk without switching on the lamp.

The first three drawers yielded nothing of interest, unless raising cattle turned you on. There were feed bills, stud books, stock inventories, vet bills, sales vouchers, transport charges, slaughterhouse fees and a pile of publications aimed at stockbreeders.

The second drawer on the left was locked. James forced it open with an ivory-handled letter opener. There was a manila file at the bottom of the drawer with nothing written on the cover. James took it out and opened it. Inside were a couple dozen invoices all from the same source. James flipped through them. Each was similar. "Account for month ending Jan. 31 ..." The same for Feb. 28, March 31, and so on. Monthly bills that came to an average of fifteen thousand dollars each, give or take a couple of hundred. There was no indication what they were for. Neither was there any address or telephone number. Just the name WESTFIELDS, CEDAR CITY, UTAH, printed discreetly at top of each invoice. James slipped one of them into his pocket. He closed the folder and was putting it back in the drawer when he saw something else. It was a snapshot of three people. Everly, Wally and the blonde Glenda whose photograph had been on Everly's nightstand in Mammoth. They were dressed for riding and Wally was holding the lead reins of three horses. It looked as though it might have been taken somewhere on the E-Bar-E. James put this in his pocket too.

By the time he got up from behind the desk, it was almost fully light outside. The sun wasn't up yet, but it wouldn't be long. It was different in the passage beyond the room. Here was almost total darkness.

He felt his way along the passage until he came to the door that he remembered led into Everly's bedroom. He located the door handle and gently turned it. The door opened without a sound. Everly hadn't drawn the drapes so there was a fair amount of gray light spilling in from outside. A gentle snoring came from beneath the covers of the king-size bed to the right of the door.

James crossed the room quietly and peered into the bathroom. He came back into the bedroom, chose a chair facing the side of the bed and sat down. The rhythm of the snoring remained unchanged. Outside the dawn chorus was starting up in the trees around the complex, and James thought he heard the sound of voices from the direction of the bunkhouse. Still Everly slept undisturbed.

After a few minutes, during which time James attempted to reduce his pulse rate to something resembling normal, he reached out from the chair and slid a hairbrush from the dressing table. It hit the carpeted floor with a quiet thud. It was sufficient to get through to Everly. The pattern of his snores changed, he grunted a couple of times then he woke up. He rolled over to get a look at the clock on his nightstand. It was then that he saw James.

At least, he seemed to see James. Then he must have decided it was a figment of his imagination, a hangover from a bad dream perhaps. He rolled over, preparing to go back to sleep. He was motionless for about five seconds, then he rolled back and looked at James again. Finally, he struggled onto one elbow and started to reach for the bedside light switch.

"No lights," said James.

Everly paused, his hand still in midair. Then he struggled to a sitting position in the bed. He was wearing plain dark blue pajamas, the kind you could buy in any department store; in Everly's case, they probably came from Turnbull & Asser. He continued to look toward James as though he was beginning to see him for the first time. The silence lengthened. It would have gone on longer but James realized that the wider awake Everly became, the less advantage he would have.

"You and I have got some talking to do," he said.

Everly said nothing. If there was going to be any talking, James was going to have to do it. At least for the time being.

"I figured you'd have some questions for me," said James.

Still nothing from Everly other than a flat, sleepy-eyed stare. Not only was James going to have to provide the answers, he was going to have to pose the questions he was expecting Everly to ask.

"How about this one for openers?" he said. "Who's dead if I'm not?"

Still nothing.

James tried another. "Or, if I'm not dead, how come I'm letting everybody think I am?"

Another silence.

"Let's move on to the sixty-four-dollar one," said James, finally. "Actually, it's going to cost a lot more than that, but we'll discuss terms later. What do I want?"

Finally, Everly felt he was sufficiently together to open his mouth.

"Can we go back to number one?" he said.

"I've forgotten what it was," said James.

"Who's dead if you're not?"

"A guy named Spruce. Hank Spruce. I loaned him my car."

Everly thought about this for a time. Then he put question number two, quoting James again.

"If you're not, how come you're letting everyone think you are?"

"Because the moment they know I'm alive, they're going to arrest me for murder," said James.

"You can't play dead forever."

"Long enough."

"Which brings us to question number three. What do you want?"

"From you, Everly, I want a whole lot of things."

Everly started to get out of bed.

"Where are you going?" asked James.

"I need to take a pee."

James shrugged his acceptance. He watched Everly get out of bed and over to the bathroom. He stayed in his chair, hearing Everly pee and the toilet flushing. A moment later, Everly came out of the bathroom dragging on a robe.

"I need a cup of coffee," he said.

"Later. Why don't you get back into bed?" said James. "You'll be more comfortable."

Instead, Everly chose a chair across from James and sat down.

"Okay," he said. "You're calling the shots." Then he added an ominous sounding postscript. "For the moment."

"Talking of shots," said James. "What do you think of these?" He pulled the Polaroid copies from his pocket and threw them toward Everly. They landed on his lap and slipped to the floor before he could grab them. He bent to pick them up, then because there was still insufficient light in the room, he stood up and walked over to his nightstand and turned on the lamp.

He stood looking at the photos of the Mammoth house. He went through them once, then he went through them again. Finally, he bunched them all together neatly and put them on the nightstand. He returned to his chair.

"Very enterprising," he said.

"That's what I thought."

"No need to ask you whether you found Charlie's stash."

"No need."

"Wally figured you weren't that smart."

"He figured I was smart enough to run Charlie to ground and make a lot of noise doing it."

"He was right."

"At which time he moved in just ahead of me and blew them away."

Everly said nothing.

"Or was that you?" asked James.

Everly didn't bother to answer. He wasn't going to commit himself to anything. James was going to have to continue making the running.

"Let me tell you what I've got on you," he said. "Then we'll discuss what we're going to do about it."

Everly started to stand up, changed his mind and sat back again. James, who had braced himself suddenly, relaxed once more.

"Poor old Charlie could be a sloppy worker at times. Sure, he had the photograph of the Garcías children. He knew the Garcías came from Bishop and he knew you had a house in Mammoth. That's all he knew. He didn't have a tie-in. I guess he figured he didn't need one. Show you the photograph and you'd roll over. Didn't it ever occur to you that the photograph by itself didn't mean diddlyshit? All you had to do was redecorate that bedroom of yours or burn the house down, if you like, and nobody could ever have made a connection."

Everly was staring at him flatly through narrowed eyes. Maybe he had realized it, maybe he hadn't. James couldn't tell.

"Anyway, all that's hypothetical," he continued. "I've got the evidence that puts those two kids into your room in your house." He nodded toward the photocopies on the nightstand. "Tell me something, Everly, I'm really fascinated. Without going into the whys and wherefores of a deformed libido, why would anyone be dumb enough to take photographs?"

Again, Everly said nothing.

"I'll go one stage further. Having taken a photograph, how could this friendly neighborhood child molester be twice as dumb and keep the photograph around to be found by the first little floozie who moves in with him?"

Everly continued to watch him in silence.

James was beginning to find the silences getting to him. "Maybe you still get your jollies looking at it," he said.

Everly looked away for a moment, as if he was unable to hold James's eyes, then he looked back. Still he said nothing.

James got to his feet and moved over to the windows. He drew the drapes closed. It was fully light outside by now and there were sounds of the ranch stirring into a new day. He didn't want to risk the chance of one of the hands walking past the window and seeing into the boss's bedroom. Not yet.

When he turned back, Everly hadn't moved. God knows what was going on in his mind, but he certainly wasn't giving anything away. James took the chair again.

"Let me just run things past you once," he said. "You don't have to say anything unless I'm wrong. Charlie puts the bite on you and you decide he's going to have to go. Maybe you've already worked something out, but then along comes James Reed, hell-bent on getting even with Charlie. A heaven-sent patsy. Bright enough to run Charlie to ground, not bright enough to see what he was getting into. You wait until I'm about to pay Charlie a visit, then you kill Charlie and his wife, plant the gun in my car, and arrange for me to have a fatal accident."

"That's exactly the way it was, son." It was Wally.

He was standing in the door to the bathroom, a cup of coffee in his hand. Now he came into the room and handed the coffee to Everly. He nodded back toward the bathroom door.

"I got me a room the other side of the bathroom," he said, by way of explaining his entrance. James wondered why he hadn't noticed the door when he peered into the bathroom earlier. But it didn't much matter. He knew that Wally was going to have to be brought in sooner or later. He would have preferred it to have been later, but there wasn't much point in worrying about that now.

"You'd most likely be wanting a cup of coffee yourself," said Wally.

Before James could answer he disappeared into the bathroom again.

James had a feeling that, with Wally's arrival, the initiative was slipping away from him. There was something about the tall, skinny old man with his weather-beaten face and cold blue eyes that he found intimidating. He couldn't imagine any situation that Wally wouldn't be on top of.

The two men sat in silence until Wally returned, Everly watching James steadily over the edge of his coffee cup. Wally came back in carrying another cup of coffee. He handed it to James.

"I slipped in a couple of shots to give it some muscle," he said.

He moved away to stand by the open fireplace where he started to roll himself a cigarette with the makings he took from his shirt pocket.

"What happens now, son?" he said to James.

"What do you think happens now?" said James.

"If I knew, I wouldn't be asking. I'll take a couple of guesses if you like."

"Do that," said James.

"You don't want to stay dead, for one. So, me and Hal here have got to come up with a way you can get resurrected."

"Go on," said James.

"Same time, you don't want to be locked up for no murder."

James glanced toward Everly, but he seemed to have dropped out completely since Wally arrived.

"Then, no doubt, you'd be wanting some cash money," Wally continued. "Kind of to compensate you for your trouble."

"And … ?" prompted James.

"Hal told me all about you being a vindictive sumbitch. I guess you want someone to get their comeuppance."

"You're doing fine, Wally," said James.

"That's where we might have a small problem," said Wally. "The first two can be handled without much sweat. You report your car was stolen and you didn't hear about the accident till just now. Me and Hal here will give you an alibi to cover the shooting. We were all in Vegas whooping it up. As for the money, that's no problem at all. How much do you want? A million? Two?"

"We'll discuss terms later," said James. "Let's get to the comeuppance bit."

"Like I said, that's gonna be a problem. Me and Hal here ain't going to admit to no killing. I was the one that did it, by the way. I ain't got no regrets 'bout it. I'd do it again. And if I couldn't, then Hal would. But that's just between us three. There's no way we're gonna let you pin it on either of us."

"You're right," said James. "It's a problem."

"Only if you say so," said Wally.

"I do," said James.

Everly and Wally exchanged a quick look. Maybe Everly was going to take over, thought James. After all, he was the boss man, even if he hadn't said a word when Wally offered James a couple of million dollars. But he was wrong. It was Wally who continued.

"Maybe I was right, and you ain't very smart, son. A smart feller, in my book, would look at the facts before making a decision like the one you're gonna make."

"What are the facts, Wally? Tell me!" said James.

"Fact one, Charlie Fisher was a snake. That wife of his weren't no better. A lot of folk are gonna sleep much easier knowin' they're dead. Fact two, the guy who was killed in your car, that was an accident, plain and simple."

"You killed him, you should know," said James.

"I'm not talkin' 'bout who did what. I'm talkin' 'bout the facts as I see 'em. Now we come to the choices. You can walk away from here a rich man. Or you can listen to that worm in your gut that's tellin' you you've gotta get even. That way you don't walk away from here at all."

He had rolled himself another cigarette. He lit it from the first, which was still burning.

"I sure know which way I'd go," he said.

"Let me get this straight," said James. "You're willing to pay me two million dollars and give me an alibi providing I keep my mouth shut about the Fishers and Hank Spruce."

"You've got it, son," said Wally.

"Aren't you forgetting one thing?"

"If I am, you're sure going to tell me."

"The García children."

Another look flashed between the two men.

"That was a long time ago," said Wally.

"Tell that to the parents."

"It's over and done with."

"Have you got any kids, Wally?"

It was a rhetorical question but its effect on Wally was out of all proportion. His pale blue eyes suddenly went even colder. He straightened up from his lounging stance, seeming to gain a couple of inches in the process.

"Take it easy, Wally," said Everly, opening his mouth for the first time since Wally had joined them. He turned to James. "Wally and I need to talk," he said.

"Somebody needs to," said James. He got to his feet. "I'll tell you what. I'll get on back to Vegas. Soon as you two have worked out what you want to do, get in touch."

Wally took a couple of steps forward as though to stop him from leaving. For one moment James thought he had miscalculated.

"Forget it, Wally," said Everly. He turned to James. "Where can we get in touch?"

"Be at the Grand, just inside the main entrance at seven this evening."

"I'll be there," said Everly.

"Me too," said Wally.

"I thought you couldn't go into Vegas," said James.

"I'll be there, son," said Wally. "I'll walk you to the door."

"No need," said James.

Wally walked out with him anyway. James was expecting him to say something, but he didn't open his mouth until he had opened the front door and stood aside for James to go out.

"You're treading on dangerous ground, son," he said.

"Then I'll need to keep on my toes," said James. "See you tonight."

Wally looked at him steadily for a moment.

"What happened to the hair?" he asked finally.

"I felt like a change," said James.

Wally continued to stare at him as though he wanted to say something else. Whatever it was, he changed his mind. Instead he reached into the pocket of his jeans and pulled out James's car keys. He held them toward James.

"You'll be needing these," he said. "Your car's parked back of the bunkhouse. Y'all take care now." He closed the door gently.

Some of the ranch hands were saddling up outside. If they were surprised to see James coming out of the main house at five thirty in the morning, they didn't show it. Neither did they react when James opened the front door and went back in.

He could hear Wally and Everly talking in the bedroom without being able to make out what they were saying. He started to move toward the bedroom when he heard a soft *ping* of sound from a phone on a table close to where he was standing. Cupping the receiver, he picked it up carefully. He listened for a couple of seconds, then he replaced the receiver gently. A moment later he let himself out the front door again and started toward the rear of the bunkhouse to pick up his car.

He checked the trunk and the glove compartment, not sure what he was expecting to find. But if somebody had brought his car in from where he had so carefully left it, they were obviously two or three jumps ahead of him. Bearing in mind what had happened to Hank Spruce, he would have liked to check the brakes too, but he had no idea what to look for. What went on under the hood of automobiles had always been a complete mystery. He resolved to change the car as soon as possible. In the meantime, he'd keep his speed down and hope he didn't encounter any steep hills between here and Cedar City, Utah.

"Me and Mr. Everly are driving over to Cedar City. We'll need the car about nine thirty," he'd heard Wally say over the phone to Harvey, the young guy who took care of the Bentley Mulsanne. James figured Cedar City as about two hours' drive in the Bentley. It would take him three. That would get him there between eight thirty and nine, a good two and a half hours ahead of Everly and Wally.

In fact, he reached the outskirts of Cedar City just before eight thirty. Located, as it is, close to Bryce Canyon and Zion national parks and Cedar Breaks National Monument, tourism provides one of the principal industries in what used to be an old mining town. The college of Southern Utah is here also the site of the Utah Shakespeare Festival, which James had attended once when he was married to Katherine and she had been invited as a special guest of honor. But right now, he wasn't interested in Shakespeare or national parks. He was interested in a place that called itself Westfields and provided a service which cost around fifteen thousand dollars per month.

He pulled into a gas station at the edge of town. The car had given him no trouble during the drive. He decided that his concern about the brakes had been unwarranted, perhaps even a shade paranoiac. Nevertheless, after gassing the car, he asked for a mechanic to check under the hood. Leaving him to it, he went to the pay phone and started leafing through a local telephone book. Westfields was listed. Just an address and phone number. No indication as to what business they were in. He tore the page out of the phone book and went back to collect his car.

The mechanic had found nothing untoward beneath the hood. Yes sir, he'd checked the brake pressure, no problems. James paid him fifteen dollars for five minutes' work and asked him how to get to Westfields. The guy had never heard of the place. James gave him the address and the guy hadn't heard of that either, but he'd ask the station manager, he'd lived round these parts all his life.

He came back with the information that the road James was looking for was outside town. In fact, James must have driven past it on his way in. James turned the car and headed back the way he had come. He spotted the road sign and turned off. Five minutes, later he reached Westfields.

There was a high stone wall fronting the road, impossible to see over. Two hundred yards along the wall were the main gates.

Ornate ironwork between two recessed pillars. Just inside the gates was a small lodge. The driveway swung up between trees that screened whatever lay beyond. A discreet sign on one of the gate pillars read WESTFIELDS. Nothing else. As he slowed past the gates a uniformed man appeared from the lodge. He was well over six feet tall and his uniform bulged around his chest and shoulders. He had a walkie-talkie strapped to his belt. He moved to the gate and peered out at James as if he was begging him to drive in so he could turn him away. James speeded up again and drove on past.

The wall continued unbroken for another 250 yards. There it turned at right angles to the road. James drove a couple of hundred yards further on. He pulled off the road onto the shoulder. He locked the car and walked back to the corner boundary of the property. There, he turned with his back to the road and started to follow the wall.

After fifty yards, he was completely masked from the road by trees. Now there was just the wall. Another twenty-five yards and there was a tree whose branches overhung the top of the wall. They looked strong enough to bear his weight. He clambered up the trunk of the tree and got his first proper look beyond the wall.

Well-kept parkland, studded with trees, rose gently toward the building at the crest of the rise. It was a large house. James estimated it must have at least forty rooms. It looked as if it had been standing for fifty years, probably built originally for one of the forefathers of the town who had made an early fortune in mining. Apart from the main house, there was a building that looked like a large stable block obviously built at the same time. There were three fairly modern-looking extensions connected to the rear of the house by covered walkways. The place was about a quarter mile from where James was sitting astride a branch of the tree and he could see at least a dozen figures moving around in pairs close to the main house. A couple of them were in wheelchairs.

At this distance, it was impossible to see whether they were young or old, but each couple included a person dressed in white. They looked like nurses overseeing their patients. Okay, thought James, it's a hospital or a retirement home. How the hell can it be so important that Everly and Wally should want to visit here when all the shit in the world had hit their fan only three hours earlier? He was going to have to find out.

Fifteen thousand dollars a month and a uniformed gateman who was built like a refugee from the Chicago Bears sounded like the kind of place where privacy was the number-one requirement. He didn't feel he'd have much success knocking on the front gate and just asking in. Seeing as he was already halfway over the wall anyway, he wormed his way a little further along the tree branch and lowered himself gingerly onto the top of the wall. Then he dropped down the other side.

He realized straightaway that he had no means of getting back, not unless he could find something to stand on so's he could reach the top of the wall from this side. On the other hand, the guard he had seen at the gate had looked large and strong enough to pick him up and throw him over the wall. Hoping it wouldn't come to that, he started to walk up toward the main buildings.

He was halfway toward the house and beginning to feel vulnerable when he spotted the wheelbarrow. Somebody had left it parked under a tree. It held a rake, a shovel and a gardening fork. He collected it and, trying to look like somebody who was minding nobody's business but his own, he continued up toward the house.

Whatever this place was, it wasn't a retirement home. Not unless people were taking a very early retirement. There were a couple of old guys, the ones in the wheelchairs, but the others varied in age between early twenties and about fifty. Most were men, but there were also a couple of women. Most of the nurses were male. They didn't seem to be tending their patients so much as just keeping an eye on them. And if they were, in fact, patients, they were certainly a healthy-looking bunch. There wasn't a bandage or a plaster cast or a crutch to be seen.

James parked his wheelbarrow close to a flowerbed and started to rake the bed industriously while he tried to get a fix on the place. That was when somebody threw a rock at him.

It hit him on the back of the neck. A couple of inches higher and it would have laid him out. He turned quickly and saw one of the nurses taking another missile from the hand of the thirty-year-old guy who had just tried to brain him. The guy didn't seem to mind much. After a moment, the nurse left him and walked over to James. He was a large, sleepy-faced man who looked as though he might be running to fat beneath his white smock. He could also have been running to muscle.

"You know you're not supposed to work around here when they're out," he said.

"Sorry," said James.

The nurse stared at him for a moment. "I haven't seen you before," he said.

"I'm new."

"Didn't they tell you?"

"Not a word."

"Yeah, well beat it before one of the others gets any bright ideas. This area is out of bounds to the help when the patients are taking their exercise."

James picked up the wheelbarrow and started toward the side of the house, away from the inmates.

That's what they were. Inmates. This wasn't a hospital or a retirement home, it was a fruit farm. And at fifteen grand a month, it obviously catered for the top-grade nut cases. Dangerous top-grade nut cases, if the nurse-to-patient ratio was anything to go by. Maybe he'd been lucky just getting a rock thrown at him.

He parked his wheelbarrow at the back of the house close to one of the covered walkways that connected the main building with one of the newer ones. The walkway was mostly glass and

James could see nobody inside. There was a door a few yards down. He tried it, but it was locked. So too was the door at the end of the walkway where it led into the newer building. But from here he could see inside the place. It was an office. There were three steel desks, a lot of filing cabinets and a couple of computers. To one side two young women were busy chatting over the coffee maker. Neither of them wore uniforms and both of them looked sane. The place was probably an office handling administration. Maybe it was here that the fifteen-thousand-dollar invoices were sent out. If so, this was the place that James badly wanted to get into.

He could hardly bang on the door and ask to go through their files. He needed a diversion, something that would get the girls out of the office long enough for him to do what he had to. He looked around. The second extension to the main house was about fifty feet away. There was always the chance of an unlocked door over there. He started around the back of the office extension. That's when he spotted the fire alarm.

There was a large bell and junction box fixed to the wall about eight feet high. He went back and fetched the wheelbarrow. The girls, he noticed, had quit the coffee maker and returned to their desks where one was busying herself painting her nails.

He positioned the wheelbarrow against the wall beneath the fire alarm and clambered up into it. Using a prong of the gardening fork, he prized the lid off the junction box and got to work on the wiring inside.

Thirty seconds later, the alarm started to clang loudly. He climbed down from the wheelbarrow and went back around to where he could see into the office. The girls had gone and they'd left the door to the walkway open. James walked in.

At the far end of the walkway, where it connected to the main house, he could hear excited voices. Hoping that everyone knew their fire drill, he went into the office and straight to the filing cabinets. He estimated he had about five minutes before somebody came around checking that the place had been evacuated.

As it happened, he didn't need five minutes. He found what he was looking for in three minutes. He would have liked to have made a copy but the machine next to the coffee maker looked as if it would take an advanced degree in electrical engineering to operate. He didn't figure he had the time to experiment. So, he took the originals from the files. He folded them quickly and stuck them in his pocket. As he left the office, a male nurse appeared at the far end of the walkway and called up to him.

"Anyone left up there?"

"Everyone's out," James called back.

The nurse disappeared back into the main house and James walked out of the same door he had entered by.

James should now have made for the nearest way out of Westfields. He'd learned all he needed to know. But everything had been so easy. He felt he could afford the luxury of confirming his findings before he left. He was pretty convinced he knew the answer, but what the hell, he'd gotten away with it so far, what could be the harm? He was going to need all the ammunition he could come up with tonight. So, instead of beating a hasty retreat he walked around to the front of the house again.

People were still coming from the main building. Nurses, doctors and inmates. There was no confusion and very little excitement. The authorities certainly knew how to run the place efficiently. James mixed in with the crowd, even helping a vacant-eyed young man disentangle himself from the strings of his own hospital gown.

"There you go, fella," said James, as he retied the tapes at the back of the gown.

The young man looked at him, empty-eyed, before shuffling away. James looked around him. Everybody seemed too involved in the evacuation to even give him a glance.

Three of the inmates had been brought out in straitjackets, a male nurse on either side of each one. The person he was looking for wasn't one of them. He moved toward a small group of women patients who were being shepherded by a couple of nurses, one of them female. She was as large and hirsute as her male counterparts.

"Everything all right here?" he said.

"Who are you?" asked the female nurse.

"Fire department," said James.

"We're okay," said the nurse. "Where's the fire?"

James nodded vaguely in the direction of the house. "It's gonna be all right," he said.

Four of the five women patients were looking at him. The fifth was staring off into the distance a thousand miles inside her head. James didn't recognize her immediately. Apart from the fact she was wearing no makeup and her hair was a mess, she seemed to have aged at least fifteen years since the photograph on Everly's nightstand had been taken. He moved over to her.

"Are you okay, Mrs. Everly?" he said.

She turned her empty eyes toward him.

"Stay away from her," said the nurse. There was an edge to her voice that James assumed was plain bad temper.

He persisted. "Mrs. Everly. Glenda? Are you okay?"

Maybe there was a flash of something in her eyes. It was hard to tell.

"I'm a friend of your husband..." he started to say. As he did so he felt his arm being grabbed like a vice, turning him.

"Didn't you hear Nurse Kenyon? Stay away from—"

The owner of the iron grip recognized James. It was the male nurse he had encountered earlier, the one he had thought might be running to fat or muscle. It was muscle. The grip tightened on James's arm, just above the elbow. He was going to have a bruise there for a week.

"You're the new gardener, aren't you?"

Nurse Kenyon put in her dime's worth. "He just told me he was from the fire department."

James didn't know how the guy managed it, but the grip tightened even more.

"Okay, buddy. Just who the hell are you?"

It was a good question. One to which James had no answer. He debated for a second whether to get physical. But this guy was no pushover. He was trained to take care of fruitcakes and a good part of that training had to be the ability to handle himself. But James didn't see that he had any alternative.

He turned sideways to the guy and tried to pull his arm free. At the same time, he brought his knee up hard aiming for the crotch. He'd been right. He shouldn't have tried it.

It was a wrong move on both counts. First, the grip on James's arm remained just as tight, and second, the man turned sufficiently so that James's knee caught him on the thigh rather than where it was aimed. The next thing James knew, he was flat on his back looking up at the sky while the man standing above him wasn't even breathing hard.

Now the male nurse turned, looking for somebody. He called out.

"Dr. Canby!" Then back down to James. "Up!" he said.

James climbed to his feet, surprised that nothing was hurting other than his pride.

"What is it, Harlow?"

Dr. Canby was an elegant-looking man in his early sixties. Iron-gray hair, clean-shaven, slim, wearing a beautifully cut tweed suit and Gucci loafers. His eyes were partially obscured by tinted spectacles which, out here in the sunlight, appeared almost opaque.

"You oughta talk to this guy, Doctor," said Harlow. "He doesn't seem to have any business here."

The doctor looked at James. "I suppose you're another newspaper reporter," he said. There was a certain tired resignation in his voice as though he was about to deal with a recurring problem.

"*Los Angeles Times*," said James, ready to grasp at any straw.

"What is it this time? Something specific or are you just nosing around in general?"

"I thought I'd find a good story here," said James.

"I think he's lying, Doctor," said Harlow. "I wouldn't be surprised if he's the one tripped the fire alarm."

"Did you?" asked Dr. Canby.

"What do you take me for?" said James indignantly.

Canby shook his head. "I can't understand you people. What is so newsworthy about Westfields?"

"You tell me, Doc," said James.

"Westfields is a hospital for sick minds. Nothing more, nothing less."

"Rich sick minds," said James.

"Even the rich are entitled to their privacy. What is your name?"

"Marvin Compact," said James.

"The *Los Angeles Times*, you said?"

James nodded.

"Whether or not you feel you have a story, Mr. Compact, rest assured it won't be printed. We have powerful friends in California. Also, after I make a couple of telephone calls, I doubt seriously whether you will have a job any longer." He turned to the male nurse. "Throw him out, Harlow." He turned away, moving off to continue tending his flock.

"You gonna give me any problems?" Harlow asked James.

"No," said James.

He followed Harlow to an electric golf cart and climbed aboard. The cart started down the drive toward the main gates. James looked back once. Glenda Everly was being led toward a group of inmates by a female nurse. If she'd even been aware of James, she gave no sign.

"How did you get in?" asked Harlow.

"You work it out," said James.

Harlow took his foot off the accelerator and as the cart slowed, he pulled on the brake.

"Out," he said.

"What for?" James figured he already knew the answer.

"Doc Canby told me to throw you out. He didn't say nothing about in one piece. How did you get in?"

It was okay to try to hang onto one's pride, but there came a time when only a complete idiot continued to push for trouble.

"I came over the wall," he said.

"Where?"

James pointed vaguely in the direction where he'd climbed over. "There's a tree overhanging," he said.

"There won't be tomorrow," said Harlow.

He dropped James at the main gates. The heavyset young man James had seen from the road walked over to the golf cart.

"What's going on up there, Ted?" he asked.

"The fire alarm tripped," said Harlow. " 'Cept up to now nobody can find a fire."

"Who's this?" asked the young man.

"He says he's a newspaper reporter."

"What are we supposed to do with him?"

"I know what I'd like to do to him," said Harlow. "But the doc says to throw him out." He turned to James. "This is a good job. What we don't need is guys like you coming around and trying to fuck things up. The doc's a good man. He's bright. But he's also too trusting. You tell him you're a newspaper man and right away he believes you. I'm not like that. I don't believe anything. I don't know what you thought you were pulling, breaking in here, but you try it again and I'm going to drive you out into the desert, break both your legs and leave you there. You hear me, boy?"

James heard him loud and clear. He also believed him.

The young guard unlocked the gates. James walked out as sirens announced the arrival of the fire department. The gates were opened the rest of the way and three units from Cedar City swung off the road and headed up the drive. James walked back to his car, turned around and headed back toward Cedar City.

James pulled off the road before he reached the main highway. He drove for twenty feet and parked the car in among a grove of trees. He got out and walked to the road and looked back toward his car. To anyone driving by, heading in the direction of Westfields, it was almost invisible. He walked back to the car and got in. It would be at least an hour before he could expect to see the Bentley. He spent that hour considering his options in light of what he had discovered at Westfields.

He was still wrestling with various permutations when he saw the Bentley. It turned off the highway onto the side road, passing twenty feet from him. Wally was driving, Everly sitting beside him. Maybe when they talked to Dr. Canby, he would mention this morning's intruder, the guy with the two-tone hair. But in the long run, it wasn't going to make much difference. He started the car and headed back in the direction of Las Vegas.

Once he had parked his car, he collected the package he had left at the front desk of his motel and went up to his room. He hung a *Do Not Disturb* sign on the door, set the alarm for five P.M. and went to bed. In five minutes, he was sleeping like a baby.

CHAPTER EIGHT

The Grand is almost indistinguishable from the Palace. The same gamblers losing their money playing the same games. The same lines patiently queuing for the showrooms. The same background sounds. Pit bosses and dealers looking as though they had been cloned. James walked into the vast casino area at a quarter to seven, fifteen minutes before the appointed time.

The alarm had woken him at five, he'd showered and shaved and checked out of the motel. He hadn't even given them an argument at the front desk when he was told that checkout time was noon and he would have to pay for another night. He'd gone back to the same Chinese restaurant where the staff looked like they were playing the same card game they had been playing yesterday. He'd ordered a bottle of wine with his supper which had turned out to be warm and sweet when it should have been cold and dry. He'd asked for some ice and drank it anyway.

He turned right inside the Grand and found a banquette seat from which he could keep his eyes on the main entrance. Everly walked in exactly on time. He was alone. He looked around and didn't see James. He walked over to a house phone, and a couple of minutes later James heard the announcement over the public address.

"Mr. Everly's guest to a house phone please."

At least Everly had the good sense not to broadcast the name of the late James Reed. James stood up and walked over to where Everly was still hanging on the phone. Everly saw him approaching, said something into the phone and hung up.

"Where's Wally?" asked James.

"He didn't come."

Bullshit, thought James, but he let it go.

He led the way back to the banquette. It was isolated sufficiently so that nobody would be able to listen in on their conversation. Both men sat down, and for a long moment nobody said a word.

"I need a drink," said Everly, finally.

"Later," said James.

Everly looked toward the huge gambling arena. "I don't like this place," he said. "The Palace is better."

"I don't feel outnumbered here," said James.

"You think we're going to pull something?"

"Aren't you?"

"We thought about it. But you've got us by the short and curlies."

"How come Wally's not here?"

"He's got a problem in town. I told you."

"He's got a problem, period," said James.

"I'm going to take care of it," said Everly.

"How are you going to do that?"

"You tell me."

He was looking at James steadily. Maybe he ought to have the drink he wanted, thought James. Everly drunk might be easier to deal with than Everly sober.

"I want money," said James. "And I want an alibi to get me off the hook for the Fisher killings."

"That's it?"

"That's it."

"What do I get in return?"

"You get your photographs back."

"All of them." It was a statement, not a question.

"The originals."

"This is the same deal we offered you this morning."

"This morning was different."

Everly looked at him for a long moment. "So, it was you up at Westfields."

"That was the general idea, wasn't it?"

Everly said nothing.

"I suppose it was Wally who worked out I'd been through your desk."

Everly didn't bother to deny it. "You weren't particularly subtle about it."

"How did you know I'd pick up on that phone call?"

"Wally heard you come back in the house."

"Why didn't you just tell me about your wife?"

"Would you have believed me?"

"Probably not," said James.

"We figured you ought to know before jumping to the wrong conclusions."

"So, tell me about her," said James.

Everly looked out across the casino once more, then back to James.

"I really need that drink," he said.

They found a private corner in one of the bars overlooking the casino area. There were crowds of people milling around, but they were all too busy drinking up a storm and working hard at enjoying themselves to take any notice of James and Everly. Surrounded by people, the two men were as isolated as they would have been sitting in an empty room.

"You saw her?" asked Everly, once he had downed his first drink.

"I spoke to her."

"And?"

"I don't think she even knew her own name."

Everly's gaze fixed itself somewhere over James's left shoulder. He was silent for almost thirty seconds. Then he pulled himself back to reality.

"God, she was beautiful," he said. "She was bright too."

"Not too bright," said James.

Everly beckoned to the cocktail waitress, pointing at his glass. "She was bright," he insisted. "Intelligent, well-read. She spoke three languages fluently."

"You don't go from a bright, intelligent linguist to what I saw this morning in a couple of years without a lot of outside help," said James.

"They keep her on tranquilizers."

"They sure do."

"It's the only way."

"For whom? Her or you?"

Everly looked at James for a long moment. "For both of us," he said finally.

The cocktail waitress brought him his second drink. He downed half of it in one swallow, then put it down on the table without letting go of it.

"How much do you know and how much are you guessing?" he asked.

"Does it make any difference?"

"I guess not. Where do you want me to start?"

"Try the beginning," said James. "Like when you were childhood sweethearts."

Everly looked surprised. "How did you know that?"

"According to the records at Westfields, her father is Walter Green. That would be Wally. Right?"

"How did you get to see the records?"

"Is Wally her father?"

"You're the one who set off the fire alarm."

"Stick to the subject," said James. "Wally's your father-in-law."

Everly nodded. "You're a lot smarter than we figured."

"If I was smart, I wouldn't be sitting here talking to you," said James.

Everly finished his second drink and caught the eye of the waitress once more, signaling for another. James waited for him to start talking again and, when he didn't, James continued.

"Wally's been part of your life from the word go. A friend of your father's from way back. So, you and she were together a lot when you were kids."

"Wally and my father were very close. Like brothers almost. He spent all his time on the ranch. That's where Glenda was brought up."

"What about his wife? Glenda's mother?"

"She died when Glenda was a baby."

"How did she die?"

"She killed herself."

"Why?"

"Shit. Who knows why a person blows her brains out?"

"I'll take even money you do."

Everly looked around the bar, as though he was wondering when his drink was going to arrive. James realized he was going to have to continue to make the running.

"I told you, I saw your wife's medical history. Her mother was mad. Maybe her insanity didn't run to torturing little kids. Then again, maybe it did and that's the reason she killed herself. Whatever, she was as mad as a hatter and she passed it on to her daughter."

"They never told us," said Everly. "Neither Wally nor my father. Not till after we were married and we were talking about having kids. That's when they told us. They said perhaps it wouldn't be such a good idea. I guess it was after that I first started noticing things about her. I mean, I'd noticed them before but I'd just ignored them."

"Things like what?"

"She used to have violent swings of mood. One minute up in the clouds, then, for no reason, she'd be almost suicidal."

"Manic-depressive psychos aren't interested in killing other people. Only themselves," said James.

"She's a paranoid schizophrenic as well," said Everly, peering around again. "Where's that fucking drink?" Then, back to James. "That didn't develop till later."

"Symptoms?"

"She nearly killed a horse that threw her once. Beat it half to death. We used to go on safari together, to Africa. She was a first-class shot but she never killed anything cleanly. Stomach wounds, leg shots, enough to bring the animal down, not enough to kill it outright. Then she'd get furious when I tried to finish the job. It took me some time, but eventually I realized she got a kick out of seeing things hurting."

Everly's third drink arrived. He swallowed it like a man dying of thirst and called the waitress back before she'd walked half a dozen steps. This time, James ordered one too..

"What happened to the Garcías kids?"

"I don't know," said Everly.

"Bullshit," said James.

Everly considered this for a moment before making up his mind to continue.

"Okay. We came back to the house, me and Wally. We'd been out on the mountain all day. Glenda didn't like to ski. We found them in the bedroom. She'd left them there after she'd got through."

"Dead?"

Everly looked around the bar again, searching maybe for some kind of salvation.

"Were they dead?" James persisted.

Everly nodded. "Yes."

Goddam it, thought James, he's lying. But he let it go.

"Wally and I buried them up on the mountain. Then we had a long talk, the two of us. Then we talked to Dr. Canby at Westfields and he agreed to take her."

"How did you talk him into that?"

"I told you. I'm a rich man."

"You didn't tell him what she'd done."

"Christ, no. At least, not about the children. I told him about everything else."

"Whose idea was it to feed her enough dope to make a zombie out of her?"

"It was better than having her stand trial for murder," said Everly, defensively.

"It was better than having yourself stand trial as an accessory too."

Everly's eyes flicked away from James, looking for something else to light on. Then they returned. "What would you have done?" he asked.

James thought about it for a time. "I sure as hell wouldn't have kept the photograph," he said, finally.

"I kept it to remind me," said Everly. "And to remind Wally, just in case he tried to talk me into getting her out."

"Did he?"

"Once. After she'd been there a few months. She's his daughter, for Christ's sake."

The waitress brought them their drinks. It was James's second, Everly's fourth. James almost felt sorry for him. "Let's discuss business," he said.

"That's what we're here for," said Everly.

"As soon as the cops realize I wasn't the one burned up in that car, they're going to come looking for me. Maybe they're looking already. I don't know. But as soon as we're through, I'm driving back to Los Angeles. There I'm going to discover that I'm supposed to be dead. I'm going to do what any law-abiding citizen would do in the same situation. I'm going to the police and I'm going to tell them I was here in Vegas with my old buddy Harold Everly on a five-day bender and I didn't even know my car had been stolen. You and Wally are going to back me up. That's the way it's going to go. Right?"

"Right," said Everly, nodding his head. The booze had started to get to him.

"You're also going to give me fifty-five thousand dollars," said James.

"I'm sorry," said Everly. "I thought you said fifty-five thousand."

"I did. I'm going to send fifty thousand to Daphne Spruce whose husband Wally killed. The other five's for me, to cover my expenses."

Everly stared at him hard. "You're crazy," he said. "Either that or you're planning a double cross."

"Is it a deal?"

"Sure, it's a deal."

"I want it in cash."

"No problem. We'll go over to the Palace and get it right away. Where are the photos?"

James tapped his pocket. "When I get the money," he said.

Everly started to get to his feet, then he sat down again, looking at James.

"You could have asked for a million," he said. "I don't get it."

"I didn't expect you would," said James.

They left the Grand and walked to the Palace. There, they mounted the moving walkway that carried people from the sidewalk to the hotel building. All along the covered walkway, a persuasive voice over the public address exhorted arriving customers to have a wonderful time. As they stepped off the walkway and headed toward the main doors, James saw the liveried doorman, who knew Everly, reach for the internal phone.

Milo met them almost as soon as they were inside. It was as if he spent his entire working day just hanging around the lobby waiting for Everly to arrive.

"Good to see you again, Mr. Everly." His eyes flicked across James. If he was surprised, he didn't show it. "Mr. Reed. Didn't I see your picture in the newspaper?"

"Mistaken identity," said Everly. "James has been with me for the last five days." He put his arm around James's shoulder.

"Right, old buddy?"

"Right," said James.

If Milo formed any opinion, there was nothing in his flat, gray eyes to show it. "Are you gentlemen going to be playing tonight?"

"Later, maybe," said Everly. "First, I need a favor."

Ten minutes later, Everly joined James in one of the bars at the edge of the casino area.

"You want to show me what I'm buying," he said.

James figured Everly must have downed at least two more drinks. His voice was beginning to slur around the edges.

"Sure," said James, reaching toward his pocket.

"Not here," said Everly quickly.

James, who'd had no intention of taking anything from his pocket, decided that Everly wasn't as drunk as he wanted to appear.

"Where do you suggest?" he asked.

"Upstairs. My suite," said Everly.

They went up in the elevator to the same suite that Everly had occupied the last time he had been here. Once inside, Everly made straight for the bar and poured himself a stiff drink. James said he didn't want one.

"Okay," said Everly. "Let's see it."

"It's a two-way street," said James.

As if on cue, there was a tap on the door. Everly crossed and opened it to Milo, who handed him a large manila envelope and received a signature in exchange.

"Enjoy yourselves, gentlemen," he said.

James counted the money while Everly went through what James had handed him, the original photograph of the Garcías children and the shots he had taken in the house at Mammoth.

"How do I know you haven't taken copies?" Everly asked, as he slipped everything back into its envelope.

"You don't," said James.

"You could come back and hit on me again."

"If I'd wanted more money, I'd have asked for it."

Everly thought about this for a moment. "You're right," he said. He walked with James to the door.

"I guess we won't be meeting up again," he said.

"Providing my alibi sticks," said James.

"It'll stick. Pity about all this," said Everly. "I like you. You're my kind of a guy. We could have had some good times."

"No, we couldn't," said James.

James walked back to the motel he'd been staying at. His car was still parked out front. He went into the front office and asked the clerk for a large envelope. He transferred fifty thousand dollars in hundred-dollar bills into this envelope and addressed it to Mrs. H. Spruce at the address he had taken from the registration slip of Hank's pickup. He slipped a note in with it. "Here's the money I owe Hank."

He didn't sign a name. Sometime in the future, Daphne would be returning home, even if it was just for the funeral of her husband. She'd get the money, and she'd keep quiet about it. He bought some stamps from the front desk and asked the clerk the location of the nearest outside mailbox. Five minutes later he had mailed the envelope, and was back at the motel unlocking his car. He estimated that if anyone had followed him from the Palace, they'd had about ten minutes with his car. Enough time to search it, not enough to disable it.

Once you get on the freeway heading west out of Las Vegas, the highway is dead straight as far as the state line. It continues in a straight line for another five or six miles until it starts to climb in a long curve. At nine P.M. there isn't much traffic. What there is bowls along at a nice steady seventy-five miles an hour, only slowing to fifty-five when there's a chance that the lights in the rearview mirror might be the highway patrol or state police. If it is the law, then their car will overtake you and, in a few minutes, you can build up to seventy-five again. But if the lights behind you slow when you do, matching your speed, and then remain there, then it's got to be because you're being followed. James wasn't one bit surprised when this is what happened.

He checked, just to be sure. He slowed gradually to around sixty. A couple of cars swept past him. The one he suspected of tailing him, two hundred yards back, stayed in the same lane, slowing as he did. Then, when he picked up speed again, the car behind did the same thing. Wally might have been a whiz at following a guy on the back of a horse. Behind the wheel of a car or a pickup or whatever he was driving, he didn't know his ass from a hole in the ground.

There weren't many turnoffs from the freeway. James could have taken any of them and lost Wally inside five minutes. But that wasn't the way the game was to end. He kept his speed to a steady seventy so that Wally wouldn't lose him. He drove this way for the two hours it took him to reach Barstow. Then he made sure to use his turn indicator well in advance in case Wally's attention was wandering.

It had to be Wally. There was just no way he and Everly could afford to have James around any longer. It made no difference whether or not they believed him when he said he'd turned over all the incriminating material. Maybe they even believed he would keep his word and nothing would ever be said. But there would still be the law to contend with.

Once James turned up alive and kicking and reported that his car had been stolen while he had been on a five-day bender with Everly, the questions would start.

How could you be partying it up in Las Vegas when we know you were in Needles? We know you were there because you gave a ride to the young widow, Daphne Spruce.

Apart from her, there are other people who can identify you. There is the black guy at the motel where you stayed. There is the doctor who treated you for snakebite.

You want to know what we think, Mr. Reed? We think that Charlotee Fisher dropped the charge of rape against you because you made some kind of a deal with her. A deal you had no intention of going through with. Instead, you drove out to the Fisher place at Needles and blew them both away. Now, talk your way out of that, my friend.

James would talk his way out of it the only way he could, by telling the truth.

They wouldn't believe him, of course. Not at first. Not until he'd told them about Everly. Not even then, maybe. But, by then, Everly and Wally would be implicated up to their armpits. The García case would be resurrected. Somewhere, somehow, the bodies of the children would be found. Even if they weren't, they would be able to put a case together.

Okay, so Glenda Everly would get the blame. Psychiatrists would get up in court and testify as to her madness. In all likelihood, she'd be returned to Westfields and that would be an end of it for her. But before that, while she was waiting for trial, she would be transferred to a state institution in the care of state-appointed doctors. There was a good chance they would take her off the tranquilizers for a time. If they did that, she might start to remember. She might remember that the children weren't dead when her husband and father came in from skiing. After all, she never killed anything. There was no fun once a thing was dead.

James wondered for a moment if she had got angry at the two men when they decided that there was no way they were going to be able to let the children go.

⚜ ⚜ ⚜

He parked close up against the wall in almost the same place he had parked last time he was here. As he got out of the car, he deliberately avoided looking across the road to where a pickup had pulled into the forecourt of a self-service gas station. The lights of the pickup were extinguished but nobody got out.

James opened the trunk of his car. His carryall was still there. He didn't even need to open it to know the shotgun he'd been toting around the past few days was missing. That would be the gun that Wally was going to use on him.

He went into the bus station and straight to the men's room. There was a young guy shooting up in one of the cubicles. He hadn't even bothered to close the door. He was about nineteen, with a fresh, open face and a shock of light brown hair. He looked as though he should have been windsurfing or skiing. He glanced up at James from clear blue eyes, then continued about his business.

James went into the next cubicle and stood on the toilet. The key to the luggage locker was still taped to the top of the partition. James peeled it off and stuck it in his pocket.

As he came out of the cubicle the young guy next door emerged. It had been a quick hit. His eyes were sparkling.

"Hey, man!" he said. "What's doing?"

"That stuff'll kill you," said James.

"I know it, man. But what a way to go."

"You got your next fix?"

"Nope."

"What are you going to do when you fall off the edge?"

"Don't talk about it, man. You're depressing me."

"How does a hundred sound?"

"Like Herbert von Karajan."

The kid's educated, thought James.

He pulled a hundred-dollar-bill from his pocket and told the boy what he wanted done.

The boy left the men's room, his feet not even touching the ground. He was on cloud nine for the next hour or two. James almost envied him. He took a pee and washed his hands. When he figured the boy had had sufficient time, he walked back out to his car.

One quick look showed him the pickup still parked across the street. The lights were still turned off and James could just make out the silhouette of somebody sitting behind the wheel. Making sure that anybody watching him could see that he was empty handed, he walked to the far side of his car and unlocked the door.

The kid was leaning up against the wall, feeling no pain. James got into the car.

"Okay, let's have it," said James.

The boy detached himself from the wall as if he'd just remembered something he had to do. As he walked past the open door of the car, he slipped the package onto James's lap.

"Stay cool, man," he said quietly.

"You too," said James.

"Bang, bang," said the boy as he walked away.

James closed the car door. He started the engine and backed out of the parking place slowly enough to give Wally plenty of time to get his act together. He pulled out of the lot and headed back in the direction of the freeway. In his mirror, he saw the pickup lights go on and, a moment later, it pulled out, back on his tail.

James drove slowly, hoping that Wally was paying attention. He had told Everly that he was heading straight back to Los Angeles. He didn't want Wally to get confused and lose him when he did no such thing.

He drove past the freeway on ramp onto the highway heading toward Needles. There, he stepped on the gas until the needle hit seventy. He checked the following lights in his rearview mirror. They had settled into a position about three hundred yards back.

Driving one-handed, he started to unwrap the newspaper from around the rifle on the seat beside him. Five minutes later, after he had nearly run off the road twice, the rifle was lying across the front seat.

He drove through the darkened town of Needles without stopping. He wondered briefly whether Daphne had returned home or whether she was still testing the delights of the big city, unaware that she was a widow. When she did finally arrive home, she'd be a rich widow.

Ten miles past Needles, he turned left at Indian Wells, heading into the desert. For the past five miles the only other car he'd seen on the road had been the one that was tailing him. Even Wally wouldn't be dumb enough to keep his headlamps on for this next stretch of the journey. Sure enough, once he made the turn at Indian Wells, the headlamps behind him disappeared. Knowing that Wally would have guessed his destination by now, he didn't bother slowing down.

He almost missed the sign to the Fisher place. He caught a glimpse of it in his headlamps and just managed to swing the wheel and turn off the track, sending up a shower of sand and gravel. He swung left at the fork, and two minutes later he pulled up outside the shack.

He got out of the car quickly and, taking the rifle and a flashlight, headed for the front door. As he stepped up onto the stoop, he kept his fingers crossed that the rattlesnake was off doing whatever it was rattlesnakes did at night.

Once inside, he used the flashlight to locate a kerosene lamp. He shook the lamp to check it still had fuel in it, then he lit it. At first glance, the place looked the same as it had the last time he was here. It was a good bet that the police had given the place a thorough going over after they had discovered the bodies, but they had been tidy about it, putting everything back into the same disorder it had been in before.

He set the lamp down on the small table in the center of the room and walked over to the kitchen sink. He reached across and pushed open the window that opened out back. He stood the rifle against the side of the window and started to climb out.

It was a tight squeeze, but he made it. He landed on his feet close to the water tank that had held the mortal remains of the late owner and his wife. He reached back in through the window and brought out the rifle. Then, moving as quietly as he could, he started back around to the front of the house.

He was assuming that Wally would be curious enough to want to find out why he had come to the shack instead of going straight to Los Angeles. He was right. Wally had parked his pickup well away from the shack, and as James peered round the corner toward the front, he saw the long, skinny cowboy making his way carefully toward the front stoop.

He was wearing a Stetson, and a heavy thigh-length coat. James expected to hear spurs clinking. In the gray-blue light of a half moon, he looked like a reincarnation of John Wayne. This impression was reinforced by the gun he was carrying. It was the shotgun he had stolen from the trunk of James's car. It looked as large as a cannon and twice as destructive.

James watched as Wally mounted the stoop and moved sideways so that he could peer through the front window. He looked left and right, trying to take in the whole of the inside. Then, when he couldn't see James, he moved back to the door. He brought the gun up, stepped back, and lifting his left leg, he kicked hard at the door with the sole of his boot. The door crashed open, and Wally followed it. James moved onto the stoop and along to the door. As he looked in, Wally was over at the kitchen sink peering out through the open window, wondering where the hell James had gone.

"Don't turn around," said James.

He saw the tall, lanky figure stiffen momentarily, then relax again.

"You tryin' to fool me you've got a gun, son?" said Wally.

James shifted the barrel of the rifle away from Wally and pulled the trigger. The sound of the shot was monumental in the confines of the cabin.

"I'm not trying to fool you, Wally," said James. "You want to put your gun down."

Wally started to turn. "Gun first," said James quickly.

Wally did as he was told, putting the shotgun down on the countertop next to the kitchen sink. Only then did he turn to face James, who had shifted the aim of the rifle back.

Wally glanced at the rifle then back up to James. He shook his head.

"You're sure full of surprises," he said. "Where in hell's name did you get that?"

"Maybe you didn't do too good a job searching my car in Vegas."

Wally shook his head. "It weren't there, that's for sure."

"You'd have recognized it if it had been. It's the one you used to kill the Fishers."

Wally thought about this for a second. Then he shook his head again. "You're something else, son."

"Like you said. Full of surprises. You want to move away from there?"

Wally did as he was told, moving out of reach of the shotgun.

"We should have killed you right off," he said.

"It wasn't for lack of trying," said James.

"Yeah. Pity about the Spruce kid." He said it in a flat expressionless voice. James doubted Wally had ever felt pity in his life.

"What happens now?" asked Wally.

"I've given it a lot of thought these past few days," said James. "To tell you the honest truth, I don't know."

It was a lie, but James needed to give Wally a little breathing space. He waved the rifle barrel toward an overturned chair. "Sit down," he said.

Wally set the chair up straight and did as he was told, stretching his long legs out in front of him. He looked relaxed, without a problem in the world. His eyes were shadowed beneath the brim of his Stetson, unreadable.

James dragged the other chair back against the wall and sat down. He rested the rifle across his lap, turning the barrel away from Wally and taking his finger off the trigger. For a long moment neither of them said anything. It was Wally who broke the silence.

"What did you come back here for, son?"

"I thought it would be a good place for you and me to talk."

"Is that what we're gonna do?"

"I figured there'd be some things you wanted to tell me."

"Like what?"

"Like what's going to happen to your daughter when you and Everly aren't around any longer?"

"She's taken care of. Besides, we're gonna be around for some time yet." When James didn't say anything, he added a question. "Aren't we?"

"That's what we agreed," said James. "I take the money, you get the photographs and give me an alibi."

"It could still be that way."

"You blew it, Wally. Was it your idea or Everly's?"

Wally crossed one outstretched leg over the other. James couldn't be sure, but he thought he saw Wally's eyes glance toward the shotgun, just out of his reach.

"I don't know what you're talkin' about, son."

"Sure, you do. I'm talking about following me out of Las Vegas so's you could blow me away first chance you got."

Wally didn't say anything.

"Tell me about you and Everly, Wally. What makes you tick, you two? Is it that poor crazy lady up at Westfields? Maybe she didn't turn out the way she did through her momma. Maybe her father passed on some pretty weird genes."

"Her mother was mad," said Wally, flatly.

"But how did she get that way?"

Wally remained silent for a long time. He uncrossed his legs and then recrossed them the other way. Without seeming to have moved his position, he appeared much closer to the shotgun.

"It's a long story, son," he said finally. "You wouldn't be interested."

"Maybe you're right," said James. "So, tell me about Everly's old man. Your bosom buddy. Why were you two so close?"

"We were good friends."

"You sure were. His son married your daughter. One big happy family. How would he have handled all this?"

"Better."

"One tough hombre?"

"He was twice the man his son is."

"That's not saying much."

"Harold's okay, providing he's not drinking."

"That's like saying a blind man's okay providing he can see."

"There's a lot of things you don't know, son."

"Tell me."

"You could still walk away from here a rich man."

"I've thought about it."

"Think on it some more. As far as most people know, you're already dead. A couple of million dollars can buy a pretty fancy new life someplace."

"I like the one I've got."

"You're a beach bum courtesy of your ex-wife."

"You guys sure did your homework."

"You don't try to hide it."

"It has its advantages. I don't have to go around killing people like you and young Harold. How many is it now? The Fishers. The Garcías kids. Hank Spruce. Between the two of you, you're racking up quite a score."

"You're dumb, son," said Wally.

"I'm the one holding the gun," said James.

He was talking now mainly for the sake of it. He wanted Wally to believe he was just rambling on with no particular direction or plan. Suddenly Wally reached up and tipped his Stetson back on his forehead. It was an innocent enough move, but made sharply enough to test whether James was completely alert. When James didn't react, Wally glanced around the room casually. This time James was sure that he was measuring his chances of going for the shotgun.

"What did you have planned for me?" James continued. "A nice deep grave someplace in the desert?"

"It wasn't anything like that."

"So why follow me? We'd made our deal."

"We wanted to make sure you kept your part of it and headed on back to Los Angeles."

"You can do better than that."

Wally tried. He suddenly tipped right back in the chair, sending it over backward. He rolled over and onto his feet, as agile as a seventeen-year-old.

Because it was expected of him, James started to fumble with the rifle, bringing it back to bear on Wally, who was already grabbing up the shotgun. Wally swung the gun toward James, crouching low. He pulled the trigger and was rewarded with a dull click of sound. He grabbed at the second trigger. Another dull click.

"Two tries is all you get," said James.

Wally straightened up slowly. James shook his head.

"An old hand like you not checking his shooting iron. You ought to be drummed out of the cowboy's union."

Wally relaxed, holding the shotgun loosely.

"What did you do, son? Mess with the gun or the shells?"

"What difference does it make?" said James.

"Curiosity," said Wally.

"The gun," said James. "You might have used your own shells."

"Yeah. I might at that," said Wally. He remained standing where he was, still holding the gun. "Looks like what we've got now is a Mexican standoff."

"Not to me it doesn't," said James. "My gun works."

"But you ain't gonna use it."

"What gives you that idea?"

"It takes a special kind of man to shoot a sittin' duck. You ain't got the stomach for it."

He was right, of course. There was no way James could pull the trigger unless he was forced to. He was relying on Wally to help him out. Wally obliged.

He allowed the shotgun to slide through his hand until he was holding it by the end of the barrels. It was a movement designed to look as though he was putting the gun down. James pretended to relax, allowing the barrel of the rifle to swing away from Wally. Then Wally let the shotgun fall to the floor. Instinctively, James looked toward it, taking his eyes off Wally for a split second. He almost missed Wally's next move. But, because he had been waiting for something like this, he caught enough of it to make the right moves himself.

Wally's right hand had reached beneath his jacket. Maybe he was wearing a shoulder holster as opposed to a six-shooter on his hip, but the speed of his draw would have impressed a Wyatt Earp. The pistol was halfway out before James eased the rifle back the necessary fraction and pulled the trigger.

He was aiming low. He didn't want to kill Wally. The shot smashed Wally's kneecap to hell and gone. The force of the bullet threw Wally backward. At the same time his leg gave way beneath him and he ended up sprawled on the floor. Instinctively he grabbed for his shattered knee. Then, just as quickly, he snatched his hands back before he could do further damage.

James got up from his chair and walked over to where Wally had dropped the pistol. It was a .38 revolver with a short, stubby barrel. He stuffed it into his pocket and then walked back until he was standing over Wally.

Suddenly, Wally looked his seventy-odd years. His tanned, leathery face had lost all its color. His skin looked like the Dead Sea Scrolls. His Stetson had come off when he fell, the first time James had seen him without it. His white hair was thin and wispy. Only his eyes reminded James of the old Wally. Although they were clouding in pain, there was still room for plenty of venom.

"You figured I'd do something like that," he said. His voice cracked slightly.

"Yep," said James.

"Would you have shot me if I hadn't tried anything?"

"Like you said, I don't have the stomach for it."

A spasm of pain shot through him. He managed to struggle to a sitting position where he could look down at his knee. The front of his jeans had been plowed into his leg. The whole thing was a mess of blood, bone and fabric.

"Shit!" he said.

"You won't die from it," said James. He tried to keep his voice flat and cold. Remembering the Garcías children helped a little. That, and the fact that Wally had already tried to kill him twice.

He picked up the shotgun from the floor and started toward the door.

"Where are you going?" Wally had slumped backward, resting against the kitchen counter.

"I've got things to do," said James. He propped the rifle against the wall just inside the front door.

"You just gonna leave me here to bleed to death?"

"I'll be back before dawn," said James. He started out.

"Hey!"

He turned back. "What?"

"What am I supposed to do? I can't move, goddam it."

"That's the only reason I'm not tying you up, pardner."

"You sure you'll be back before dawn?"

"You can depend on it."

He walked out. He stopped for a moment by Wally's pickup. He thought he heard Wally shout something else, but he ignored it. He climbed behind the wheel of his own car, started the engine and headed back toward Indian Wells.

He put in a call to the Palace. It seemed that Everly wasn't there. He asked to speak to Milo.

"This is James Reed," he said, when Milo came on the line. "I thought Mr. Everly was staying over."

"He changed his mind," said Milo.

"Did he go back to the ranch?"

"I've no idea. How can I help you, Mr. Reed?"

"You can tell me where I can get in touch with Everly."

"I'm sorry. I can't do that."

"Can't or won't."

"It's the same thing." The line went dead.

James fished around in his pocket for more change. He dialed the E-Bar-E. Everly answered the phone himself. He sounded sober. James identified himself. If Everly was surprised to hear his voice, he disguised it well.

"You calling from LA?" he said.

"I'm calling from Indian Wells."

"Near Needles?"

"That's the one."

"I thought you were going straight back to LA."

"So did your father-in-law."

There was a short silence on the other end of the line.

"I don't know what you're talking about," said Everly, finally.

"You didn't know he was following me?"

"Why should he follow you?"

"He's probably asking himself the same question right now," said James. "I just shot him."

This time the silence was longer. Finally, Everly asked the inevitable question.

"Is he dead?"

"Not yet," said James. "I'm not a very good shot."

"Why are you telling me this?"

"Seeing as how close you two are, I thought perhaps you'd want to help him. Or is that a one-way street?"

"What's that supposed to mean?"

"He's the Big Daddy in your life isn't he? No matter what, Wally will fix it."

"How badly hurt is he?"

"He's not jumping up and down."

"What the hell am I supposed to do?"

"Maybe stop him bleeding to death. Take him home. Fix him up. Whatever."

"You could call an ambulance?"

"Then I'd have to tell everyone why I shot him. I didn't figure you'd want that."

There was another long pause. Somewhere, there was a crossed line. James could hear a woman's voice so far away it seemed to be coming from another planet. Then Everly spoke again.

"Where is he?"

"The Fisher cabin."

"I've never been there."

This was exactly what James wanted to hear. "I guess I'll have to show you where it is then."

He told Everly how to get to Indian Wells from Las Vegas. "There's a gas station at the crossroads. I'll be waiting for you there. See you in about three hours. Just before dawn."

There wasn't much he could do while he was waiting for Everly, so James climbed into the back of the car and tried to get some sleep. Usually he could drop off anyplace, anytime, a faculty he had developed when he had been a cop in London and been sharing a stakeout with a partner. This time, it didn't work. He would have liked to think it was because the back of the car wasn't particularly comfortable. In fact, it was because he was thinking of all the things that could still go wrong.

The Bentley pulled into the gas station just after four thirty. Already there were thin fingers of light on the eastern horizon. James checked the revolver he'd taken from Wally, then stuffed it back in his pocket. He got out of the car and walked over to the Bentley. Everly lowered the window as James reached him.

"How much further?" he asked.

"Fifteen minutes," said James. "Better use my car."

"Why?"

"It's a rough ride. The Bentley might not make it."

If Everly wondered how James's car could cover ground the Bentley couldn't, he didn't say anything. He was probably too tired to argue anyway. He got out, locked the doors with the central switch and walked with James back to his car.

"You drive," said James.

Everly climbed in behind the wheel. James walked around to the other side of the car and got in beside him.

"Head south," said James.

"Which way is that?"

James pointed the direction and they took off.

James figured he wouldn't have much more time to talk to Everly. He wanted some last things straightened out before they reached the cabin.

"Are you guys going to stay off my back this time?" he asked.

"Yes," said Everly.

"You believe me when I tell you I'm not going to come back and hit on you again?"

"Have we got a choice?"

"If you'd taken my word for it last time, Wally wouldn't have got himself shot."

"He wanted to take out insurance."

"Just Wally?"

"I went along with it," said Everly, reluctantly.

"Seems like that's the story of your life. I'll bet it was his idea to kill those two kids."

Everly didn't even bother to deny it any more.

"After all," James continued. "She was just your wife. You could have handled it. Sure, you might have felt shitty for a time, but you'd have gotten over it. But not good old Wally. This was his baby daughter who'd been doing these bad things. He wasn't about to have her stood up in court for the world to hear about. Better to finish what she started. Dump the kids and send her away someplace nice and quiet where maybe they'll turn her into a vegetable, but at least she'll be taken care of. Hell, son, you can afford fifteen grand a month." James shook his head. "That's some father-in-law you've got."

"I've known him all my life," said Everly.

"Great," said James. "That explains everything."

"How much further?" asked Everly.

"A few minutes."

They drove in silence for a couple of minutes before James spoke again.

"What did you do with the photographs?" he asked.

"I burned them."

"That's the first sensible thing you've done since this whole mess started."

Everly didn't argue with him.

"I may be wrong," said James. "But this time, I'm going to believe you."

He reached into his pocket and produced the printout he'd made from Charlie Fisher's floppy disc, the one that gave dates and places, a summary of Charlie's investigations subsequent to him finding the photograph.

"Like Wally, I took out some insurance too," he said. He handed the printout to Everly.

"What is it?"

"Something that Charlie Fisher put together. The original is in a mailbox in his name at a Venice post office. How you go about getting hold of it is your business. Once you've got that, you've got everything."

"So you *were* holding out on me?"

"Most of the stuff in there is just guesswork. Enough to make people curious but nothing that can hang you."

Everly maintained a precarious grip on the steering wheel with one hand while unfolding the printout with the other.

"Read it later," said James.

Everly glanced at him, then stuffed the printout into his inside pocket.

James pointed out the Fisher turnoff well in advance. As they headed toward the shack he looked toward the horizon in the east. There was still some time to go until sunup, but it was definitely growing lighter. He crossed his fingers it wasn't going to be *too* light.

The final two hundred yards to the shack, James slumped low in the front seat. Everly glanced at him.

"What the hell are you up to?"

"I've been sitting in this car, on and off, for the past six hours," said James. "My back's killing me."

It was a dumb excuse, but it was the best he could come up with, and Everly was too worried about what he was going to find at the shack to get suspicious.

The pickup was parked where Wally had left it. James would have been surprised if it hadn't been. The distributor head was in his pocket. In the thin, early light, the shack looked like something dreamed up by Charles Addams.

"Pull up over there," said James, indicating a spot next to Wally's pickup. He slid a fraction lower in the front seat.

Everly pulled up where James told him, thirty-five feet from the shack. He switched off the engine. The silence wrapped itself around them like a quilted blanket.

"Inside?" asked Everly.

"That's where I left him."

Everly opened the car door and got out. James eased himself up in the front seat sufficiently to watch Everly walking toward the shack, but not far enough to be seen by anyone who might have been watching the arrival of the car.

I'm crazy, thought James. Maybe Wally has passed out altogether. Maybe he still thinks he can make some kind of a deal. Maybe he's still propped up against the kitchen cabinet and hasn't been able to reach the rifle I conveniently left for him. Maybe it's already too light and he'll recognize Everly, who doesn't really look anything like me.

Too many maybes, thought James, as he watched Everly approaching the shack. Shit, why hadn't he taken care of Everly himself instead of concocting this crazy scenario? What the hell difference did it make who pulled the trigger? Better still, why hadn't he just gone to the law when the whole mess started?

Everly reached the stoop and mounted it. He glanced back toward the car once, perhaps wondering why James hadn't come with him. Then he pushed open the door and stepped inside.

James estimated the shot hit him dead center just below the ribcage. It plucked him two feet off the ground, hurling him backward off the stoop. He landed flat on his back, his arms and legs spread wide. He looked like a large spider that had been stepped on.

Wally would have been at the window, watching and waiting. He had to have been at the window because that's where James had left the rifle. He would have seen James's car drive up and one man get out from behind the wheel. Then he would have edged his way around so that he was facing the door. That way he could get a clear shot the moment James came in.

There was always a chance that he might have recognized Everly at the same moment that he pulled the trigger. For this reason, James kept the body of the pickup between himself and the shack while he replaced the distributor head. He got back into his car and started the engine. He backed out fifty feet before making a U-turn. As he headed away from the shack, the sun started to edge its way up over the horizon.

Three hours later he called Mossman at his shop in Westwood from a downtown Los Angeles phone booth. He told him where he could pick up the rented car. He told him to check under the front seat before turning the car in. He'd find an envelope there with his name on it.

"Make sure your wife's not around when you open it," said James.

"I thought you were dead," said Mossman.

"I told you not to believe all you read in the newspapers," said James.

Five minutes later, he walked into police headquarters in downtown Los Angeles.

If he'd known what it was going to be like coming back from the dead, he would have tried it before. Everybody was so goddam glad to hear about it. His poker buddies, Bee Kendrick, Gloria, his creditors, even Amy and Carlotta. Katherine, whom he hadn't spoken to for over a year, called to say she'd shed a tear when she read about his accident and if he'd like to come up to the house for lunch, she'd love to see him. The police had accepted his story about his car being stolen just as they accepted his reason for not coming forward earlier. When you're backpacking in the Grand Canyon, you don't get to see any newspapers.

It was four days before he spotted the newspaper item he had been waiting for. Dateline, Needles. It seemed a group of kids desert backpacking out of Indian Wells had called at a cabin to ask for a refill for their water canteens. What they discovered there really screwed up their trip.

There was a follow-up story the next day. This one gained more prominence, finding its way to the front page. It stayed on the front page for three more days.

Harold J. Everly might have been a private kind of a guy, but he was extremely rich, and rich makes good newspaper copy in California. Also, the media had other things to go to town with.

DOUBLE HOMICIDE ON CALIFORNIA DEATH RANCH
THE CURSE OF THE FISHER RANCH

Nobody assumed the two cases were related, other than by coincidence of geography. That would come later when ballistics showed that the rifle found at the scene was the same one used on the Fishers. What was plain right now, was that Walter Green had killed Harold Everly, probably after Everly had shot Green in the kneecap, rendering him immobile and thus preventing him from leaving the scene of the crime.

It was estimated that Green died approximately forty-eight hours after killing Everly. Cause of death, loss of blood, and general trauma. James wondered briefly why Wally hadn't used the last shell in the rifle on himself. He must have known he was going to die. Motive was assumed to have been blackmail. Evidence to back up this theory was found on the person of Everly in the form of a computer printout. There would be follow-up stories, of course, but with no murderer on the loose, public interest died fast.

James spent one hundred dollars having his hair dyed back to its normal nondescript color. He drove into Beverly Hills and had lunch with his ex-wife, an experience that he found vaguely depressing. When he got back home, there were three messages on his machine. Would he please call Bee Kendrick, she would love to see him. There was a similar request from Gloria. The third message was from Carlotta. Amy had flown back to New York for a couple of days on business, would James be interested in coming over to the main house for dinner tonight? He called her right back.

"Before I commit myself, which way is your libido pointing right now?"

"Would it make a difference?"

"I like to know what I'll be eating."

She told him. He said he'd be over at seven thirty.

ABOUT THE AUTHOR

Jimmy Sangster was an acclaimed screenwriter (*Curse of Frankenstein, Deadlier Than the Male, The Legacy*, etc), director (*Lust for a Vampire, Banacek*, etc), TV writer (*Wonder Woman, Cannon, BJ and The Bear, Kolchak*, etc) and novelist. His many books include *Touchfeather, Touchfeather Too, Snowball, Hardball, The Spy Killer* and *Foreign Exchange*. He died in 2011.

GUILDERLAND PUBLIC LIBRARY
2228 WESTERN AVENUE
GUILDERLAND, NY 12084
518-456-2400

Made in the USA
Middletown, DE
23 December 2019

81877904R00161